JOE TAYLOR

Bad Form

BAD FORM
A HUMOROUS FANTASY NOVEL

Dedicated to Stephen Slimp and Tricia Taylor,
both of whom helped immeasurably with this novel.

A Celestial Preface: Chez Snelling

"She knows. You hear me? She knows." This voice punctured the air.

The old man being addressed stood on a diminutive ladder befitting his diminutive size. Instead of answering, he bit his lips while pressing a glittery blue plastic sign against a wall. He leaned to sniff the wall's timbering, and with his free hand he tugged a six-inch cord constructed of glued rat vertebrae. The sign began to blink, *Chez Snelling, Chez Snelling, Chez Snelling* in glowing bone-white. Nearly slipping off the ladder in glee, the old man exclaimed, "The blinking and the French—they add continental flair, don't you think, dearest?"

A dwarfish woman, who could have passed for the old man's twin except for her mop of white hair, narrowed her eyes. "Mis-ter Snel-ling. I . . . just . . . said, '*She knows.*' Don't try to sidetrack me with French frippery. And where'd you get the batteries?"

The old man nudged the still blinking sign to his right. He'd been searching out the perfect spot for half an hour. "Of course she knows. That's her job as Lady Sophia, remember."

"I just don't want her around, messing with my turn in the roost. *Where'd you get the batteries?*" The woman's voice came strained, tense.

"I found them on the front porch, can you believe? Just what do you propose to do about her—is it more centered here, dearest?"

"I like off-center best. Move it back. What I propose to do is lock her away in some far-off, god-forsaken—" both of them cackled at that phrase until their plenteous wrinkles jiggled—"some sightless room that even the cobwebs have forgotten."

"Bad form, the extremest of bad form, dearest. You simply cannot do that to Lady Wisdom. Say, let's compromise. How about here?" The old man scooted the sign back where it had been thirty minutes before. His legs wobbled. Pressing his forehead against the sign, he pulled a hammer from his waistband and a nail from his right shirt pocket. He favored right pockets; his dearest favored left.

His dearest winked at a muscular orange cat on the plank floor. The cat sprang just as the old man's arm swung. Cat met elbow, hammer met thumb, sign and old man met floor. . . .

"My sweetest fluff, let *me* take care of hanging signs for the next century or so," Mrs. Snelling intoned, petting Mr. Snelling's silky white hair as he howled.

"My thumb! And the sign's broken. It doesn't blink anymore."

"We wouldn't want people getting ideas from those batteries, my fluff. About electricity, I mean. You really *do* need a long vacation, don't you? *Two* centuries? And surely you know that everything looks immensely more real when it's broken."

"Bad form," he mumbled.

"No doubt. Still, you are right about one thing: there *is* something suave and continental about the French, so we'll keep it. But remember: when I'm in the roost, bad form will be quite *au courant*, not to mention the cat's meow." She gave a fulsome wink at the orange cat, which purred and rubbed against Mr. Snelling's side as he moaned. The cat winked back, and Mrs. Snelling climbed the ladder to nail up the sign's three pieces, leaving a gap so that they blinklessly read:

Snelli Chez ng

"There. Perfect," she said.

First Leg: Quest, Schmest

Chapter 1

Causal relations amongst rattlesnakes
offer nary enough strife
to alter one's life.
Riddle me.

Billy Wise coughed and re-read the newspaper's lines. They were printed in hot pink, boxed by obituary black. He looked out to the surrounding farmland. Quests—didn't they always start with a riddle? The hot pink might be modernity's twist.

He was sitting on his back deck having breakfast: instant coffee mixed with cream and sugar until it bogged into swamp, plus one piece of whole wheat toast, Puritan and plain. Taking a sip of swamp, he realized there must be a typo in the hot pink lines.

"Casual," he laughed, looking up at the clear sky as if it had inspired him. "Casual relations."

He imagined rattlesnake underbellies tingling with forbidden joy, slithering over one another beside cool farm ponds, rattles tickling rattles, poison sacs nuzzling poison sacs. With sudden morning chill, he fretted the Freudian implications of snakes caressing snakes. Was he a repressed homosexual? Re-re-reading the newspaper, he realized that "casual" didn't make a world of sense either. How could casual relations among rattlesnakes possibly change one's life? Presuming rattlesnakes even have casual relations—or more to the point, presuming one even has a life. *Quest? Who am I kidding?*

A vulture swooped onto a rotting fencepost marking the end of the yard, then shook its throat as if contemplating a back flip.

"Who am I kidding?" Billy shouted at the vulture. His coffee sloshed, the vulture stared.

Billy envisioned an old *Playboy* centerfold hidden in his desk drawer at work. It too had stared, though not with eyes. He'd received it in the mail two weeks ago, a greasy red lip-print smacked across the centerfold's bountiful bosom and staring nipples. It was Linda's last sick joke celebrating the paperwork of their divorce, a divorce finalized through no conscious fault of Billy's own.

He flicked toast crumbs off the newspaper, as if that would clarify the pink rattlesnake sentence. It was probably one of those weird info bits journalists use to fill space they aren't bright enough to fill any other way. "Causal relations amongst rattlesnakes offer nary enough strife to alter one's life." That's what it said, all right. Hell: causal, casual, who cared? Quest, schmest; nary, schmary; Linda, Schminda; riddle, schmiddle, who cared?

Walking inside, he phoned the marvelous Purchasing Department at the University of Alabama, where he'd accumulated fifty-one marvelous leave days, since he'd called in sick zero times when he was married. *Maybe,* he thought as he punched numbers, *I should have called in like this then. Maybe I'd still be married and paying mortgage in the city, instead of rent in the country.* Did that make sense? As much as causal or casual relations amongst rattlesnakes.

"Janet? Hey there. This is Billy, uh, Wise. I don't feel so uh in the pink today so I better not come in and spread whatever I've got. No, nothing serious, a uh stomach virus or something. Yeah, thanks. You too." *Bad boy,* he thought on hanging up, wondering if his tongue were elongating. No, it was the nose that grew with lies. Pin-nose-io. He felt his nose: the usual Billy Wise gristle. He turned to zap water in the microwave, and soon deluged another cup of instant coffee with floods of cream and tidal sands of sugar. From the kitchen's back window, he spotted a deer just beyond the fence, wearing a damned hot-pink harness. Can people tame deer?

When he tapped the window, the deer simply looked up then returned to licking the salt block the landlord put there a week back. Billy reached for a machete he kept handy, since his landlord had warned that rattlesnakes and copperheads abounded, speaking of casual relations. Walking through dewy grass toward the gate, coffee in left hand, machete in right, Billy realized that he'd reversed battle priorities, for he was left-handed. Some brave warrior, dumping milkish coffee on a rutting reindeer. Even when he spilled half the coffee on opening the rickety gate, the deer kept licking, unconcerned about the approaching be-weaponed human terror. Hearing a jingle, Billy suddenly wasn't so sure the animal was a deer. A 4-H goat? He grasped his warrior apparatus, a.k.a. his machete. To his left, the vulture flapped noisily off the post, and flew to knock down a distant rotten branch. Everything else, including the deer, kept lickingly quiet.

The animal's pink bridle—surprise!—had brass bells. And the animal itself sported a single, three-inch horn. Had it lost the other in a fight? It looked too young for that. Well, what did he know? Daniel Boone with a left-handed machete in his right hand. Or was that a right-handed in his left?

"Uh," Billy droned, as if to start a conversation with the doe, for he thought of it as a she despite the single antler/horn. He thought this because of its big eyes and the hot-pink sleigh bell harness. The doe started off in a trot that jingled the bells, heading down a dip in the field. She entered the woods under the same spot where the vulture had clipped the limb. A great morning for omens, not to mention quests.

Mist swirled. Billy looked back to the white house that had been his gay divorcé home for two months. He tried tried tried to imagine, imagine, imagine someone waving, say a pale Civil War belle in a gray dress and white apron. He saw only a garbage can. Hearing a jingle he turned to spot the doe framed by dark trees. Her head cocked at him, as if she were waiting. Lambent daylight wavered through cottony mist, which was forming droplets on his arm hairs. In nearby trees, three squirrels chased one another. Better than three vultures, anyway.

What the hey.

Billy walked. When he stepped over the rusty barbed wire separating meadow grass from a blanket of fallen leaves, the doe walked too. Billy gripped his coffee mug for its heat, then took a sip. His wife—ex, never forget that prefix—his ex-wife had made this habitual swampy mixture the focus of her frustrations. "You're just like that instant morning pabulum you guzzle: no gumption, no imagination." She'd said this thirty-six times. Counting them had become his weird obsession during their divorce. He wondered if her lawyer, a frizz-haired woman from Kentucky, had gotten as sick of hearing it as he had. "You're just like that instant morning pabulum ... blah, blah." Talk about no imagination, Linda.

The deer neared a small crest in the woods, the other side of which descended to the pond, Billy's favorite farm spot. Mist thickened, so Billy gripped the machete as dead leaves and rotting branches melded to a patchwork. What if he stepped on a poisonous snake? He'd called in sick, so no one would have reason to worry. He eyed two mottled sticks; each hissed: "Billy Wis-se, Billy Wis-se." Maybe a lack of imagination wasn't his problem; maybe it was too much imagination.

He glanced back, but the mist hung as thickly behind. Ahead, the bells jingled, so on he walked, feeling damp leaves underneath his boots and mist thickening against his cheeks until his pupils dilated with a dull ache. He couldn't make out more than the heavy shapes of tree trunks.

"Uph!" Something caught his crotch. Another barbed wire fence marking useless, old boundaries. A jingle? Oh yeah, the doe's bridle. Funny how you forget minor matters when snakes, divorce, and barbed wire occupy your mind. Maslow's hierarchy tugging in the wild just as it does in the big cruel burg of Tuscaloosa.

The jingle again. Well? Forward or backward?

Curiosity won. Keeping hold of his coffee, Billy tossed the machete over the fence and pulled the top wire to crouch between strands. A twang vibrated electricity through his palm and he let go with a curse. Thirty yards to his left, a third of a football field but more than close enough, two fuzzy red eyes glared, disembodied in mist. He caught his breath. Operating lights for an electric fence his landlord had rigged to keep the cattle out? That didn't make sense; the landlord had dammed the pond to give them water. Why keep them out to dehydrate?

Again, the jingle. The red eyes disappeared. Or turned off. Or ... Billy gingerly set his cup down, then dove through a sag between the wires and grabbed his machete.

"Billy!"

He jumped, knocking over his cup. His ex-wife, dressed in a bridal gown that oddly both blended with and stood out from the mist, wagged a finger from the opposite side of the barbed wire. Way too close now.

"Uh, what are you doing out here, Linda? How'd you know I was here?"

"They told me you'd called in sick."

"But how'd you know I was here?"

"Where else would you be? Billy, want your pabulum? Look." She thrust his coffee cup forward, full now and steaming.

Billy blinked. Something about her voice, as if it were scritching through homemade walkie-talkies of two tomato soup cans, connected with wire. And that fairy-tale wedding gown. Was this an elaborate, sick joke? Even if the department did tell her he was sick, she couldn't drive here that fast. He backed off. "No, I don't want it."

"Take your pabulum, Billy. Take it."

"No!" After his shout, only mist, vines, and trees surrounded him. Linda had disappeared. His coffee cup lay empty on its side under the barbed wire. Nothing else. Then,

The bells. From their echo, they were by the pond. "No imagination, huh, Linda? Linda?" Nothing. He walked on, warily watching left and right, for several minutes.

Chapter 2

The doe was waiting by the pond, where she shook her tawny head, causing a jangle of bells. Billy stopped on a slick bank and watched the doe step into the pond. As water lapped her legs, mist formed a corridor to loom like bleached dinosaur ribs. Billy gawked: at the corridor's end, a woman sat on the pond's tiny island, under its single sycamore. Dressed in a satiny blue gown she appeared to be reading something in her lap. A book, was it? She looked up, beckoned with a lithe arm, and smiled. Then her attention returned to her lap. The now-swimming doe shook her harness. Ripples raced along the pond's dark surface, along with syrupy jingles. Billy stepped in.

The water wasn't as cold as he expected; in fact it was warm, which explained the rising mist. Up to his calves, then his knees, while he kept his eyes on both doe and woman. Up to his thighs, his groin, his belly button, his ribs, his nipples, his neck. Just when he thought he'd begin swimming he kept walking, as if the soft muck were taking him prisoner.

"Billy!" He glanced back. It was his w—his ex wife, with that same voice like a hiss of rainwater, with that same cup of steaming coffee, unspilt. But now she was dressed in vulture-black widow's rags. Anything was better than going back to her, even suicide. He kept walking. Water pleasantly warmed his lungs, being only marginally harder to breathe than air. In fact, it offered immense release and cleanliness when first emitted from his nostrils.

My nostrils? Have I lost my mind? Am I really committing suicide?

His ex-wife's calls abated. He could hear only himself, breathing silt and water. Under the pond's surface, morning light retained surprising strength and he walked gingerly to avoid stirring mud. Three or four feet above, the doe swam awkwardly; he spotted the disked outline of a large turtle swerve to avoid colliding with a lunging hoof. As he continued his descent along the mucky bottom, the doe floated, now maybe ten feet overhead. Billy's own mouth was open and he was "breathing" water, taking it in fully and blowing it out in a pursed whistle. For some reason this didn't surprise him, though he did laugh when silt tickled the back of his throat.

An old trunk lay to his right. He'd inspect it on the way back. All around, fish swam their fishy business. Ahead on the pond's floor, a huge catfish, maybe ten pounds, was sorting through algae. It passed him, then headed toward the trunk. Before it was halfway there, an even huger snake swallowed it whole. He could swear the catfish stuck out its tongue and made a raspberry before being swallowed. Or was it the snake? *No way. Imagination.* Water expelling from his lungs made a bone-and-flesh sound, a pleasant in-out rhythm. The snake, which was pig-fat, nudged the trunk's latch, then shimmied back to charge it, full force. The impact barreled through the water.

Billy tiptoed. Peering over stirred silt, he laughed, water merrily sloshing his teeth. The broken trunk held an old clawfoot bathtub, which the snake slid into, though its head and tail hung out either end and catfish whiskers drooped ridiculously from its mouth. Bingo! The hot-pink newspaper riddle became crystal clear, as clear as the silt-water around him. *Causal relations among rattlesnakes are none of your damned concern: Keep your mind on your mind; keep your vision pure.* Billy breathed in water: he was a washing machine; he was cleansing himself. He looked from the lounging snake to see the doe wading up the thin shore of the pond's single island.

"Lassie, wait." His words bubbled. The doe turned and jangled its harness, which barely sounded down to Billy in the water.

Soon Billy was also ashore. Water poured from his mouth, his nose, his ears, his hair, leaving him so light that his toes curled to clutch the ground lest he float off like a World War I dirigible.

"You're early," the woman in blue said, closing her book with a melodramatic gesture. *So it was a book I saw,* Billy thought stupidly. The woman gave her golden ringlets a shake. Each ringlet bounced as if it might take flight if the sun ever broke the fog.

"Early?" Billy spewed a quart of water with that word.

The woman laughed a lightsome laugh that glided like a child's bamboo glider. Spewing more water, Billy noted that her lips were shaped incredibly like a stylized Cupid's heart.

"Yes, five years early. Did you experience some life crisis?"

Billy watched her blue eyes bulge—no, that wasn't the right word—he watched their wet blue *soft* from her stark face as if impatient to see what the world might offer. Well, no poet he. Still, feeling dangerously pulled by their oceanic blue, he studied the tiny island. Hanging in two persimmon trees was yellowing fruit, nearly camouflaged by leaves. His mouth puckered as if he'd swallowed alum. The fabulous swimming doe was not to be seen. He felt the island's sand under his boots. The woman said something. Though her voice came teasing, Billy felt his dripping clothes and took stock of what had happened. Why wasn't he cold? He looked to the young woman's bulging, alluring blue eyes and shivered.

"Five years early? Are you Death, then? Have I killed myself?"

"Death?" She giggled, giving a twist to her shoulder and pulling at her dress to reveal a dark blue bra strap. As her body shifted with the strangely compelling feminine anorexia of *Cosmopolitan* cover models she said, "Do I look like death to you?"

To Billy, she looked like many things, none tending toward death. He shook his head and grinned. She returned his grin with those heart-shaped lips. Lately he'd been trying to focus on his instincts, something the marriage counselor had advised. He'd gone to the counselor eight times, though Linda had gone only once, more out of humoring him than any real prospects of "plastering up"—her phrase—the relationship.

"No." He coughed out what he hoped was the last of the pond's water. What had been easy to breathe underwater proved laborious on land. "No, you look lovely, too lovely to be true."

She smiled, twisting with a rustle of her satin/rayon/silk dress. Was she sitting on a stump?

"Who are you?" he asked finally. "Where's your pet doe?"

"Doe?"

"Well, she's got a single antler—"

"Antler?"

"Like a horn."

"As in unicorn? If you're talking about Alexandra, she's . . ." The woman's flourish was graceful, like a conductor's baton, and despite the early morning, Billy felt himself aroused on seeing her bare arm. Her lips curved even more like a valentine heart, and her blue eyes caught the mist. She managed to look like a sophisticated princess while sitting on a fifty-by-twenty foot island.

"Alexandra?" Billy blinked and turned toward where the slender arm indicated. Leaves in the farthest persimmon tree rustled, accompanied by a faint jingling.

"Doubting Thomas," the woman teased.

"Uh, unicorn. Are you a, uh, witch then?" Billy could barely believe he asked this.

The woman tsked.

Billy tried a new tact. "Why am I five years early?"

"Who knows?"

"No, what I mean is, what am I five years early for?"

"Ah." She tapped the book on her lap with her fingernails. "Look to your hand."

Billy did. In his left and proper hand was the machete, covered with a layer of moss from the water. "I've been appointed to harvest the pond," he said.

"That's good. You wouldn't have made a joke two months ago."

It was true. He'd made four or five jokes in his life until this morning, and no listeners had ever done more than grit their teeth at any of them. He looked to the blue, blue eyes and recited stupidly: *"Causal relations amongst rattlesnakes offer nary enough strife to alter one's life."*

She smiled. "Perfectly correct, I'm sure. But here's something else: *When in the pond, don't ponder. Eh?"* With that, she gave a flick of her wrist toward the persimmon tree.

Billy heard a plop and turned to see the tail of a beaver slap the water. The beaver wore a hot-pink harness.

"Come on! Don't waste time staring, now that you've made it this far." The delicate woman in blue rose to a height not so delicate, something over six feet, the same as Billy. She stepped into the water.

"Hey wait! What's your name?"

She turned coyly. "Soapy," she answered, giving her clean, heart-shaped grin.

"I'm—"

"Hurry, Billy Wise, or you'll miss the entire show." Leaving the image of her blue, blue eyes gazing over her bare shoulder, she turned and waded heavily downwards.

Billy gave a salute with his machete and followed.

Chapter 3

Underneath the pond, Soapy's dress took an ultramarine hue and her hair looked more emerald than blonde. She too walked on the bottom rather than swam.

"I've started a fad," Billy thought he thought. But on hearing words bubble back, he realized he'd spoken. Tiny fish swam by.

Soapy was walking toward what remained of the trunk. The snake still lounged in the tub, and catfish whiskers still lounged from its mouth. Billy saw a fry nipping at one whisker, but the whisker seemed always to foresee the fry's lunge. Once at the tub, Soapy rapped it briskly.

"Whadya want?" the snake asked, twisting.

Billy burbled water, but otherwise kept his composure.

"Let me in."

The snake gave a whiplash in the direction of Billy. "You know you're being followed."

"He's the one."

"Him? I've watched that ninny sit by this pond for two months now, moaning over his lost love, evidently a real shrew. He's worse than E.A. Poe. Praise the moon this one don't write poetry too.

'Once beside a pondside dreary, while I mumbled weak and weary
   Lenore, Lenore, oh make me snore!'

And talk about brave! Three times he's jumped from a garter snake. Once a crawdaddy scuttled too close to the—"

Soapy rapped the tub again, and the snake swallowed both whiskers. "You're going to be sorry. You're making a ridiculous mistake, all of you." With those words, the snake undulated from the tub directly toward Billy as if to ram him. Billy jumped, not away but into the snake's path, except it swerved right at the end. Some great matador.

Was there a billowing of laughter or was the snake noisily raising silt? Billy couldn't tell, so he gave an angry swipe of his machete in the snake's direction before jingling bells brought his eyes back to the tub. The harnessed beaver was hovering over the tub's white porcelain, looking from it to Billy. Soapy balanced on the tub's rim, her blue dress flipping slo-mo in the water; then she dove. The beaver gave an expectant shake; then it too dove into the tub. Billy walked forward, feeling pond silt squishing under his boots. Reaching the tub, he looked down on white porcelain turning lemony from the morning sun creeping along the bank. With a shrug, he stepped in

—and immediately landed on his head in the middle of a meadow.

Soapy and a young girl laughed as he fell, nearly chopping himself with his machete. The girl, he thought, was wearing a hot-pink necklace with bells.

"Bravo! Bravo!"

"Encore!"

Sitting spraddle-legged, Billy looked at the two females. Soapy's dress was as flowing and dry as if she'd never been in water. And he hadn't been mistaken: the young girl did wear a pink pearl and cinnabar necklace with tiny brass bells that jingled as she laughed.

"You're supposed to dive in, not step in," the one called Soapy taunted. "You're lucky the passage worked at all, O ye of little faith."

"Passage? So you *are* witches," Billy said, laying the machete flat and safe. He gave it a nervous tap then looked up quickly. "Both of you. And this is a witchland."

"Braaaanck! Say the secret word and win a hundred dollars."

Though only Soapy had spoken, both of them vanished, leaving two pieces of green paper flapping down. Billy looked about the field, which was similar to the one he'd left not an hour ago, except this one was sunny, and nearing midday, from the feel of the heat. Not very witchy, now that the two females were gone. He leaned for one of the green slips of paper: a fifty-dollar bill. He scrambled for the other and heard mocking laughter from a swampy clump of trees.

What the hey, let them laugh: he wasn't about to look two gift horses in the mouths. Stuffing the bills in his pocket he stood to look in the direction his house should have sat. Instead of its familiar white siding, there was only a flowing green hill—lush with grass and scattered poplars. Turning, he saw more undulating hills and could make out a large stained wood house—maybe two stories tall—about a half-mile away. It was the type of house he'd always dreamed of, one of those cool-in-summer, warm-in-winter log jobs that blended with the earth.

"Go on," a musical voice from the nearby poplars urged. Billy thought it might be Soapy, though he was confused now, with this younger girl. There was motion to his left: a fat brown and tan snake nudging grass aside, the same one from the pond. His machete! He'd left his machete to pick up the fifty-dollar bills. Backing away, Billy stooped for his machete and held it forward. The snake, ten very close feet near, coiled to the height of Billy's waist, with a businesslike triangular head atop a well-fed body. Instead of a warning buzz, two small catfish whiskers twirled on either side of its mouth and its lips parted in a Theodore Roosevelt grin revealing goofy flat teeth, not fangs. He expected it to either burp or hiss "Save our national parks!" at any moment.

Instead, it said, "Hi y'all! Done any lusting in your hearts lately?"

The lousiest Jimmy Carter imitation Billy'd ever heard or seen. He looked about him. Where were the speakers and hidden wires? But the snake was crawling off—too late to inspect. Its slinking skin shook spasmodically with a deep, smoker's laugh.

"Very funny!" Billy reached down for a rock to toss, finding nothing other than a tuft of grass, which he threw anyway, watching the blades billow.

He looked at the sky, a normal enough blue. "No imagination, huh, Linda? Then what do you make of all this?"

The fat snake was undulating toward the distant log house. Billy looked to the trees to see if he'd have any more company, but the sun beating his forehead convinced him to move toward the house. *That makes okay sense,* he thought. The house's golden wood glow would contain all the answers. Any house looking like that would just have to.

A bird whistled as he started out. *Twee-oh-wee. Twee-oh-wee.* A clipped, three-note ditty. He imagined it was one of the small, iridescent blue birds he'd seen around his own house, but he couldn't be sure, for every time he thought he'd pinned the bird's location, a mockingbird would distract him from a nearby limb. Down the first hill, up the second. The house stayed visible, though this second hill was lower than the one where he'd landed headfirst. *Twee-oh-wee. Twee-oh-wee.* Between the bird's calls, he heard voices, thin and barely perceptible, like voices he'd heard when he went to sleep as a child. Not that he was schizophrenic kid, for those voices had a rational explanation: he'd built a crystal radio kit that picked up tinny, thin broadcasts from the local radio station. So hearing voices wasn't that odd, was it?

Well okay, maybe it was. And now he heard tinny, disembodied sounds like that same running patter as he walked toward the house—except now he could make them out:

"You aren't going to just let him walk in there, are you?"

Twee-oh-wee, twee-oh-wee.

"I agree. I think we should . . ."

"But they've reached a consensus already. . . ."

"Why?"

"If *he's* five years early, then maybe something else will be too. Something bad."

The snake had disappeared, but the voices and the bird continued, as did the sun's heat whenever it cleared through trees on Billy's right, which was often enough to keep his temple tingling. At the top of the fourth hill, noticing that the house didn't seem to be getting larger, he realized it was much farther away than he originally thought. *It must huge,* he decided. *It very well could be three stories. Why build a three-story house out here where land was so cheap?*

The bird was still terwilliping, the voices still arguing, when he topped a fifth small rise to be stopped deader than a moldy boulder thudding against an oak. A blue telephone stand with small yellow flowers blooming around its base faced him. The phone rang.

"Natch," Billy commented, looking for the snake or the witchy women or Linda. He saw no one. Again, the phone rang. Chewing on his upper lip and wishing he had a waxed moustache, he walked to pick up the receiver.

"Billy Wise? This is Mr. Schroeder. You told Janet you were sick. What are you doing gallivanting around your neighbor's farm?"

Billy held the phone before his face and stared at it. A breeze twitted his non-Pinocchio nose.

"Well, what do you have to say for yourself?" the voice asked, metallic now that his ear was no longer against the receiver.

Billy stretched the wire against the phone book hanging from the stand. He imagined it to be the snake's neck (its shoulder? its spinal column?) and gave a hard whack with the machete, cutting directly through the line. The phone stand whooshed into a tall, thick dog fennel plant, or at least the bottom half of one, for he'd decapitated it with the machete.

"Causal relations amongst rattlesnakes offer nary enough strife for laughter," Billy shouted, addressing his words to the grass ahead, which was rustling.

In answer, the bird gave a *twee-oh*, forgetting to finish.

The rest of the walk to the house was uneventful and long, and would have offered someone—someone other than Billy—time for reflecting about hiking back and standing on his or her head to return to the tub in the pond, from thence to return to the bank of the pond, and from thence to his or her rental home, and from thence to the refrigerator for a cold beer and some reality therapy. This especially might have occurred to someone other than Billy when, on finally nearing the house after eleven hills and calling out to its empty front porch and windows, its front door opened to spew (with an ominous drafty rattle) a newspaper page upon which were printed obituary notices.

Maybe it *was* lack of imagination that kept Billy from jogging back when this happened. Curious, he first peeked into the dark door from where the paper had blown: nothing. Then he picked up the page to read tomorrow's, yes, *tomorrow's* obituary column. The first name, in bold black, was his. *Billy F. Wise,* the notice read, *survived by no one, formerly employed by the University of Alabama, died late yesterday evening at his home after falsely calling in sick to work. His funeral will be held this Thursday at 1 p.m. Friends may visit Jack's Drive-thru Funeral Parlor. University employees will not be excused for attendance. His ex-wife has requested that donations to SPCA be made in lieu of flowers. Closed casket, nose too big.*

"This is stupid. No one would write a notice like this." Billy looked about for the snake, but couldn't find him. He folded the paper and placed it in his hip pocket. A sudden whiff of garlic made him sniffle. Did it come from the house?

"Hello! Anyone home? Uh, hello!" Billy cautiously ascended four wooden steps onto the huge porch. A rocker to his right, the only furniture on the porch, was placed between two outcropping bay windows. The three-story house was indeed just the type of home he'd always dreamed of, only grander: stained wood exterior, a grand porch wrapping around the front and half of a side. He peered through the open door into the house's interior: the first floor might even have a cathedral ceiling.

"Hello! Hello! Uh, anyone home?"

A scurrying that could indicate anything from an opossum to an axe-killer was the only answer. Billy stepped back nervously, then forward curiously. There didn't appear to be any furniture inside. Who in his right mind would abandon a dream like this? A dream, of course! A dream. He laughed. Then he felt the obituary notice pressing in his rear pocket. This was no dream. Calling out once more and shrugging, he walked inside.

"I told you he would," a tinkling voice said, obviously pleased with Billy's decision. Billy jerked about, but saw no one. He looked up. There *was* a cathedral ceiling, of sorts. A carpeted staircase led to a loft bedroom. Over the bedroom hung part of that ceiling, segmented differently, as if suspended by wires. But wasn't that impossible architecture?

"Soapy? Alexandra?"

To his left in the living room sat an ivory couch that he hadn't seen, placed before a fireplace big enough for several people to sit in. Otherwise, there was only a dark wooden sideboard with a washbasin in its center, neither of which he'd noted before entering, since they blended with the shadows. On his direct right was an immensely long hallway, paved with flagstones. It looked ominous; it looked dark. A breeze eased from the comparatively short hall running alongside the staircase, and he walked in its well-lit direction after a glance upward to what he still presumed to be a bedroom. At the hall's end after five closed doors was a window. Peeping out Billy saw an immense drop, which he instinctively backed from. On his left, a kitchen tiled in sandstones showed empty except for a green counter and a large wood table. Directly ahead in the kitchen, a door led to the outside. On the table stood a bottle of Maker's Mark whiskey and a glass, stiff as a salute.

"Anyone, uh, home?" Billy gravitated toward the table. On the kitchen's inside wall was another fireplace, this one large enough to contain a huge old iron pot hung over a grate. He thought of cauldrons and witches and walked to the door that led outside, opened it and looked onto a large meadow, occasionally interrupted by outcropping boulders. No, not boulders, but roughly hewn and half-fallen gravestones.

"Easter bunny, Easter bunny, give me a wish," he whispered, gripping his machete and looking over his shoulder back into the kitchen. He didn't get his wish: Soapy didn't appear, and the tombstones remained. So he closed the door and walked to the whiskey. Opening the bottle, he gave a sniff—no telltale almond hint of arsenic—so, after calling out once more he poured a jigger's worth and belted it. His stomach curdled and he ran to the fireplace to spit.

"God, how do alcoholics stand this stuff before noon?" he asked the iron cauldron.

"Just what makes you think it's before noon?" the cauldron answered.

Or was something inside? Billy rubbed his mouth and tiptoed, ready to run. "Uh—"

"There's nobody here but me. I'm alone in this house and have been for seventy years. Of course seventy years my time might be about seven thousand or so of your time. Look at your watch and see."

Billy did as he was told, keeping a firm grip on his machete and peripheral eyes toward both doors. The tombstones didn't seem so bad now, since they were outside and not inside with a talking cauldron. His watch read five o'clock, the p.m. indicator enclosed with lines.

"What happened to the day?" Billy asked.

"Beats me. You're the one who wasted it." With these words the snake, all sooty now, lifted its head out of the iron pot, catfish whiskers back in place.

"Where's Soapy? Where's Alexandra?"

"Whats-sa matter? You want a wet nurs-se or s-something?" the snake said.

"You didn't hiss like that before." Billy leaned to examine the whiskers, thinking they were remote control antennae.

"Special effects. Thought you'd like it. So why'd you spit out the whiskey? I put it there for you and me, figuring we'd have a man-to-beast while the girls are out—well I'm not supposed to tell you what they're doing. Buying you a birthday present maybe?"

"It's not my birthday."

The snake began swaying the cauldron on its hinges, evidently enjoying the ride. "Pity. How many people do you figure there would need to be in this room for the odds to be in favor of one of them celebrating a birthday?"

"A lot more than this room can hold."

"You'd be surprised what this room could hold. It's a magical room, you know."

"I figured," Billy said dryly. "Is it magical enough that the rusty hinges to that pot won't break if you keep—"

But one hinge did break, and the pot fell onto the floor and the snake spilled out. Billy jumped away, partly because of instinct, partly because the tombstones were still on his mind, and partly because he didn't trust a talking snake.

The snake arched, shaking off the fall. Then it looked to Billy, standing against a far wall, machete raised. The snake's ridiculous whiskers twitched and it disappeared under the table. Before Billy could lean, it was rushing him, rattling loudly. Billy raised the machete and gave the snake a hard thwack.

But the snake was quicker so Billy only chopped off several rattles, leaving the snake to slither away and cough heavily.

"Murderer!" it croaked, whiskers giving a last twitch before disappearing. Billy leaned forward as the snake's breath labored and its sides heaved. It lay on its back, its mouth opening slowly, emitting dirty water in a sad trickle.

"Oh crap," Billy said. "Why did you rush me?"

With a flip of its tail the snake righted itself by somersaulting. It gathered into a coil and bobbed its head with a toothy grin. "Agility drill. Now how about that whiskey?"

"You're okay then? You aren't hurt?"

"Hurt? I'm tickled as pink as a snake can be. I've been hoping to break off those rattles for ten years. I just wish you'd gotten them all. Damned nuisance. Who else in the big, bad world rattles before striking, eh? Politicians?"

"Uh, why didn't you just chop or bite them off?"

"Bad form. Extreme Bad Form. Hey, would you mind lifting me onto the table?"

"Uh, how do I know you're really a snake, and not a machine?"

"That's odd. I was just wondering the same about you. Heard of Descartes and his evil genius?"

Billy shook his head.

"Ptoo! I can't believe they think you're the one."

"Uh, if you're real, then how do I know you won't, uh, bite me?"

"Uh, if you're real, then how do I know you won't, uh, machete me?"

"There's only one glass," Billy said, stalling.

"That's okay, I'll drink from a puddle. You know, Crawl on thy bellybutton, serpent, and drink till you're stoned. Come on, now. Lift me up, so I can fulfill the Maker's will." The snake grinned, showing those flat Roosevelt-rabbit teeth again.

With a sigh, Billy lifted him up onto the table and poured a puddle of whiskey out. Noticing the resultant soot on his hands he felt queasy, so as the snake slurped, Billy filled his glass and drank, not spitting out a drop this time.

"Good stuff for the soul, huh?" the snake said, nudging the bottle for Billy to replenish the puddle.

Chapter 4

"What'll we drink to?" the snake asked as Billy poured more Maker's Mark onto the table. "Adventure? Plunder and pillage? The five oceans? The seven seas? The four winds? A drink without a toast is like a pig without a roast."

Billy raised a cynical eyebrow. Already the snake had slurped two to his one, and Billy'd suffered through at least three homespun, rhyming homilies like the last for each slurp. Oblivious to Billy's silence, the snake slithered another trail of soot over the table and greedily lapped the latest puddle of Maker's Mark.

"Well then, you tell me," the snake said, taking a breather. "What do people in America toast? The President? Education reform? A victorious nuclear war? An undefeated football season? You tell me; I thought all my toasts were fine."

Billy hesitated. "A long and, uh, healthy life."

"Ptoo! You sound like an insurance salesman. I thought you were a computer programmer." The snake glanced slyly, its already thin eyes slitting more. "Or maybe there isn't any difference."

"You sound like my ex-wife."

"Hey! Let's toast her." The snake nudged the bottle with a clink from one of its rabbit teeth.

"Don't you think you'd better go easy on that stuff?"

"So you admit I'm not a machine, eh?"

Billy shrugged. "I, uh, suppose."

"He, uh, supposes. Well as beast to beast, how about just one more—a good bolus before we go exploring, sort of like a combo typhoid, tetanus, bubonic plague, cholera, and flu vaccine before shipping out overseas, you know? Whiskey's not risky, it keeps you immune and in tune."

Billy grimaced, but poured a small fifth puddle. When snake nudged his wrist, Billy turned puddle to lake, noticing the snake's soot had transferred to his forearm.

"That's better," the snake said, grinning with his ridiculous teeth. "Now, what's your lassie's name?"

"Who?"

"Your ex-wife. The one we're going to toast, remember?"

"Linda."

"Here's to Linda, beautiful Linda in any language. Avast, ahoy, drink up, me hearty."

"Why are you talking that way, so old-fashioned, all of a sudden?" Billy asked after sipping his drink.

The snake coiled and Billy stepped back. Even those two flat goofball teeth couldn't ease his mind about the snake's triangular head—or those disconcerting dusky brown hourglass patterns, for that matter.

"In a previous life I was a sea serpent swimming the Caribbean. Pirate talk was all the talk unless you wanted to take a walk—on the planks. No thanks."

"Right," Billy said. "And I used to be an Apple computer; that's how Eve and I started our new business and quit being just tuber rooters."

The snake's remaining two rattles buzzed as it revealed its bunny teeth. Billy backed against the door to look out at the tombstones. "Do you suppose that's a family plot out there?"

The snake dropped its cheerful front to mutter something.

Billy asked, "Say what?"

"I said, 'I just hope we don't become part of the family.' How about one last drink before we start nosing around?"

Billy remembered the obituary notice in his pocket. If this snake could talk, why couldn't it read? "Uh, if you're afraid of something in this house, or out there in the graveyard, don't you think it'd be smarter to keep a bit of a head? The way you've been drinking, you won't be immune *or* in tune, you'll just be on the moon." Billy gave a grin. Two could play the lousy platitude and rhyming game.

"Oh, all right." The snake took a last lick from the table. Billy could swear he heard a slurp as the forked tongue flickered.

"Uh, what kind of nosing around do we have to do, anyway? I'm supposed to be sick at home, you know, so I can't—"

The snake laughed in a belch. "Haven't you ever called in for a mental health day before?"

Billy shook his head.

"Man, has your boss that Schroeder fella ever got you brainwashed. You'll see what kind of nosing around we'll do, soon enough, don't worry. Hey, your boss doesn't have ESP, does he?"

Billy shook his head, though he wasn't so sure, the way Schroeder seemed to know everything that went on in purchasing two minutes before it happened. The snake swung its triangular head to stare into the kitchen's hall entrance, so Billy turned too.

"Is Soapy somewhere back there, in the house?" he asked. "Are she and Alexandra coming with us? Whose house is this? Hers?"

For answer, the snake slid down a leg of the table in a slo-motion that turned the whiskey in Billy's stomach and made him dizzy. Then, giving a body-twitch that resembled a fat, beckoning finger, it slithered toward the hall but turned to speak in a low, whiskey voice. "One thing: you might want to start whispering once we're walking about. And don't forget your sword."

"My—oh my machete."

"Call it a *sword*. They're scared of swordplayers, and they'll be petrified when they see you're left-handed. Superstitious, you know. It comes from the olden days."

Olden? They? Billy counted the dusky brown hourglasses on the snake's body as each one slipped through the doorway. Eight, nine, ten ... grabbing his machete off the sink, he remembered to switch from his right hand to his left as he followed the thirteenth or fourteenth hourglass into the hall.

In the hall, the snake made a point of darting its thin crimson tongue at the second door on the left and then the remaining three closed doors, as if checking for body heat. Its sooty trail was thinning on the polished wooden floor, which might be just as well. No need to leave telltale signs ... for *them*.

"It would have been just like them to hide in one of those rooms," the snake whispered, looking back, its tongue lashing its lips.

Billy nodded as if he knew who *they* were. Then he glanced to his left. Why hadn't the snake checked the first door? Was he drunk? No sooner thought than the door banged open and what seemed to be a shiny, twisted black coat hanger with legs spun out, thrashing and spiraling in Ninja fashion to connect with Billy's calf above his boot. Billy screamed, slicing his machete down, cracking the creature and sending half of it against the wall in a clatter. Two more inky coat hangers bound out, but on seeing their comrade's fate, skittered on looped heels, clacking against one another, their looped but otherwise empty faces contorted with a weird, shiny film, like soap bubbles.

"Use your sword!" the snake yelled.

"Swford! Swford!" the wiry black creatures huffed in a reedy whistle, their filmy faces pulsing. With the machete, Billy swung a backhand and snapped three of the four legs. The swing carried his machete with a biting chunk! into the door's frame. Reedy shouts of "Swford! Swford!" mixed with clattering, as if a closet full of coat hangers were falling; then the door slammed, popping the machete loose from the frame.

Billy spotted the remaining one-legged black coat hanger just as it lunged and sliced through his jeans. With a kick he pinned it against the wall until it cracked and joined its two comrades on the floor. Their looped, flat heads were about the circumference of peaches. The one that had just fallen blew a soap bubble that popped, leaving an oily film. Hollow, shiny black reeds lay scattered like Halloween drinking straws. Lifeless white splinters showed underneath the black, so they were wood, maybe painted bamboo and not coat hanger wire.

With a groan Billy looked at his legs, bleeding through torn jeans. He caught movement and nudged the nearest still-shivering black torso with his boot. The creature made a feeble lunge at his ankle, so Billy swung his machete down heavily, splitting the looped head into half-circles and leaving a watery imprint on the yellow wood floor. Despite the dishwater bubbles, the face's skeletal structure was as hollow as the rest of the body.

"It's good to break their face bones like that. I was just going to warn you. They play possum. Their bones can cut like razors."

"Bones?"

"Of course. They're alive."

Billy grimaced, feeling his throbbing left leg, the deepest cut. He squeezed it, hoping to staunch the bleeding. He then looked from scattered black bamboo bones to the closed door then to the snake, which had slithered near the stairwell. Hadn't its flat teeth been real fangs for the slightest moment? More clattering emitted from behind the first door, so Billy pressed against the wall while moving toward the stairs.

"Don't fret," the snake whispered. "They've seen your sword. We won't have to worry about them for the rest of the day, maybe even part of tomorrow. That's how long their memory lasts. Even though they're alive, you may have noticed they're short on brain cells."

Billy looked at the remaining full loop. The soap water film had nearly dried, leaving a salty glaze. Was their soap water equivalent to blood?

"For one day, and then you'll have to remind them. If you give your sword a flashy name and shout it as you kill them, fear may grip them one extra day even. That would be to our advantage, obviously." The snake grinned, its Roosevelt teeth in full bloom now, fangs forgotten. "Guess we need to go back and pour some whiskey on those wounds, eh?"

Billy stared at the scattered bamboo bones. "They look like coat hangers."

"That's exactly what they are, the old hotel type made of bamboo, but alive. It's sort of a House joke."

"A house ... I don't understand." Billy tried to catch his breath, but pain wasn't making that easy.

"A joke. You know how everybody hates coat hangers, how they're always tangling and getting in the way? These do that, all right, but they're alive and razor sharp to boot. A real House yukker. Those blank bubbly faces and their soap-bubble lisps just add to it."

"I still don't understand."

"Stick around, you will. 'The House giveth in play, The House taketh away.'" The snake gazed at the cathedral ceiling. "Seems I've heard something like that before—hey, how about the whiskey for your wounds?"

Billy ignored the suggestion. "Uh, you checked all the doors but this one, the one these three came from." As he bent to squeeze his leg, he watched for the snake's reaction. "How come?"

The snake twitched, and a lump moved several inches down his body. Otherwise, the lump would have passed for a shoulder. It was the catfish from the pond, digesting, no doubt.

"I dunno," the snake said. "A whiskey oversight. Sorry."

"You didn't do it on purpose, say to test me? More agility drills?"

The snake just grinned.

"Uh, you won't mind if I return the favor then, will you? I'd like to see how those two goofy Teddy Roosevelt teeth are going to handle anything, even something as brittle as this." With his machete, Billy scooted two bamboo legs across the floor toward the snake, which merely slid out of their way.

"The teeth were Soapy's idea. She said you'd be too nervous otherwise. Said they'd remind you of Jimmy Carter, though, not Theodore Roosevelt."

Billy looked up, keeping pressure on the worst wound. "I was a history major before I realized I'd never get a job that way. So what are you telling me, about your teeth? That your true fangs are heart-stoppers?"

The snake simply threaded through the stairway's banister. When it reached a position close to Billy's height, it whispered: "The bamboo clackers, by the way, aren't the real problem. They're more or less mindless aberrations, like say a spell of bad luck sprinkling your world. Modern, up-to-date gremlins, you could call them."

"Well, they're a real enough problem for me. My leg is aching."

The snake gave a shrug that sequentially passed through the four balusters it had intertwined. "Hey, I'm not saying they're not bad, I'm just saying they're like coat hangers, too stupid to be evil, if you get my drift."

Billy wasn't sure he did, and he wasn't sure he cared to. He looked at the still open double doors leading to the front lawn.

"Hey, hey! Don't get faint-hearted now. The whiskey's back there," the snake added. "Maybe that'll straighten things out for you."

"I'll go get it. Alone. You stay here and yell—hiss—if any more doors open."

Billy limped back to the kitchen and poured Maker's Mark on his legs, grabbing the table in pain as he did. Outside, in the cemetery, someone had been digging a grave. He hadn't noticed that before. For a good reason, he realized: it hadn't been there.

Back in the hall he tiptoed warily by the first door and over the bamboo splinters then told the snake, who had wound fatly and rather idly through the banister, what he'd seen outside the kitchen door.

"Urban renewal," the snake commented. "Come on, let's go before they get another idea."

Billy walked around the stairs and glanced down the expansive corridor, the one he'd avoided on first entering the house. At its far, far end loomed two regal doors, wide open now. He turned to stare the snake in its two golden eyes, as it clumped on the steps. "Uh, who are *they*, and just what *is* the real problem then?"

"We don't know. I guess you might say that's the real problem."

"We?"

Giving a twist, the snake plucked something from its skin. On turning, it held a fuchsia business card between its teeth. Billy took the card and read:

ARISTOTLE B. RIDDLE,

  foundling member

  * + * The Society Of * + *

"The society of what?"

"If we knew that, we wouldn't have any problems, now would we? But notice how we left plenty of space for contingencies. Very open-minded, don't you think?" When Billy didn't respond, the snake continued, "It was your gal Soapy's idea, leaving all that space; she thought we might need to fit a couple of Latin words or even some ridiculous German compound in there. Come on now, tuck the card away; you can be an honorary member. But we need to begin searching. If we're not going to drink Maker's Mark, we might as well be productive." The snake stretched to murmur "teetotaler," then gave a wink and continued up the steps, half-singing, "The Great One of the Universe will bless you Americans for distilling Maker's Mark, I predict. Maybe you'll discover a microchip mine in Kentucky."

Billy rolled his eyes and tucked the fuchsia card in his shirt pocket, then followed the snake upwards, wincing at each step.

"What's the B. in your name stand for?" he asked, watching the snake clumsily negotiating the steps. "On the business card, I mean."

The snake turned and hissed. "Shhhhhhh! You trying to get us killed, landlubber? Changing rooms in this house can be deadly."

"I just wondered," Billy whispered.

"Bogus," the snake answered. "It's the moniker I really go by, not 'Aristotle.'"

Billy arched his eyebrows. *Bogus. That figures*, he thought. "My name's Billy. Billy, uh, Wise. Pleased to be working with you, Bogus."

The snake wagged its head. "You s-sure pick dumb time-s-s for s-social amenities-s-s." It shook its two-rattle tail and turned to slither upwards.

Chapter 5

Once they were firmly on the second floor landing, Billy drew in a sharp breath. A tan wooden door directly faced him, blocking farther ascent. The door was closed, but through a glass transom Billy saw another flight of stairs. The loft bedroom to his left showcased a Victorian four-poster bed with a blue velour canopy, but the "room" to his immediate right really got his attention. It consisted of an expanse of sand and rock, expanse meaning maybe half a mile. Obviously some mirror trick. Most of the light for the second floor was coming from this room. Mirrors would explain that too. Billy glanced at the blue-canopied bed, thinking of Soapy, but the snake slithered into the much larger room, leaving a track in the sand.

"Come on, she's not over there. Get your mind out of the gutter."

Impossible, Billy thought, looking down at the sand, barely registering that the snake had read his mind. With a last look at the blue bed he stepped inside the room. Instantly he felt hotter and drier—water was almost sucked from his cheeks. He poked his machete into the sand. By leaning with all his weight, he plunged it to the hilt . . . into never-ending sand? Withdrawing it, he walked to a large rock and curiously rubbed the machete against it, producing a grating. He pushed the rock and it didn't budge, so there was little doubt about its being four or five hundred pounds' worth of real. And no doubt about the temperature change, either, for he was sweating from heat rising off the sand. In the distance loomed what seemed to be cliffs. How could a house hold this much weight? How could—

He jumped back. Bogus the snake had struck hard at something under the rock and was now shaking it like a dog shaking a raccoon. Billy realized Bogus had clamped on a Gila monster about the size of his forearm. The Gila twitched several times then turned belly-up as Bogus dropped it on the sand.

"Damn things taste worse than cow paddies," the snake commented. "But you never can tell where the next meal's coming from in this wretched house, so excuse me while I snack."

Bogus extended his mouth to enclose the lizard, then work it slowly, as a moving lump, toward digestion, say a point about one-third along his length. Sweat popped from Billy's forehead and his stomach quivered.

"Gwhen gwhe get to gknow one hnother better, I'll be ghasking you to cu-hut out the venom sac." Bogus gulped; then he spoke clearly, "I've always thought they might taste pretty good without that sac."

"You eat a lot of those?"

Bogus grinned with his rabbit teeth. "Oh no, pardner. I haven't et one in nigh on a hunderd years. You just cain't perdict what these rooms'll be from one time to another, you know. Amazon forests, moonscapes, deserts, cities—"

"Cities?"

"Well, I ain't never seen no skyscrapers, but I wouldn't put it past them."

"*Them* meaning the capital T them you've been talking about?"

"You got it, Poncho."

Billy cocked his head. "I guess you just passed your test under fire. I guess the Gila monster would have stung me if you hadn't stopped it, because I was just getting ready to sit on that rock."

"Bit you, not stung you. They bite to inject their venom, like me. Hey, you humans can do it just by speaking some sweet sarcasm, though. Man, does that make me jade-green jealous. It must mean we're your ancestors and that you're our improved biological version, eh, Darwin?"

"Ha." Billy rubbed his eyes, for sand was blowing about in a wind gust.

"I don't like the looks of those clouds; there's a storm coming up."

"Clouds?" When Billy looked, he could see, sure enough, that the roof had either receded or disappeared, and that there were indeed storm clouds forming. "My God..." He quickly turned. Instinct.

The door was still there and he could still see the top baluster of the staircase and the open bedroom's blue canopy bed, though he stood much farther from either than he would have expected, about forty yards off. It was as if the room had grown since they'd entered, for he'd taken only a few steps. He looked about: other than that door and its connecting walls, the room was no longer a room but a bona fide desert. Even as he looked, the walls shimmered and seemed to disappear, giving way for more sand, more desert. He looked again at the clouds—had the roof simply rolled back, like in a superdome? But that wouldn't explain the disappearing walls...

Bogus nudged his leg. "Those cliffs will have caves. We should head over there."

Cliffs. Billy didn't even want to look. "Uh, why don't we just go back downstairs?"

The snake hissed and two humps—the half digested Gila monster and the catfish too?—performed jumping jacks under its skin. Billy squeezed his eyes shut.

"Bad Form to enter a room and leave it without spending a night. Very Bad Form. You wouldn't want Soapy to hear you suggest that."

Soapy, the magical word pulling him on, despite a snake with a Gila monster bulging one-third along its gullet, despite gathering storm clouds, despite newly formed cliffs a half-mile away. Yes, cliffs. And now the door leading to the blue, blue canopy bed had receded to a small dark spot. Billy stomped his boot in the sand, watching it form a small crater.

"Is this an illusion they produce? Are we under some sort of drug?"

For an answer, the snake belched, though a rising wind covered much of the sound. "Damned Gila monster, already souring my stomach. Come on, we can talk later. Illusion? Ha, stand out here in a thunderstorm and you'll find out just how real things in this house can be. Illusion. Frankly, that's just part of what * + * The Society Of * + * has always worried over." The snake belched. " 'What is truth, said jesting—' " another belch—" 'Pilate.' "

As they headed for the cliffs, Bogus refused to talk anymore, arguing that talking and digestion didn't jibe in snake physiology. Billy replied that was fine, that he needed time to think anyway. His reply for some reason struck

Bogus as amusing, and the snake alternated belches and chuckles, continuing to do so for half the distance to the cliffs. *Talk about bad form*, Billy thought. But he kept that to himself, remembering how quickly the snake had struck the Gila monster.

He really never had much chance to think, for the heat made him woozy. His cheeks felt like sponges dropped into The Great Salt Lake, his stomach tossed like a small boat on top of that same lake. His feet became swollen and his hot skin grew taut. Other than an occasional blast of frighteningly cold wind from an increasingly dark cloud, he imagined himself the Pillsbury Dough Boy trapped in a Dutch Oven—baked dry and forming a deep brown crust. He mentally cursed the snake for convincing him to drink whiskey so early in the morning—or whatever hell time it was in this crazy house. He looked at his watch. It had stopped. If only he could do the same.

When Billy estimated two hours had passed, they were within a hundred yards of the cliffs. He spotted the dark opening of a cave, on a section of the cliff's face he'd already scanned at least a hundred times. Maybe the softer light of the gathering clouds revealed it. He pointed mutely and Bogus changed directions, heading upwards. The lumps in the snake's gullet had shrunk to nothing more than a small beer belly, so Billy decided to ask a question:

"What did you call those black things that cut me?"

"Huh? Oh, the clackers." Bogus easily slithered up between two boulders. Billy had to find footholds to climb. When Billy's own winded body finally appeared over the top, the snake was lounging in a pile of head-sized rocks. "Clackers. But like I said, we don't need to worry about them for a while. Have you thought of a name for your sword yet?"

Billy rolled his eyes. Before them lay a dusty path. It sloped harshly, so maybe it would pass the cave. Looking down from the boulders he'd just climbed, Billy could barely make out a small dot in the distance, which might or might not be the door to the second floor of the house and stairwell. He was so dehydrated he couldn't even wipe sweat from his brow. The blue Victorian canopy bed and Soapy seemed ridiculous to even think about.

"There's a chance we could get lost in here, isn't there? I mean lost and separated from the house."

"Oh no," the snake answered. "That could never happen. We might be killed, but I don't think we could be lost."

"That's comforting."

"Isn't it. Have you thought of a name for your sword yet?"

"Uh, no."

Bogus stuck a forked tongue out at Billy, as if reading his temperature. Then they climbed until the cave came in sight. Bogus turned to hiss, "Shh. Let me go in first."

"Gladly."

"Oh you'll have your turns, don't worry."

Billy waited outside, tightening and loosening his grip on his machete, which wasn't even wet from his palms. He was that dehydrated, though discrete raindrops did occasionally hit his face, accompanied with the same cold gusts he'd been feeling as they'd trudged the sands. The clouds were so dark now that shades of green peppered them. Another chilly wind hit him and he shivered. Peering into the cave revealed nothing.

"Bogus? Is everything okay in there?"

No answer. Because of the heavy overcast that had set in, Billy couldn't see very far into the cave. Suddenly he felt the hairs on his arm rising and a tingling in the machete. He tossed it in the air and dove into the mouth of the cave just as lightning struck a nearby boulder, sending rock shrapnel blasting the cave roof over him. The air smelled like a frazzled light socket. His machete, which must have acted as a lightning rod, glowed greenly. Wind arose then abated. The smell of ozone was so strong that Billy wanted to spit it from his mouth. Licking his lips he looked at the green and black sky.

Lightning never strikes twice, right? So he crawled toward his machete when it dimmed. Gingerly touching it, he ascertained no static electricity remained; then he noticed a hot pink piece of paper near what was left of the boulder, which had crumbled like an overdone oatmeal cookie. Keeping himself and his machete as close to the ground as possible, he crawled to the paper. Grabbing it and keeping his nose nearly on it, he read as he crawled back to the cave:

MEMORANDUM
DATE: TODAY
TO: PURCHASING EMPLOYEES
FROM: MR SCHROEDER
RE: ABSENTEEISM

IT HAS COME TO MY ATTENTION THAT SOME EMPLOYEES ARE USING SICK TIME FOR PURPOSES OTHER THAN IT WAS INTENDED, THAT IS, BEING SICK. NEITHER THE UNIVERSITY NOR THIS DEPARTMENT WILL ENDURE SUCH ACTIVITIES.

"Come on, come on, you ninny! Get inside and quit reading the funnies. Where in the world did you find them, anyway?"

Billy looked to the snake in the mouth of the cave. After another crack of lightning, he scrambled inside, keeping on all fours, much to the snake's amusement.

"What? Did the Almighty Bearded One catch you doing something naughty too? I thought he'd run his gamut with us snakes and the 'Crawl on thy belly' stuff. You humans got the rainbow, right?"

"Lightning, Bogus. Lightning struck out here. That's why I'm crawling. Didn't you hear it? It turned Frazzle green."

"Frazzle?"

"That's what I just named my sword. And I'm not reading funny papers. Look at this, would you?" He showed Bogus the memorandum, and the snake chuckled.

"You can't deny it: they've got a dandy sense of humor." Then Bogus hissed darkly. "I wouldn't let their sense of humor fool you, though, or you might wind up permanently absent from work, if you catch my drift, Poncho."

"What's with the Poncho bit? That's twice you've called me that."

"We're in the desert, aren't we? When in the desert, do as the deserters do. That's my motto."

"You know," Billy said, "All these little homilies you come up with—BDs, that's what I'm going to call them, though they're closer to BMs."

"I give. What's a BD? Or a BM?"

"BM's medical shorthand for Bowel Movement. A BD is Bogus Dictum."

Bogus grinned, revealing his teeth, clearly Teddy Roosevelt style. "BDs or BMs, you've got to admit that they pass the time. 'A dictum in rhyme passes some time.' Soapy tells me that one of your philosophers named Pascal built a whole philosophy around passing time. Too bad he didn't have Maker's Mark around, eh?" The snake twitched violently as hail pounded his hide. He and Billy retreated farther into the cave. The storm passed as quickly as a BD, and once it was over, the snake laughed wildly, looking at the ground outside the cave's mouth. "Great! Ice, just what we need to complete my little surprise." Arching in a Mary Lou Retton twist Bogus dragged a pint of Maker's Mark forward between his teeth. Billy couldn't be sure, but it looked as if Bogus had removed the pint from his own skin. Was a secret pouch sewn in?

"You fetch us some hail, and I'll fetch a glass and a bowl." As Bogus spoke, Billy stared gape-mouthed at a rocks glass and soup bowl that Bogus produced. "A rocks from under a rock. Don't dally, Poncho. Gather ye icebuds while ye may."

They spent the next hour drinking whiskey and watching hail alternate with rain. Billy spotted a funnel cloud bouncing toward where he remembered the door standing and pointed. "What if it crashes into the door?"

"It won't. Besides, there's always more than one way out of these rooms."

"This is some room. Even Vanderbilt couldn't top this for a mansion. What is it we're looking for, again? I forgot what you told me down in the kitchen."

"Ha. Nice try, Poncho, but I didn't tell you anything, because I don't know what we're looking for. I can barely know myself, as my old buddy Socrates so strongly recommended doing.* + * The Society Of *+ *, remember? And I'm a bona fide card-carrying, dues-paying member. A foundling member, truth be known. But you want to know what I know right now? Here it is: I know that we just found a rocks glass under a rock. So. So maybe we could be looking for a Piece of the Rock, or maybe the big Rock Candy Mountain. Will either of those do for our quest?"

Billy didn't even roll his eyes. Instead he thought about the weird newspaper factoid back at his own house. After all, it had made him think of a quest, it had made him call in sick. He watched the funnel picking up sand and slinking like an Indian fakir aiming a rope toward heaven. "Uh, if we're going to get blown away like Dorothy and Todo, I'd at least like to know why I'm here, where here is, and what I'm supposed to do."

"Who are Dorogy and Kodo?" the snake asked, holding the pint tightly between its upper and lower teeth and pouring two more strong drinks.

Billy caught the drunken lisp and looked back. What the hell, maybe the snake was right. Pass the time. Billy took his whiskey and commenced a long rehearsal of the Wizard of Oz, forgetting about why's, where's, and what's, forgetting the house and its desert.

The snake drank Maker's Mark and listened enraptured—at least until it began to snore.

Chapter 6

Hypnotized by the spectacular lightning, Billy had nearly dropped into R.E.M.s when he heard a rustling. For a moment he couldn't tell if he were dreaming or awake, for Soapy's swishy skirt was just what he'd been fantasizing. He straightened, bonking his head against a protruding rock on the cave's wall. Despite that pain, he smiled in the direction of the rustling and motioned at the sleeping snake. Soapy stepped out of the shadows to be lit by lightning outside. She grinned when Bogus let out an exceptional snore. The white dress she wore flashed bluish with each sheet of lightning as she tiptoed and bent to blow softly on Bogus's head, who gave a snake-sigh and curled even more.

"I missed you," Billy said, watching her golden ringlets brush against Bogus.

There was shuffling in the back of the cave.

"Alexandra?" Billy asked. Soapy nodded, placing her fingers to her lips.

"Sleep, sleep, Alexandra. It's been a long, hard day. Sleep, sleep, Alexandra," Soapy whispered.

Oddly, she seemed to be directing her incantation more at Bogus, though Billy felt his own eyelids drooping at her melodious voice. The dress she wore was split along the legs to reveal her thighs. It was just the dress he would have ordered up in his dream.

"You're beautiful," he murmured stupidly. He could smell a light peach perfume. After rustling more crinoline or silk, she sat beside him in a type of glide, holding her bare legs with her arms and rocking as the wind blew outside. Looking into her smile and that heart-shaped mouth, Billy again felt drowsy.

"Look what I found outside," he said, showing her the pink memorandum.

But she didn't look, she only continued that hypnotic rocking as the storm lit her dress and her face. Billy yawned. "It's a note from work. Bogus says it's a joke by *Them*, but he won't tell me who *They* are." Billy placed heavy emphasis on both the mysterious T words. Soapy's rocking continued.

Rocking, rocking, rocking.

Billy blinked.

Rocking, rocking, rocking.

What had at first been sensual turned spooky. She was now humming and leaning ever closer.

Her eyes, something about her eyes. Billy scrambled aside and grabbed the machete, just as she lunged where he'd been sitting, breaking off splinters of rock with elongated nails. What had been Soapy was grunting like a pig while trying to free its nails, which had embedded in the cave's wall.

"Kill it! Kill it! It's not Soapy, it's a phantom! Kill it before it frees itself."

Billy recognized Bogus's shouting, just as the thing tore its right hand free and turned to slash at him. One look at its spattered red eyes told him Bogus was right: it wasn't Soapy, for those eyes sparkled with flames and those teeth flashed metallic. As another sheet of lightning filled the sky, a purple tongue snaked out from the creature. Billy sliced hard with his machete, cutting the tongue and sending slivers of crystal onto the cave's floor. With a heavy back swing he hit the creature's head. More crystal shards scattered. The creature still struggled to free its left hand from the wall, slashing all the while with its free right one. With one more downward swing of his machete, Billy stopped the struggle and left only a death throe.

Bogus, meanwhile, had coiled and was testing the air with his finely forked tongue.

"There's something in the back of the cave, I think," Billy said, gasping for air. "I heard a noise and thought it was Alexandra before ... this."

Without comment, the snake slithered in that direction. Billy backed against a wall and watched as best he could whenever lightning reflected in the clouds outside. Where the false Soapy had been now lay a mound of broken, shimmering glass.

"Nothing that I can sense or see," Bogus said, crawling back. But when he got near Billy, he shook his head and twitched in the lightning. A signal?

"Care for a drink after all the action?"

"No thanks," Billy answered, raising his brow at the bravura of Bogus's voice. "I don't think that would be particularly smart for either of us."

"Sure it would," Bogus continued loudly. "Relax our nerves, Poncho. Make hair grow on our chests anyway. Or at least yours—I keep rubbing mine off by crawling on the ground. Hey, I *insist* we have a last drink."

Again, in the lightning, Billy could see the snake twitch. Didn't his voice sound awfully brash? For a moment, Billy wondered if the snake were another phantom, but no—that grin was too churlish to belong to anyone else. The snake coughed. *Ah, a signal*, Billy thought, giving himself the boulder-head award.

"Come on," Bogus insisted, clinking the bottle against Billy's glass and knocking it over. "Straighten that up for me, would you, Poncho ol' doggie?" Billy leaned to straighten the glass. "You're right, there's another phantom back there," Bogus whispered. "I saw it for just a minute, behind a rock where I couldn't strike. It's smaller than this one, but just as deadly if its claws are poisoned. It's waiting for us to go back to sleep. They're all scared mindless of fire, though, and for good reason, so pour a good dollop of Maker's Mark in your glass and I'll light it."

Billy did as he was told.

"That's good, Poncho," Bogus said, resuming with his loud, cattle-call voice. And why don't we share a cee-gar, sort of a male bonding ritual since we don't have any spears to toss." Somehow, Bogus pulled out a Bic lighter from his skin and tossed it to Billy, who lit it and held it to the whiskey, warming it nearly a minute until it caught with a blue flame. "Follow me," Bogus whispered, his tongue flicking in Billy's right ear, "and toss glass and all at the rock I point out."

They tiptoed about twenty feet into the cave and stood still, waiting for another flash of lightning. The glass was becoming hot and Billy was afraid it was going to break before he could throw it. As lightning flashed, though, he spotted a bluish glimmer behind a stone about the size of a wastebasket. Bogus said, "Give it a toss, Poncho." Billy did, and ghostly blue flame covered the rock. There was a scream then a fiery yellow bursting, like hundreds of ladyfinger firecrackers popping.

"What a waste of good whiskey," Bogus commented when quiet took over. A strange, dusty ozone smell filled the air.

"What are we going to do? Could there be more back there? Or could there be other things?"

"Nothing else tonight, anyway."

At the sound of that voice, Bogus and Billy both whirled about. Standing in the cave's mouth were Soapy and Alexandra. Billy squeezed the hilt of his machete.

"Don't worry, we're real this time. That's how we found you: when they stole a patch of our secondary essence, we tracked it down."

Billy watched Soapy's outline as she danced large, slow-mo gestures against the stormy sky. Blue sparkles trailed wherever her arms went. The bells on Alexandra's harness jingled softly. To Billy's right, Bogus stuck out his tongue. In the lightning, Billy saw curved, inch-long fangs slowly morphing into Roosevelt teeth.

"It's them, all right," Bogus said. "Soapy and Alexandra. They're giving off heat. That's why I never woke when those phantoms entered the cave: they don't give off heat because they're made of crystallized saltpeter and metal."

Soapy finished what looked like a solo ballet, and a bluish glow hung along the mouth of the cave. Though lightning lit the sky outside severely, thunder was nearly non-existent, or at least it barely penetrated past that blue glow.

"We'll be okay now," Soapy said, walking into the cave. Alexandra's bells jingled in agreement as Soapy approached Billy to sit down exactly as the phantom had, holding her legs close to her body with her arms and rocking.

"What's wrong?" she asked as Billy scooted away.

"Uh ..." He explained his reserve, more to Bogus than to her or Alexandra, as he was still uncertain.

"That makes sense." She gave him her reassuring valentine-heart smile.

"They captured a patch of my secondary essence after all, so we would act and look alike."

More lightning sheeted outside, and Billy peered into Soapy's eyes—so moist, so soft. Though he couldn't quite make out their blue in the dark, they certainly didn't emit any glowing red.

Bogus burped. "Told you once they were real. Told once is gold, told twice is mold."

"Okay, okay," Billy said, moving closer to her.

Soapy touched his hand and he jumped, not from fear, but from passing amperage. Her smiling teeth reflected a pure, pure white when another display of lightning lit the cave. Billy stared, entranced; for just a moment, he'd seen that oceanic blue...

"Ahem. Don't mind me, you two. I'm going back to sleep."

Bogus immediately let out a snore. Somewhere off in the back of the cave, Billy could hear Alexandra's faint, happy jingling. Or was that his heart?

Chapter 7

"The phantom might have folded its legs and it might have rocked like I do, but I bet it couldn't kiss like I do..."

As Soapy tugged him downward, all Billy could think of was the tingling on the crown of his head—that and the soft, soft lips touching his. Lightning danced outside ... soft, soft, electrical lips. Had this been what went missing from his and Linda's marriage? No, the physical side was fine. What then? The omnipresent and mysterious "basic personality conflict"? If that was the case, then just what had bring-brung-brought them together in the first place? ... Soft, soft, electrical lips working his own, like they were fluffing a pillow. He felt Soapy's breasts brush his arm and chest, he felt the angular bone of her hip, he felt heat rising in his body despite the storm howling outside the cave, and with a flash like lightning he knew the answer to his question, about what had brought him and Linda together in the first place. Duh. The obvious.

I can't believe I'm going to do this, he told himself on realizing that answer.

"Wait." He pulled from Soapy and removed her clasping hands to set them on his knobby knees, which had already scrunched defensively. "Uh, we need to get to know one another first. After all, I'm not even sure that you're human. Maybe you're a ghost or witch or something."

"Something," she repeated ambiguously. But no inhuman ambiguity dotted her heavy breathing. Since the lightning outside suddenly abated, Billy had to accept her statement in the dark of the cave, or rather in the dim of the bluish glow still etching the ceiling and walls from whatever incantation she'd performed at the cave's mouth. In that blue glow, her hair reminded him of spun decorations used on Christmas trees. And under the tree, a present he so wanted to open. Still, he repeated what he'd just said,

"Wait."

Hearing her sigh, he sighed in response. The word "wait" suddenly seemed the stupidest word in the English language. But when she moved her hands along his thigh, he persevered, for he wasn't going to open himself to another ridiculous Linda affair based on lust. Even witchland lust.

"Wait. Soapy, what were you doing when you first came into the cave? With your arms, I mean, and with that bluish glow."

Her hand twittered a dance on his leg. "A banishing ritual to protect us for the night. At sunrise tomorrow it'll disappear and we're on our own."

"What's a banishing ritual? You need to remember that I'm a computer programmer working for the purchasing department of a university. Anything beyond a binary yes or no confuses me." He expected her to grunt some low curse just as Linda always did when he announced something like that. Instead, she laughed amiably.

"A banishing ritual offers protection. This specific one—" she stretched to motion toward the blue glow—"calls upon the aid and protection of lesser elementals." As he shifted, she added, "Elementals are beings that aren't quite rational, but not completely irrational either."

"Sounds like most humans I know. Including myself," he added.

She laughed again. "Some banishing rituals can call on angels and higher, more powerful beings, but phantoms and clackers are really small fry, so there was no need for that. I watched you dealing with the clackers in the hall, by the way. Very well done, my hero." She gave his knee a squeeze and her breath floated warmly about his body.

This wait business, he thought, *can be tough*, but then he focused on what Soapy'd just said. "You saw? You mean you were close by in another room, testing me just like he—" Billy gave a nod toward the sleeping Bogus curled about a rock—"like he was?" Billy grimaced, though he knew his facial contortion was wasted in the semi-dark.

"Of course I wasn't testing you. Billy, you need to remember that the house can work *against* us as well as for us. I was in another room, all right, but no closer to you than we are to the staircase right now. You saw how far away *it* was when there was still light outside this cave, didn't you?" After an assenting Billy-grunt, she continued, "So there was nothing I could do but watch."

"I don't understand this house. It's like a maze, it's—well, what is it?"

"We've been trying to learn the answer to that for ... for a long time."

Billy noticed the catch in her voice. A long time. Was she as old as Aristotle Bogus Riddle claimed to be? Centuries? Millennia? He rubbed the back of her hand and felt elastic veins. *Take me to your spa, fraulein.* She shifted and he felt warm skin not so terra firma, and its soft-soft-soft sent amperage flowing. But before his first inhalation was completed, he remembered his grand mission of "Wait." *Damn that word anyway. Who can stay pure in a dark, cold cave?*

When his arms moved to clasp her, Soapy spoke: "Let me show you something about the house. The knowledge will come in handy."

He could feel her shift off the blanket that had somehow spread beneath them, and in the blue glow he saw her on her knees gazing about. Focusing, he could see outlines of the walls. Soapy tugged his wrist, so he crawled after her, scraping his knees on outcropping, sharp rocks. In a kind of compensation her hips bumped his shoulders. She was humming something that reminded him of the time he'd attended a Catholic Church service with a girlfriend. Any minute he expected to smell incense and see four or five cassocked, castrati boys. Then she stopped crawling and clapped her hands softly. A harsh light popped over their heads, yellow like a mosquito bulb. Billy stiffened at its intensity.

Directly before them, under the globe's light, the cave's wall ascended in perfect smoothness, almost like wood paneling. Billy edged forward to sniff: it even smelled of musty wood. Then he spotted two porcelain knobs. The wall mimicked a drawer—no, it *was* a drawer, he was sure of that, though Soapy didn't open it.

"See? There are always parts of the room remaining just as when you first entered, parts hidden away in any eventual landscape that develops. You just have to stay alert to find them."

He remembered Bogus saying the same thing, so he leaned to touch a cool knob, though Soapy stopped him from pulling the drawer open. "Bad Form to do that unless it's absolutely necessary." The way she enunciated the phrase "Bad Form" left no doubt that its words were chiseled in capital letters. Billy squatted back onto his heels.

"Bogus is into Bad Form too. What's Bad Form supposed to mean? Is the house alive? Will it get mad if I open the drawers ahead of time? Will the mysterious *they* kill us?"

Soapy touched his cheek. "I don't know. But we'd lose our self-respect, and that can be as bad as being killed, can't it?"

Billy wasn't so sure of that, but he let the knob go and simply leaned to sniff the drawer. It was wood all right, but even in the yellow light from the globe hovering overhead, any seams separating the wooden drawer from the cave's rock wall remained invisible. The house certainly held surprises. He thought of the pink slip, then patted his pockets and straightened.

"Look at this, speaking of Bad Form." He handed Soapy the memorandum, which looked more green than pink under the yellow light.

She frowned after reading the note. "Listen to me, Billy. You can't let them get to you this way." She grabbed his face to turn it toward hers. "Don't worry about your job. Time doesn't run the same here in the house. Only hours pass outside, when days or weeks pass here. The job outside will be there when you finish here. If you even want it then … or … or if you ever finish."

"*If* I ever finish? Hold on. It's not like I enlisted in the House's Homeland Security for this, you know. Maybe I don't even want to fin—"

Soapy covered his mouth with her palm, which was moist and hot. *So she's scared, too,* he thought.

"Let me guess," he said, removing her hand. "It's Bad Form to say what I was going to say."

"That's right. You're learning."

Just looking into her large eyes made him once more regret saying, "Wait," for their blue took on a luxurious luminescence and the yellow globe overhead easily passed for a full moon in his romantic mood.

Letting go of his face, Soapy lightly clapped her hands and the burning globe vanished. "You've learned something from our little talk. You should be happy about that. Like I said, it might come in handy."

In what seemed sudden total darkness, he heard her shifting, once more opening her body language to him. He stiffened at her warmth, even though they weren't touching, and he could smell a fruity perfume. Were they going take up where they'd left off? *Oh boy, oh boy, the hell with waiting.* He closed his eyes and leaned for a kiss. When he opened them, she was gone.

Chapter 8

"Ahem. A-ahem."

Back on the blanket Soapy left, Billy awoke to Bogus's fake coughing and the smell of greasy cooking. The snake was lounging on a low flat rock near the cave's mouth, evidently supping coffee from an indentation, for Billy could now smell brewed coffee too.

"Let me ask you something," Billy said, propping himself up on an elbow. "How come you ate that nasty Gila monster yesterday if you can get Maker's Mark, coffee, and breakfast anytime you want?"

"I can get coffee and Maker's Mark anytime I want. Those were my two wishes."

"You had two wishes and those were what you wished for?"

"You got better suggestions?"

Billy rubbed sleep from his eyes and noticed a cup of coffee by his leg. He lifted it and smelled the aroma, halfway wishing himself into the warm cup, since the storm had left the cave chilly.

"Well, I might wish I was out of here and back at work."

"Better think it over. Have to leave Soapy if you get that wish. That's why I kept mine simple. Otherwise the wish can backfire." Bogus cleared his throat and sang operatically: "When you wish up-on a star, you can wi-ind up real-ly marred."

Billy looked at the blue blanket he lay on and was quiet. "Your BD's are bad enough when you say them, but when you sing them in a fake Disney voice they for sure turn to BM's." Outside, Billy saw that the sun ... well, *a* sun or something *like* a sun was shining and the rain had stopped. "But no, Bogus, I guess I don't have a better wish, not right now. But if I get an opportunity I might."

"Wish for lemon wedges. They'll go great with the Maker's Mark and prevent beri-beri too."

Sipping the coffee, Billy sat up and leaned against the wall. Something was protruding into his ribs; he twisted to see a knob to the dresser.

"She showed me this part of the house last night. She explained that it might come in handy."

Bogus smacked his snake lips. "She—Soapy—showed—you two took time to explore the house? And you question my choice of wishes? The two of you alone—for all practical purposes—in a cave on a stormy night and the best you can do is fumble with an old dresser? What? Thinking of opening an antique shop? Hey, Soapy *is* a girl, you know. You *are* a boy—*aren't* you?" Bogus angrily splashed coffee in the puddle as he swayed. Billy didn't bother to answer.

"So what's cooking?" Billy asked after a few more sips of caffeine.

"Eat first; then I'll tell you."

Billy crawled toward the fire at the cave's mouth and sleepily looked into the pan. "Chicken nuggets. Great, I'm starved."

"Go ahead, I'm still digesting the Gila monster."

Billy made a face at the snake, who looked even fatter today. Then he removed the pan from the fire and popped two nuggets into his mouth. They were so hot that he had to suck in cooling air. After several more, he grew fond of their sweetness, which wasn't really chicken, but then wasn't really not chicken. Frog legs? Turtle? Rabbit? Low-fat turkey franks cut into nibble-sized bites? Finishing the last he rubbed his fingers in the pan, justifying his crudity by the fact that he hadn't eaten all day yesterday.

"They're great. What are they?"

"Some type of larvae I found growing outside in a downed tree. Palmetto bug, maybe."

Billy dropped the pan and stared at the snake.

"Hey, it could have been worse, it could have been chopped Gila monster."

"I think I'll have another cup of coffee." Billy tried to suppress the quiver working his stomach, but couldn't, and his whole frame shook. The snake was chuckling as it took Billy's coffee cup in its teeth and filled it from the pot near the fire. Billy leaned back and sniffed the coffee, trying to forget his breakfast *haut cuisine* and wondering if he shouldn't go ahead with that first wish, the one about being out of the house and back in purchasing.

***

"What are you doing?" he asked on opening his eyes after finishing his second coffee. The snake, pencil in mouth, was carefully drawing something. Not answering, it continued to draw for a minute or so, then dropped the pencil.

"Mapping the position of the drawer for the council. We keep a central map in our library's filing cabinet."

"Filing cabinet? Don't you use computers?"

"Did you see any electrical outlets in the house? Did you? If you do, I'll be happy to learn whatdyacallit Pasquale, Cobalt, or some other computer language. Maybe invite Bill Gates to host a weekend seminar. Computers? Hell, we're lucky to sneak in a newspaper from your world. But enough gab. We shouldn't hang around in this cave too long—"

"Bad Form?" Billy asked.

"How about poor health practice. They surely have a bearing on us from the two phantoms last night."

They. Billy was getting used to the word and looked around for his machete, spotting it ten feet away. He stood and grabbed it. "No harm can come to us when Frazzle is near," he proclaimed loudly, licking his lips unsurely.

Bogus chuckled and used his teeth to fold map he'd been drawing. "Open that lower drawer, would you?"

"Is this another test?" Billy stared at the drawer, imagining all sorts of creatures springing out.

"Nope, nothing like that. You've proven yourself to me, anyway. The drawer's safe: only twice in my entire nine hundred millennia have I seen occasions where clackers have been able to infiltrate the house's passages." The snake twitched. "Of course ... both those times the people using the passage were killed."

"Uh … killed. As in permanent, I suppose." The snake shrugged in answer to Billy's query. "I don't suppose *you* want to crawl on over here and open the lower drawer then."

"Be happy to, but eventually you need to know what to expect and how to react on your own. It'll look good on your résumé."

"My résumé. Uh, I don't think so."

"Mmm. Soapy'd love to have you stay and work here. She'd give you a great reference. Mmm, how's that old Platters tune go? Let's see … dah-da-da-daah-du-da-dah … mee-ting in Soapy places, hi-ding in Soapy corners … Soapy gets i-i-in your eyes" Bogus warbled this out as he folded the map, which he tucked somewhere in his golden hide, no doubt in one of the evil-looking brown hourglasses, the same place that he kept all those somehow clankless bottles of Maker's Mark. Billy didn't exactly plug his ears, but he did flinch at several off-key snake notes.

"So, uh, you're telling me that this résumé idea is important to—" There was a flicker and Billy shook his head. "Uh, the blue glow that Soapy conjured. It just left."

"Stayed longer than it should have anyway," Bogus commented, "Sun's been up nearly an hour." Though the snake's voice stayed nonchalant, its ridiculous teeth were replaced with fangs. "That girl's a real catch. Me, I'd love to be some life form other than scaly and find a beauty like her for myself. You though, you better quit dealing in antique dressers, if you want to give all the other charmers hanging around her a run for their money."

Billy raised his eyebrows at the word *other*. Bogus coiled and looked expectantly to the wood drawer stuck in the cave's wall. "Okay, okay, I'll open it," Billy said. "I'm just not sure how to enter 'opening drawers' on my résumé."

On tugging at the wood, which slid smoothly, Billy noticed fog trickling out one corner.

"Damn! Jump back, Poncho!"

Billy did, holding his machete to the ready. The fog subsided, though, and a simple brightness emitted from the open drawer, which rested only half a foot from the cave's floor.

The snake crawled over and peeked in. "False alarm. They must have tried but were unable. Well, well. Poncho, the council might be right about you after all. The clackers certainly are going to a lot of trouble to get you. Or rather, someone's going to a lot of trouble to send them after you." Bogus nudged Billy's hand. "Here, let me go in first, just in case. This does make two times, though. Let's remember whose turn it is next." Bogus slithered halfway up the drawer and twisted to address Billy. "What's going to happen is that we'll end up directly at the top of the staircase where we first entered the room, so don't get upset. It's a Keyway, just like the bathtub in the bottom of the pond. You might want to keep Frazzle on alert, though Soapy's probably zapped the area of any evil-wishers."

"Okay, I'm ready."

"*Hasta la vista, Poncho.*"

The snake disappeared, slithering in headfirst. Leaning to watch, Billy thought he caught a glimpse of the staircase's banister in the bottom of the drawer, but wasn't sure. Then all he could see was a bright light that hurt his eyes. He lifted a foot but hesitated. There was a clattering behind, from the mouth of the cave. He turned to see a troop of clackers perched on entranceway rocks and one another's shoulders.

"Frazzle!" Billy yelled, brandishing his machete and hopping into the drawer with both feet.

Chapter 9

What seemed a myriad of arms pulled at him. He looked down briefly at the living room below and realized that he'd landed on the banister upside-down, on his head, just as he had in the meadow. But even as he teetered, he was pulled to safety by Soapy and Alexandra, who stood on either side of him, and by Bogus, who wrapped around his left leg.

"I told you he was the one," Soapy said. "Why else would They go to all this trouble?"

"Are you s-sure it was Them?" Bogus hissed. "They can't re-cast the metaphysics of the house anymore than we can, can they?"

Balanced upright, Billy looked from one to the other. Alexandra was clothed in a green blouse and shorts with brass bells attached in a belt. They were still tinkling from pulling him off the banister. Looking at her radiant face, Billy thought that this must be her true shape, that of a small, auburn-haired girl.

"Telegram for Mr. Wise, telegram for Mr. Wise."

They turned to see an overweight, pink boy with piggy eyes, dressed in a red velour suit. He stood about two feet tall.

"An elemental," Alexandra exclaimed. "How cute!" She pulled a bracelet of bells from her pocket and jangled them at the figure. The pink boy wavered, seeming to lose solidity.

"Not an evil one, or your bells would have driven it off," Soapy commented.

"Maybe, maybe not. It's-s s-still wavering," Bogus warned.

"Telegram for Mr. Wise, telegram for Mr. Wise," the pink pigboy repeated, blinking at the bells.

"Bes-st to ignore it."

"I think it's cute," Alexandra said, producing a second bracelet and ringing bells all around the pink boy now. The figure barely reacted to the sound this time.

"Telegram for Mr. Wise, telegram for Mr. Wise."

Billy freed himself of Soapy's arm and neared the boy, whose face was more piggish than human with a pink snout lifted upwards. Billy kept his machete ready, but the pigboy looked straight into Billy's eyes, ignoring the machete completely.

"Telegram for—"

"I'm Mr. Wise."

"Do you have any identification?"

Billy felt in his pocket and realized he'd left his wallet far back in his house—wherever that dwelling was now. Then he remembered the obituary and the pink memorandum. He showed the latter to the boy, who seemed to take it at face value and handed over the telegram, then waited as Billy read it:

Mr. Wise:

The great state of Alabama is *wise* to your tricks. You have two hours to get to work, or a governor's conference will be held revealing your sloth and indolence, not to mention that your desk's contents will be audited, and any missing paper clips, envelopes, jump drives, or pens will be duly noted as stolen state property. I trust that I needn't remind you that theft or knowledgeable receipt of stolen state goods is punishable by imprisonment in a booth that continually replays outdated National Public Radio newscasts. Be advised, Mr. Wise. Stop.

"Do you have a response?" the pigboy asked, brushing lint off his red velour and giving a shake to a corkscrew tail. "I'm supposed to wait for a tip and a response."

"Nuts."

"Sir?"

"Nuts. That's my response."

"And here's your tip." Alexandra leaned to kiss the elemental on the cheek and drop a bracelet into his outstretched hand. When she did this, the pink boy disappeared in a puff of smoke nearly as red as his coat.

"What a mean trick, Alexandra," Soapy said giving a tsk. "Those bells will drive all his elemental friends berserk."

For an answer, Alexandra jangled her many remaining bells.

"I've made the appointment for ten o'clock," Soapy said.

"Appointment?" Billy shook his head and displayed the note. "Uh, do you think they'll really look in my desk?"

Bogus laughed. "Aha! So you have been stealing from the state!"

Instead of missing paper clips and mouse pads, Billy thought of the *Playboy* centerfold with the lipstick print on its nipples. Linda must have rummaged three used bookstores to find it. Just how would it play with the wave of political correctness flooding Alabama's campus? How would it play with the women he worked with, period? About as well, he decided, as this house was playing with him.

Second Leg: A Loop

Chapter 10

On the way downstairs, Soapy explained that Billy was to have a job interview with Mr. Snelling, chairman of the board for the house. Before Billy could respond, Alexandra shape-shifted into a gazelle and bounded over the banister to drop fifteen feet down to the living room, her hooves skittering on its hardwood floor. In mock anger, she tilted her horns at some imaginary creature, then pranced before the over-sized fireplace. Billy stood flat-footed, then caught up with Soapy and Bogus, who were evidently used to Alexandra's pranks.

"Is she—"

"Fine, just frisky. Let's worry about your interview instead of her antics."

"Uh, how can I go to a job interview when I don't even know what job I'm applying for? Besides, I already have a job with the University of Alabama." *Which I should be getting back to.*

"Just be yourself," Soapy blithely advised.

"Plenty of job security in that," Bogus chuckled while crawling underneath Billy's feet.

"Thanks," Billy answered, nearly slipping on the steps to avoid the snake. Looking down into the living room, it seemed to Billy that Alexandra was just as far away as before, though they'd taken at least ten steps. He noticed a musty odor hanging in the air. Instinct told him that this odor had been hanging around earth forever, bothering grandmothers, pet dogs, grandchildren, cats, gerbils, and gazelles in an equally bedeviling manner. He sniffed, then counted on his fingers as he walked down the steps. It was distinctly the fourth time he'd vaguely smelled this same something.

Distinctly, vaguely? Ha. That syntax clicked with everything swirling in the crazy house: Aristotle Bogus Riddle; a changeling kid who could be a deer one minute, a gazelle another, and who-knows-what jangling, bell-bedecked creature another; and a nymph named Soapy who could create floating yellow balls or walls of blue light. Wasn't light supposed to be God's job? Maybe, Billy mused, that was the job he was applying for: Gabriel. But then why stop there? Forget horn-tooting, what about Godhead itself? Billy cringed, expecting a bolt of lightning to surf along the banister and crash gigantically against his head. Having a snake crawling between his legs didn't help. The place was getting to him.

When lightning didn't come, he remembered the telegram in his pocket, supposedly from work; he remembered years of sitting at his squeaking, armless chair in that huge open office besieged by the pale, same-same faces of eighteen accountants and purchasing agents. M/F, B/W, under thirty/over sixty, it didn't matter—they all gazed at the ledgers with the same numbness as their squeaking, armless chairs. And every single day, they all demanded some minor change in a computer program to make their lives easier. "Could you design a program that knows when to shift out of the encumbered column into the paid column? Could you design a program that audits itself? Could you design a program that turns the computer off and on at the right times? Could you . . ." Maybe a new job was just what the doctor ordered. When Sir Galahad the knight applied for a job, it was to find the Holy Grail. When Lancelot applied for a job, it was to protect the court of King Arthur. *Yes, Billy boy, and look what happened to that last arrangement, with Guinevere and all.*

Finally, they neared the bottom of the stairs. Billy shook his head at the time the trip had taken and glanced back: the staircase now stretched at least a quarter mile long. *Damn this weird house, anyway.*

"Soapy?"

She stood two steps ahead, and when she turned he forgot the stupid staircase to rivet on her eyes. *Wait? Wait?—I can't believe I said that to her. Boy, am I ever stupid.* Maybe that's the job I'm applying for: professional waiter—don't bother with tips since I won't be the kind that carries out food and drinks: I'll just stare at some clock and occasionally burp out, *Uh, wait.*

"Yes Billy?"

He shook his head. "Uh, the staircase. Why—" he turned to see the staircase had diminished to its original length—"Never mind."

"You'll get used to it, pal," Bogus said, picking something out of Billy's cuff that looked like a cave bug, then giving a crunch and a slurp.

That's exactly what I'm afraid of, Billy thought.

Alexandra remained prancing before the fireplace, but on hearing Bogus's mealtime etiquette she darted toward the long, dark corridor, the one Billy had only stepped into, the one with the regal double doors over half a mile toward its end. The corridor was still dim, to say the least, and on hearing a clatter, Billy held his machete tightly and intoned the word "Frazzle." That word echoed reassuringly off the walls. The floor was still composed of heavy-looking large cut stone, so at least one thing in the house had remained the same since he'd entered . . . last night? Billy scuffed his boot and realized this stonework was what you'd expect in an English castle.

Bogus yelped at Alexandra. From the snake's urgency, Billy figured that Bogus's teeth were no longer Jimmy Carter/Teddy Roosevelt, but had metamorphosed into viperous needles.

"Frazzle," Billy shouted again. Again, the word bounced off the stones. He couldn't believe how long this corridor was. Alexandra, who'd run ahead, looked small.

"We're late, we're late, we're late, for a very important date," the snake said proudly, like he was quoting the Rolling Stones or Lady Gaga. Well, maybe there wasn't any danger, maybe Bogus was just anxious. Still, Billy didn't relax his grip on the machete.

After twenty minutes, they'd passed maybe fifty doors on each side, hearing their steps echoing on the stone. Another architectural impossibility, given that the outside of the house could have been . . . Billy shook his head, not even bothering with the math. Still running, Alexandra butted her horns against the regal doors at the end of the hall.

"Come on," Soapy said, "Let's catch up with her."

"The catch-up never lets up," Bogus said. He picked up his pace, so Billy did too.

Alexandra butted the door again, on seeing them approaching.

"Enter, enter," replied a singsong male voice.

The ten-foot high doors opened, not with a Hollywood squeak, but with a soundful silence. Looking over Soapy's head and Alexandra's horn, Billy saw that the walls of the room were constructed of large gray castle stones that matched the hallway's floor. He also spotted an oversized maroon canopy, presumably for a bed, though there was so much junk piled where the foot would have been that he couldn't be sure. The canopy itself needed a semi-permanent visit to a dry cleaner's.

"Ah, the candidate has joined us," the singsong voice warbled as a pink cushion dropped to the floor.

Candidate? Billy was tempted to shout out, "Family values! Tax cuts! Your special interest is my special interest! Make Alabama Great!" But he only walked quietly and humbly toward the voice, trying to locate its source. The canopy indeed did cover a bed, and on that bed lay pink satin sheets, straight from some cornball country song. The clutter at the bed's foot consisted of multi-colored throws, pillows, blankets, and an occasional silver mug lying askew in the obscuring pile. A singular cough brought Billy's attention to the only other furniture in the room: a large, weather-beaten roll-top desk behind the bed. On the wall over the desk was an incomprehensible blue sign: Snelli *Chez* ng. A gnarled, white-haired woman rolled into view on a chair, pumping her fat legs. She was bent, and ridiculously reached to dip a quill into a silver inkstand, evidently to record something Bogus had just said that Billy hadn't caught. She wore a mint green suit and her right cheek bulged as if she kept a wad of chewing tobacco locked inside. There was something odd about the suit...

"Ah, the candidate himself." This voice came from the center of the bed. Billy still couldn't locate its source because of all the clutter. Then several pink pillows sloughed aside and an old man dressed in a white sleeping gown with a matching sleeping cap stretched. Vintage Charles Dickens. He stretched again and a fat orange cat in his lap looked up in annoyance. The man's hand dropped onto the cat's fur; Billy wasn't even sure that the old coot was looking at him, though only five feet separated them. The cat, though, gave

Billy an indignant glance then moved to a pillow beside the old man's knee. A second, smaller gray tiger-stripe jumped into the old man's lap.

"Mrs. Snelling!" the old guy yelped, seeming disoriented. Then he actually stood up in the bed, and Billy could see that he was a true dwarf. His eyes bulged and his lips curled at one end in a permanent ironic twist to reveal large yellow teeth. Starting to bounce as if on a trampoline he rubbed his hands together. "Are the candidate's papers and résumé in order?"

"They cl-are indeed, Mr. Snelling. Cl-would you cw-are to see them?"

That was spoken by the woman at the desk. To say her speech was syrupy would be kind; it was thicker than swampwater pabulum, to quote a famous ex-wife. This woman too was a dwarf. With a thwack she shut a small drawer in the roll-top and moved whatever she'd stashed in her mouth to the other cheek. Billy looked at her frayed mint-green suit, expecting tobacco spittle stains, but saw contorted faces sewn wil-nil into the fabric's design. Her mouth also carried an ironic twist, though that twist tended toward a snarl.

"Certainly, certainly, of course I would," the old guy shouted, pulling Billy's attention back as he jumped and landed on his butt, to the annoyance of the two cats who hissed. "Would you show our other guests into the tea room while I read the résumé and conduct the interview, Mrs. Snelling?"

Instead of responding, the old woman slipped a roll of papers into a copper tube, which she dropped into a hole in the desk, giving it a hard slam with her palm. There was rattling in the floor underneath, then a pop behind the old man's head as the copper tube shot onto a pillow to his left. The orange cat hissed, the gray tiger-stripe fidgeted.

Soapy gave Billy's hand a squeeze, winked and pecked his cheek. On that instant, his cheek burned and no less than three stars glazed his eyes.

Bogus slithered over to whisper from a half coil. "Keep a stiff upper lip with the old man, mate."

Alexandra, as usual, had skittered and already stood by a large, darkly stained oak door to the far left. She looked small there, which made Billy realize just how grand the room was, full enough to hold summertime dances for a mid-sized town. With a cough, the old woman pushed up from her desk and hobbled directly in front of him, huffing like a steam locomotive.

It wasn't tobacco she was chewing in her chugging cheeks, for her breath left a hot cinnamon ball wake as she headed toward the oak door in such a cambering movement that Billy worried she was having a heart attack. On reaching the door she gave three or four jerks that popped her bones, then yanked at a large brass handle to open the door. As the others followed her into the second room, the bed's inhabitant coughed and vaguely motioned Billy toward him, patting a pink pillow as if he wanted to tell a bedtime story.

"This," the old man said, pausing for either breath or emphasis while picking up the copper tube, "this is a crossroads in your life. Are you ready to accept the responsibility?"

Irritating how the old guy wouldn't look at him, but kept petting pillows or cats. The oak door slammed rudely to Billy's left.

"Uh, responsibility? I don't even know what type of uh job I'm supposedly applying for." Billy wondered if the old guy sucked cinnamon balls too. He sniffed, but the bed smelled like cat and old people roiling in musk.

The old coot threw the tube down so hard that the fat yellow cat jumped off the bed. Snatching at its fluffy tail but missing, he scooted to the right of the mattress and called the cat, leaving his pale rear-end exposed in a too-short sleeping gown. Twisting and giving a tiny-lipped smile, he scooted to the left, grabbed a pink cushion and crooked a finger not a foot from Billy's face. Billy stiffened, trying to peripherally see where the cat was.

"Come here, you young ninny. I'm not a phantom or a demon. Come here, I want to tell you something privately."

Billy leaned. The old geezer's teeth must have been the product of some delirious dentist. They protruded at top and bottom in a yellow parade that actually gave color to his face, for except about a million liver spots, his skin glowed as white as his bedclothes. Maybe he'd once been an accountant for Alabama, working nightshift to cook the books.

"Take the girl—what's her name, Sophia, Sophie?"

"Soapy," Billy corrected.

The dwarf gave a piercing laugh, more like a howl, evidently finding the name humorous. "Soapy. All cleaned up for a watered-down age." Then he grabbed Billy's shirt. "Take her. Why do you care *what* the job description is as long as you have *her*, eh? It could be digging ditches in drifting dunes and you'd still get a sparkle of energy whenever you slid under the sheets with that one." He let go Billy's shirt to clutch a pink pillow to his groin and laugh, "Soapy, Soapy. All cleaned up." Spittle flew from his mouth as his laugh turned into a chant and he stood to dance in the bed. "Soapy, Soapy, all cleaned up. Soapy, Soapy, all cleaned up."

Billy, figuring he was encountering his first dirty old man—why not, he was divorced and thrown among the unclean—said, "Soapy's fine, but don't you think I ought to at least know a few things about this so-called job before you hire me and before I accept it?"

"Don't you think I ought …" the old man squeaked in a mocking voice and fell back onto the bed. "Is there a scared mouse in here? Quick, Slasher, get it!" Flipping over to show his rear end again he crawled about bed to tug at the gray tiger stripe cat. "Here, help me find Pussy and I'll let you know plenty about this job."

"I beg your pardon?"

The old guy turned to face Billy: "Pussy, the orange cat, damn it. Did you think I meant Mrs. Snelling?" The old geezer raised a white eyebrow and leered. "If she heard that, she'd take that quill of hers and fill you so full of holes that you'd sink, even in air. Then she'd stitch your face into a pocket of that damnable green outfit of hers so she could prick and torture you for eternity." He leaned over the bed, sticking out his milky legs and pink rear end to call his cat. Billy backed off to help search.

"Here it is, down on the floor at the foot of the bed."

"Well, lift her up and bring her to me."

Billy did as he was told and got scratched for his thanks.

"See? You're learning about this job already. Don't trust animals. And that includes humans of all shapes." Pulling the orange cat to him Mr. Snelling began to stroke its ears. Amazingly, the tiger stripe opened the copper cylinder and unrolled the papers out on the bed. The old man glanced at them. "Your résumé says you're a computer analyst. Is that anything like an alchemist?"

"No sir, it's—"

"A joke, son. Relax. We get newspapers here. About a year ago Mrs. Snelling was going to buy ten or so thousand computers and scatter them around, brighten things and modernize the place. But she decided no. Never told me why. I think she's afraid of that Carpel Tunnel Syndrome stuff. Lord knows I wouldn't want to catch it. Couldn't pet my Pussy." He looked up slyly for a response, but Billy kept his face blank, so the old guy went on: "Besides, we don't have electricity here, so we could never have turned them on, though Tom Edison—I don't suppose he's still alive, is he?" Billy shook his head. "Sad. Death's such a sad, sad annoyance. Well, Tom did visit once. It was a fluke, something to do with an experiment he was conducting in Sarasota." The dwarf fingered what was supposedly Billy's résumé, though Billy'd never laid eyes on it. "Says in here that you're divorced. Probably didn't vote Republican, eh? Don't pray before meals, etc. Probably watch Public TV, too."

"Is this a political appointment?"

The dwarf perched his chin on top of the orange cat's head. "Everything's a political appointment, except maybe love. But I won't burden you with philosophy." A hand with enough liver spots to mate with a leopard reached under a pillow then emerged. "Care for a dog biscuit?" Seeing Billy blink, the old man apologized. "Sorry, wrong species." He tossed the dog biscuit over his back and it hit the roll top desk. "Care for a cup of coffee, then?" His fingers stretched toward an ivory mug embossed with green leaves and pink flowers, sitting on a bedside stand.

Billy jumped. The stand hadn't been there before, nor had the maroon chair next to it, not to mention the mug that was steaming and obviously full of coffee. He thought he'd heard a pop! similar to the sound the tube delivery system had made sending his so-called résumé, but where could this entire apparatus possibly have dropped from? The chair's velour matched the canopy, he vaguely noted.

"What good could I do here?" Billy asked, pointing at the coffee mug. "You said calling me an alchemist was a joke, but I can't do things like that—" Billy nodded at the table and chair— "I never even played Dungeons and Dragons. I've only watched *Star Wars* once. So what could I do here?"

"You have an odd view of magic." The old man motioned for Billy to sit in the chair.

Billy tested it with his hand before sitting, thinking that he had a healthy and normal view of magic. That is, he didn't view it at all.

"Some people might claim that your typing in numbers at one place and making them appear in another is magic, after all."

It is the old guy speaking, and not one of those cats, isn't it? Billy thought this because those yellow teeth never seemed to disappear, no matter what was said. He sipped his coffee—made just the right swamp water consistency!—before addressing the dwarf's statement. "That's just electricity and magnetic storage. There's nothing magical in that. Nothing like—" he tilted the coffee cup he'd just picked up. Was something clinking in its bottom? A coin depicting some elfin king that he'd have to serve forever?

"What if I told you the table and mug simply came from a dumbwaiter and a vacuum delivery system? Wouldn't you feel silly then, worrying about magic?"

"Did they?" Billy asked.

The old man rubbed the orange cat's ear. Billy heard a loud purring, and for the life of him it seemed triplicated, like the dwarf and both cats were all grinding out rrrrrrr's.

"Young man, my point is that life *is* magic. In the end that's what every philosopher or thinker worth his salt believes. Plato had his cave, Nietzsche his Eternal Return, Jung his archetypes and mandalas, Aleister Crowley his Supreme Will, and Einstein his Relative Time. All magical, no?"

"You're playing with the word 'magic.' "

"Am I?"

There was a long silence that Billy interrupted with a rather undignified slurp. He chuckled, remembering the job interview training he'd gone through before applying to Alabama. Number two rule after 'Always Smile and Don't Wear Purple' was 'Don't Take Coffee or any drink that may prove cumbersome or lead to an accident—or a slurp.' Well, it wasn't like he was really being offered a job—was it?

"Uh, how many hours a week will I be working at this job?"

The old man began to cackle, and his cackles grew. Billy jumped, ready to try CPR or cry for help as wet, gasping cackles emitted from the dwarf's mouth and his head sank into the stacked pink pillows and his eyes rolled wildly. Even the cats seemed disturbed and mewed deeply. Just as Billy leaned to give a Heimlich slap, the old guy inhaled and pushed himself up.

"You ... you would have done stupendously as jester in a medieval English court. You might even have inspired Chaucer to put one in his *Canterbury Tales*, like ol' Shakespeare did in *lear*. Listen, once you take the job, if you ever step into one of the house's rooms and find yourself confronted by British royalty who look vaguely medieval and brutish, do stay the night. You'll know they're medieval British because they'll be speaking bad French and blowing their noses in their shirtsleeves. It was quite the etiquette before Richard II."

"Does that mean that I have the job?"

"Certainly. I couldn't think of a person who'd do better."

Billy smacked his lips and sipped the coffee. "Uh, how much does it pay?"

This time the old man truly did die laughing and Billy jerked at what looked like a servant's cord while pounding on the old geezer's chest, trying to balance not breaking dwarf ribs and forcing a heartbeat. He succeeded in resurrecting a cough.

"Thanks, thanks," the old man managed. "Yes indeed, a real hit with the medievals. Better than the Black Death and Hundred Year's War rolled into one."

It was the strangest job reference Billy ever received. And he still didn't know what he'd be paid.

Chapter 11

"So how'd it go? You got the job, right?"

Before Billy could answer Soapy, the room grayed as if a huge factory vat had dumped hot ash around him. He collapsed from searing heat as his breath was taken, and when he sat up he found himself alone inside a stone silo some twenty feet in diameter, with an open window about as far above, directly underneath an open-beamed ceiling. To his immediate right sat . . . his desk from the University of Alabama Purchasing office, the only damned furniture in the room, for Pete's sake. He walked over to see his PC with its taped-on Dilbert cartoon. The screen directed him to

"PRESS ANY KEY TO CONTINUE."

"Soapy?" No answer besides an echo within the silo. "Soapy!" Still no answer, just a louder echo. When that ringing stopped, the screen stared, insistent as a cyclops' eye. He leaned to the keyboard, nearly touching his nose to the plastic, and pressed X. The entire computer metamorphosed into a hunched form wearing a white shirt and gray polyester trousers. Then this thin, talcum-pale dwarf unbent, as if readying to hurl a razor-sharp discus.

"Mr. Schroeder?" Billy choked.

It was his supervisor at the university, in bulldog miniature. Schroeder curled his bare foot to open a desk drawer with elongated, prehensile toes. His red nose, supposedly broken by an angry student when Schroeder worked for the bursar, twitched and then poked into the drawer to snort out a clump of pastel, plastic-coated paper clips. "What . . . I ask . . . are these doing in your desk?" Schroeder, face still in the drawer, was evidently so angered by the contraband paper clips that his nose pushed the drawer out of the desk to spill yellow, red, purple, green and blue paperclips onto the stone floor. When he did look up, a paperclip stuck to his nose caused him to sneeze. He straightened, seemingly ready to bound and grab Billy's throat.

"I, uh, use them for memorandums and paperwork."

The miniature Schroeder spewed miniature spittle: "Pink? Red? Green? Plastic-coated? Don't you realize we're in statewide fiscal crisis, Wise? What kind of frivolous image are you trying to give our beloved Purchasing Department? Another incident like this and I'll write you up to the Vice-President of Business Affairs or even ..." Schroeder's voice trailed ominously as he hunched over, transforming once more into a desktop computer. The same message on the same screen again faced Billy.

"PRESS ANY KEY TO CONTINUE."

A walnut shell hit Billy's head. He looked up to spot a bird on the single windowsill. In the sunlight Billy could see a Macaw's large orange beak. He heard a familiar jingling of bells as a second walnut shell hit his head with a pop!

"You're stuck in a loop, Billy. Go ahead and unplug it or you'll never get out," the Macaw called down. Even its thin bird voice echoed in the concrete silo.

"Alexandra?"

"That's me."

"Where are Soapy and Bogus?"

"They're below me, outside this granary. We heard you talking with someone."

"I'm in a granary?" Billy looked around at the obvious now.

"Yeah. Things are a lot nicer outside, believe me. Black shadows keep scurrying in the cracks inside here. Rats, I think. Lots of them. —Say what?" The bird crooked its head backwards then looked down to Billy: "Bogus wants to know if you've had your bubonic plague shot."

Billy heard a voice outside vaguely shout, "A shot in time saves mine." He inhaled and looked at the round wall. What Alexandra said was true: unsavory shadows *were* scurrying. He leaned toward the message on the computer screen, looked up at the bird then unplugged the machine. With a quiver part of the wall's stone facing rolled back into itself, as if on unsteady wheels, to reveal a wooden door. Billy opened the door and took a step ...

... outside onto a hillside meadow, into fresh air, sunshine, and lots of green, green grass. Bogus lay curled along the rim of a well, while Soapy was leaning against a cart with large wooden wheels. Both Soapy and Bogus grinned on seeing Billy, while Alexandra the macaw croaked from the silo's window above. Gulping fresh air, Billy realized how dank the inside of the silo had been.

"We could hear someone else's voice inside," Soapy said, looking expectantly over Billy's shoulder at the open door.

"Schroeder, my old boss. But he disappeared."

"*Old* boss? Then you got the job here?"

Soapy's choice of the word *here* struck Billy as strange, since *here* wasn't where they'd been minutes before. But he guessed it would be Bad Form to mention that, so he just said, "Yeah I suppose. But I still don't know what the job is."

When she smiled back and sunlight glinted in her hair, Billy felt his heart quicken just as if he'd sprinted a half-mile. He remembered what Mr. Snelling said, and it was true: as long as Soapy hung around, why worry about the job's description? Or the pay, for that matter.

"Do we ever get to eat on this uh job?" Billy asked, gracefully moving from one area of sensuality to another. Actually, his stomach did the moving, for it growled despite the glinting golden hair Billy's eyes were feasting upon.

"Food? About time someone mentioned that," a voice called. "There's some good-sized snails crawling inside this well." Bogus shifted his body along the well's rim.

"No thanks," Billy said.

"They go great with wild garlic. Thought I saw some—"

"No thanks," Soapy added.

"Garlic and snails make a stomach wail."

Billy and Soapy ignored the snake, who'd wrapped his tail about a post and was elongating downward into the well. "Alexandra!" Soapy called to the

Macaw still perched on the windowsill. "Why don't you locate some berries or fruit?"

"How about throwing in a few mice, if we aren't going to have snails," came an echoic voice. "These juicy babies are too far down for me to chomp."

Alexandra squawked and flapped off with a jingle. Billy, Soapy and Bogus—still muttering about snails—followed as best they could up a rolling hill with grass tufts and cow paths that seemed manicured, as if awaiting some folksy landscape artist to chance along. The artist, of course, would have left out the odor and mush, but Billy didn't, since he managed to step into a gooey paddy while gazing at some body part Soapy was swaying.

"Hey, how come you can't change into all sorts of things like Alexandra can?" Billy asked Bogus as he slithered around an abandoned plowshare. Billy asked this to distract from the fact that he had to wipe his right boot on the grass.

"I dunno, how come you can't? It'd do wonders for your complexion, hayseed—not to mention your body odor."

"Boys, boys, be nice," Soapy commented.

Alexandra flew back and informed them that not far away lay a small orchard. So, after walking over two hillsides, they came upon three apple and three pear trees. Alexandra knocked down the highest, ripest fruit while Bogus lounged. Noticing that the snake had traded his Carter/Roosevelt teeth for fangs, Billy squeezed his machete's hilt as they slumped against a stone fence.

"Is our job to fight? I mean, are we protecting the old man and woman who interviewed me?"

"Protecting those two? Some of us on the board think that they're—"
Soapy cleared her throat loudly. Bogus shivered his usual snake shrug.

"I've been here before," Bogus announced glumly. With his forked tongue, he indicated the hillside and three castle turrets just visible over it. "It's in the Middle Ages. Everyone here is nuts. Self-flagellation, public execution, and jousting to the death—as if they don't have enough problems with the Plague. They speak a dandified English-French mixture—but manage to gargle it out in the most Teutonic broth you can imagine. Near as I could make out last time, this place lies near Canterbury, England. So keep a watch for any pilgrims or clerics. They'll rob or rape us. Or talk our heads off, one."

"We've traveled to England? From the house?" Billy's brows knitted. "Uh, the old man said if I ever get to medieval England I'd be a hit. I thought he was kidding. You don't suppose …"

Soapy and the snake exchanged glances; then Bogus munched an apple that Alexandra had knocked down, though seeming more interested in whatever was living in the apple than the fruit itself. Alexandra was circling overhead. Billy bit into an apple but on pulling out a large white worm, he dropped both onto the ground. A squirrel skittered forward.

Bogus struck at the squirrel, but he was too slow and wound up with the discarded apple stuck in his jaws. The white worm crawled over his lips and wriggled.

"Sonny boy, Daddy's been wondering where you were." Bogus slurped both worm and apple down his gullet.

"You're a real jokester, Cisco," Billy commented.

"It keeps things moving along, Poncho," Bogus said, spitting out the apple's stem.

Billy started on another apple but gave up mid-bite to speak: "The old man sent us here, didn't he? You know, there's something familiar about him and the old woman in green."

"Did they remind you of anyone?" Bogus asked, twisting about.

Billy completed his bite and chewed, feeling pulp grow in his mouth. Then he swallowed and laughed. "His eyes, they shifted just like my father's, and the old woman shuffled her feet and kept hard candy in her mouth just like my mother. But my mother always sucked on a peppermint, not a cinnamon ball. She said it eased her stomach from putting up with my dad."

"Tell him." Soapy was staring at her silken slipper, straight from a fairy tale or a porn site, according to mood. "Tell him," she repeated.

Bogus twitched his heat pits as if a pair of horn-rimmed granny glasses were cutting into them. "The old man coughs like a friend I once had who smoked a pipe. He had a constant chirrup in his throat."

"But I didn't hear him cough—"

"And another thing: he chews his whiskers just like another friend always did too," Bogus interrupted.

Billy stopped mid-bite of his apple.

"You didn't see his whiskers?"

Billy shook his head.

"No one else ever hears him cough, either," Soapy added. "Uh," she smiled sweetly at Billy, as if happy to be contaminated with his slovenly vocal habit, "Once I had a very good friend who taught me everything I know—"

"Oh come on," Bogus interrupted.

"Well a lot, anyway. And Mrs. Snelling looks just like that friend, with her hooked nose and all. And Mr. Snelling's head is fat and triangular, like a skate's, just like another male friend of mine."

"But—"

"That's right. You didn't see a hooked nose. And who knows what Mr. Snelling looked like to you. Just like I never smell cinnamon, but always apples. My first friend loved apples. They give me a stomach ache."

"Stomach ache ... I bet. You and your pal Eve both should've tried the worms instead."

Until then Billy hadn't noticed that Soapy wasn't eating. A breeze dissipated mist from a nearby depression to reveal five cows and two calves previously hidden by the mist. Their mechanical munching seemed ominous.

"The bottom line is that they remind everyone of someone very important: parents, best friends, or mentors," Soapy said.

"Everyone?" Billy asked.

"Everyone."

"Now, ask if that's good or bad," Bogus said.

But Billy didn't get a chance, for three riders approached from his right. Bogus slipped behind an apple tree and Soapy moved near Billy.

"Well met, wights. Doth yonder castle control a road connecting to Canterbury? We fear we have been misled by ne'er-do-wells, if not." The man speaking was short and round, looking somewhat elfish, though he was certainly human. Perhaps a great-grandmother had slipped into midnight woods to mate with a fairy. But all three riders were more than human, for all three in desperate need of a bath. The road—whether the one they searched or not—hadn't done them or their horses any favors.

Billy coughed and took a step backwards, near the tree Bogus was hidden behind. "Uh, we're strangers here ourselves, but we didn't see any, uh, road in the direction you're heading."

The third and largest of the group urged his horse forward. "By your dress and short sword, sir, ye be a knight. How be ye y-cleped?" The man gave a wet sniff and wiped his nose on his sleeve with a smile.

"He's asking your name," Bogus hissed.

"Uh Billy."

"*Sir* Billy," the snake hissed.

"Uh Sir Billy."

"Ah. Sir Uh Billy, I am Sir Wilfred, and this gentleman is Sir John Gower, poet to the king, and yon elfish one is Sir Geoffrey Chaucer, also poet to the king."

"Where is your charger, Sir Uh Billy?" the one named Chaucer asked. "Surely the lovely damsel next to you isn't a bewitched charger, else all the kingdom would be applying to the sorcerer who changed her into such a beauty."

"Curtsy!" Bogus hissed. "And look demure. None of your snappy answers, Soapy."

Soapy did as she was told. "I thank your honor for the kindness. Our horses were stolen from us e'en last night, but no matter in this world of woe. Are you truly the great Chaucer who wrote *The Canterbury Tales*? I love it when the miller cuts the rope to his bucket and falls hollering to the floor."

The three men stared gawp-eyed.

"How can ye know that? I was just telling Honest John and Sir Wilfred about completing that very tale."

Sir Wilfred's pale face turned paler. "Mayhap they weren't robbed. Mayhap they stand in collusion with the same wights who sent us off the trail in the first happenstance."

Sir Wilfred's stallion huffed angrily, and Billy noted with alarm that the knight drew his sword infinitely better than he drew his conclusions, though just as quickly.

"Alack, think you so? Then once more I find that beauty is not truth, nor is truth beauty," said Chaucer.

It was Billy and Soapy's turn to stare at an anachronism.

"He really didn't say that, did he?" Soapy whispered. "I mean, isn't something like that line Keats's claim to fame?"

Sir Wilfred threw down a glove by his stallion, which gave a snort, as if this were some prearranged trick. "Whispering and plotting! Very well then, bandits. To the death!"

"To the death. Awk! To the death! Awk!" Alexandra circled overhead.

"Sorcery!" shouted Sir Wilfred, crossing himself, clumsily knocking first his sword's hilt, then its blade against his forehead.

"No, no," Chaucer said. "It's only a talking bird. I have heard sailor's tell of them."

Honest John Gower agreed. But this didn't seem to ease matters, for both he and Chaucer drew their weapons after crossing themselves.

"Psst. Tell noble round Chaucer that's-s how you knew about the Miller's-s Tale. Tell him Alexandra was flying over his shoulder and heard him telling it to them and retold it to you."

Soapy curtsied once more and restated what Bogus suggested. "And I can't help but think, noble sir," she added with her most glowing smile, "that a good strong woman would do your tales no harm. Say a good wife from Bath or thereabouts."

"Oh think you so, do you?"

"The very thing I was telling him," said Honest John Gower.

"Agh, you were doing no such thing. You were trying to have him turn the whole hang-it-all into a Cupid's dream-sermon. I heard you." The knight and Honest John Gower both glowered.

"And what, pray tell, is your name, fair gentlewoman?"

"Soapy."

"Soapy? Surely I did not hear the fair damsel rightly." The elfish man leaned forward on his mount and cupped his ear.

"It's short for *Sophia*."

"Ah. Lady Wisdom, of course. Marry, gentlemen, I believe we owe Lady Wisdom and her companion—and her marvelous talking bird—an apology." Chaucer looked to his friends, and Sir Wilfred sheathed his sword, dismounted and, picking up his glove, walked to kneel on one knee before Soapy.

"Will you intercede with your great lord Sir Uh Billy for me? Else take my head from my shoulders, for I swear your beauty and grace have already blinded me and will soon turn me dumb. Mercy is all I can plead."

"Oh brother," the snake hissed.

Soapy stomped her foot backwards toward the tree. She took the glove from Sir Wilfred's hand and turned to Billy. "Sir Uh Billy, can you find it in your heart to forgive and forget at my chaste bidding?"

Billy rolled his eyes, but straightened when he noticed Chaucer and Honest John watching. "Uh, marry, uh, rise up, Sir Wilfred. All is forgiven."

"But what penance shall I perform?" the knight said, stubbornly going to both knees rather than rising, then leaning toward Soapy, who held her breath as he sniffled at her hips and once more wiped his nose on his sleeve.

"Tell him to get us–s s-some food."

"We alas, verily were robbed by the very bandits you spake of and have neither food nor horses. As you see, we were eating only of this wilden fruit. Could you spare us some meager crumbs?"

"I could do with a Big Mac and a milkshake myself," the snake hissed, a bit too loudly.

"Eh?" Sir Wilfred looked at Billy, then at the apple tree, then rose to one knee.

Soapy stepped forward. "Big Mac is our faithful servant. He was changed into a snake by a sorcerer traveling with the bandits. Changed into a gentle snake, for he still keeps his smiling teeth and voice. But alack, he needs be an outcast now. But do rise, Sir Wilfred, I beg you." She held out her hand to the knight, who after one glance at her eyes promptly returned to two knees with a thud, somehow managing that sound despite the soil's softness.

"I pledge not only food, but revenge on these bandits for Big Mac and the fair Lady Sophia!"

"Bravo!" Bogus crawled from behind the tree, showing his best dentifrice.

The sight of him got Sir Wilfred off his knees and caused the horses to prance nervously.

"Recall in thine heart," Soapy said, touching Sir Wilfred on the shoulder. "This is our faithful servant Big Mac, who was cruelly transformed whilst trying to save our possessions."

"What profit a man if he gain the world and lose his shape," Chaucer said, shaking his head. He dismounted and offered Bogus, Billy, and Soapy hard bread and equally hard cheese. Bogus—alias Big Mac—made his apologies, saying his appetite had been bewitched too. Hunger had sharpened Billy's and Soapy's sixty-four total teeth, though, and they immediately sat by an apple tree to rip crust and rind.

Halfway through the meal, Billy needed to go where even kings, queens, and knights go. Heading off a polite distance and standing behind a large oak with one sword in each hand—that is, one fleshy and metaphorical sword, and one machete—while thus dawdling he spotted a clacker peeping at the picnickers from behind another oak. Tucking his metaphorical sword and raising his machete, Billy ran at the clacker, cutting it neatly in half, sending both halves onto the grass.

"Frazzle!" he hissed, though there were no other clackers around to hear.

Chapter 12

"A spy," Billy announced, carrying the halves back, looped in his machete.

"We saw a strange, bedeviled group of black reeds very like unto that on the banks of a pond over yon hill," Chaucer commented. Bogus, who'd removed to a discreet distance because of the horses' and Sir Wilfred's nerves, was sticking his forked tongue out in every direction, searching danger.

Billy tossed the pieces to the ground and Chaucer prodded the dead clacker with his boot. "Shiny black and shaped y-like a man that a child might draw. They send a shiver up a wight's very back."

"Marry," agreed Honest John. "And remember how I told you, friend Chaucer, when we spied them by the pond, that they minded me of burnt souls troubling for a space on this earth. Indeed, I think that an even more apt description now."

"Nay, Chaucer told *you* that, Gower. I heard him well." Sir Wilfred was pacing nervously, dividing his glances among Bogus, the horizon, and the dead clacker.

"Marry, they held death-still, like a legion of the very Devil's own. And that too was strange, for a breeze y-rippled the water and y-tossed the leaves of nearby trees."

"Our enemy the sorcerer!" Soapy yelped. "He must be plotting an ambush."

"Huh?" Billy asked in something of a half-belch near Soapy's face, not used to the spices in the cheese. He quickly remembered himself as the three men simultaneously wiped their noses on their sleeves in incredulous dismay at his grunting manners. Billy grabbed his throat as if some demon had inadvertently jumped out, cleared it, and then intoned highly, "Uh, I mean, think ye so, Fair Lady?"

"Sir Uh Billy has unwittingly ingested a counter-potion against your charms, my lady, else he could have never y-spoken so vulgarly in your presence."

"Mayhap the very wizard you speak of hath entangled his mind so it cannot appreciate your beauteous rose," Honest John added.

"Mayhap this is not Sir Uh Billy, but some imposter phantom created by the demon sorcerer!" Sir Wilfred clasped his sword's hilt and strode toward Billy. "The water test!"

"Yea, the water test!" Honest John Gower agreed. "Plenty of stones in yon fence line for that."

Billy's eyes bulged, for he knew enough medieval history to know that several hundredweight of stones might be tied around him before he took a hapless swim.

"No!" Soapy insisted. "No! None of your guesses are true. Sir Uh Billy is pledged to me as I am to him, but another keeps us from ever sharing our love. Hence Sir Uh Billy must publicly pretend to rudeness to cover our mutual devotion."

"Ah, thwarted courtly love," intoned Honest John.

"Nothing sweeter," intoned Sir Wilfred. "Nor more bitter." With his last statement he sighed, eyeing Soapy. Then he turned to Billy. "My friend, I give you my jeweled dagger. If ever you needs take your life to release yourself from love's pangs, use it freely. Afterwards, I, poor slave, will faithfully watch o'er this your chaste lady in your sacred memory."

"I bet," Bogus hissed.

Chaucer heard and walked over to the snake, evidently discerning a kindred cynical spirit. In unison, he and Bogus fluttered their eyes toward heaven as Gower and Sir Wilfred continued the praises of Fair Lady Soapy and unrequited love. Finally, when the syrup became too thick, Bogus nudged Chaucer's leg. "Don't forget what she just told you about the clackers—the bewitched familiars with knife-sharp limbs. There'll be plenteous more than this dead one roaming about soon."

Agreeing, Chaucer intruded upon Honest John Gower's and Sir Wilfred's flowery troths, plights, and promises by coughing harshly to say: "Our bewitched friendly Big Mac believes with this fair lady that the black reeds we saw may be in league with the sorcerer. He reminds us that legions more may well y-come this way soon."

"For myself, I have no fear, but we must needs escort the fair lady to safety," replied Sir Wilfred.

"The fair lady can ride my steed as I walk to guard her lovely foot," said Honest John.

"No, mine, as *I* walk to guard her lovely foot," countered Sir Wilfred, setting his legs apart.

The two placed their hands on their sword hilts.

"Gentlemen, I will ride Honest John's steed for part of the journey and Sir Wilfred's for part of the journey, and ..." Soapy looked at Chaucer, who instantly bent to rub his instep with a groan, just in case she was thinking of borrowing his small palfrey. "Then both those two brave gentlemen shall have my favor. My mind is set," she added.

Chaucer straightened with relief. He did offer, however, to let Bogus ride in a wicker basket tied to his mare's side. After suspiciously examining the wicker and judging that he could easily bite his way out, Bogus agreed, giving Billy a toothy smile as Chaucer lifted him into the basket.

"Big Mac, thou truly must have been a weightsome wight," Chaucer commented with a grunt.

Bogus pushed up the basket's lid and grinned at Billy, "Sorry fellow, but riding is reserved for fair ladies and battle-scarred, bewitched heroes. Dig yourself up a sorcerer to change you into a pig and maybe you'll catch a ride."

Billy started to flip Bogus the finger then decided against it. Soapy-smitten Sir Wilfred and Gower were just waiting for an excuse to dunk him in water to see if he was a warlock.

Once Soapy was mounted, they traveled west, away from the clackers by the pond and the castle, toward what they hoped would lead to Canterbury. After an hour Soapy and Chaucer spotted a dirt road. Turning onto it they saw, some distance ahead, a large group approaching.

"A royal procession from its size," Chaucer intoned. "But the King is too brittle to travel, and Lady Alice surely wouldn't . . ." His voice trailed as he stood in his stirrup then quickly sat down. "It *is* the King and Lady Alice. We must dismount."

When the royal train neared, the three Englishmen nodded gravely at several friends then knelt for the royal coach, which was something of a pig-cart. Soapy, kneeling too, tugged at Billy.

"But it's Mr. and Mrs. Snell—"

Soapy hit Billy behind the knees and he crumpled into a kneeling position until the carriage and its rear guard passed, a process which took some ten minutes, for the royal train was large.

"We'll follow at a discreet distance," Sir Wilfred said.

Behind, atop the hill from where the royal train had emerged, came a clacking. Billy noticed that Bogus, peeping from the basket, had again reverted to fangdom. . . .

Chapter 13

Near sunset, a castle loomed ahead.

"Whose is it?" Honest John Gower asked.

Chaucer shrugged. "Sir ABCD's" he said. "Who knows?"

Sir Wilfred and Billy had made much of guarding Soapy, each keeping his sword unsheathed, each claiming a lovely white foot. Alexandra, still shaped as a Macaw, had perched on Soapy's right shoulder and occasionally flapped to Billy's shoulder to whisper assurances that nothing untoward was occurring on the other side of the saddle. Alexandra's heavy flaps disconcerted Sir Wilfred, but Soapy jiggled her pale ankle and smiled at him, so being a good Englishman, he quickly forgot one bird for another.

A raven cawed nastily as Alexandra swooped down for one more report: "Her foot's still a virgin, Billy, but old Sir Wilfred did quite a stutter-step when her ankle slipped from under her gown. If you want to know the truth, I believe the old guy's lusting in his mind. I wonder if he's a distant relation to Jimmy Carter. But cheer up; at least he isn't Jimmy Swaggart."

This news turned Billy red, but the next flit back turned him to a real Crimson Tide fan, especially since Alexandra flitted long green tail feathers in his right ear before revealing her juicy tidbit: "The old boy has a foot fetish. He accidentally—ha!—grabbed her ankle when checking the horse's harness. And Gower is busy composing an allegory about a virgin's white ankle and its pilgrimage through the world."

Billy, feeling his throat thicken as the stale cheese and bread welled up, grabbed Alexandra's claw. "Why don't you, uh, just stay with me? You're enjoying this too much."

Alexandra bit his finger and he let go with a yelp. Brushing feathers in his ear she said, "I'll be back if anything else untoward happens. Pretty heavy competition, having an honest-to-goodness knight *and* a royal court poet go after your girl, huh?"

Billy snatched at a tail feather, but missed.

As expected, the king and Lady Alice's retinue rode into the castle, whose-so-ever's it was. From his vantage well behind in the horse manure gallery, Billy could discern only the tails of the last horses, swishing at flies as they entered the gate.

A mounted knight rode back, his chain mail clinking: "His Excellency Edward prays that your group will spend the night with him," the knight said.

So they were invited into the castle, even Bogus, who produced many gasps from the royal retinue upon flapping his wicker cover open while being introduced as the enchanted Big Mac. The dining hall they were led to was huge. It was also smoky—haze filled it from the ceiling downwards to hang within five feet of their heads. Sir Walter Raleigh would have been pleased, the American Cancer Society, dubious.

The king and Lady Alice Perrers were in full view on a dais, the king reclining on a couch since he was ill, Lady Alice on a silken footstool by his side. It was truly the king and his lady now—not Mr. and Mrs. Snelling. At least, Billy supposed the two people he saw were who Chaucer said they were, though he noticed an orange cat would occasionally crawl over the king's shoulder and that the king's purported illness didn't keep him from eating half a chicken and a small leg of mutton. Nor did it keep him from drinking one pitcher of wine and another of ale.

The four of them were led to a spot near the end of the tables, a good fifty feet from the royal dais. Chaucer, Sir Wilfred, and Honest John walked on toward the king himself, being more privileged.

"Hand me a bit of that rabbit," Bogus said, sticking his head out of the wicker basket after a dog sniffed its side. Billy chased the dog off just as it was hiking its leg; then he handed Bogus the entire rabbit. After eliciting a frightened look from a nearby lady, Bogus dropped under the lid. "This," he said, his voice filtering through wicker, "is the best rabbit I've ever eaten in this wretched house."

"House?" Billy asked. A bearded neighbor grunted and pointed at a stack of chickens. Billy nodded and tore the man off a leg. The man snarled at the proffered leg and leaned to grab the entire chicken.

Soapy waved a finger in Billy's face. "House. Don't forget where we really are. "See that second pillar from Mr. Snelling, the would-be King?"

Billy looked first at the king—he was again Mr. Snelling—then at the pillar. Five feet up it was hollowed out into a—"It's the kitchen fireplace, isn't it?"

Soapy nodded.

Billy then noticed Chaucer, Sir Wilfred, and Honest John talking with the king—Mr. Snelling, that is. Chaucer seemed to be reciting something privately, maybe part of a poem from the way his head bounced. The king—Mr. Snelling—looked pleased. Then he glanced toward Billy and Soapy, and Chaucer waved.

"I don't like this," Alexandra said from Soapy's shoulder. She flew off.

"Should we make for the fireplace? We've been here nearly all day, it seems to me—long enough not to worry about Bad Form," Billy said.

"If they were phantoms, they wouldn't appear to Chaucer, Sir Wilfred, and their friend as the King and Lady Alice, but to us as Mr. and Mrs. Snelling. Phantoms can't do that—appear differently to different people."

"That's-s right," Bogus said.

Billy couldn't tell whether the snake was hissing or lustily spitting rabbit bones. Billy stared at the drumstick still in his hand and grabbed a hunk of the blackest bread he'd ever seen. The bread wound up being surprisingly sweet, made from honey, and it contrasted with the chicken that was spiced with cinnamon and very gamey. He chewed on both, looking for a veggie plate: there was none. God, every artery at this table must flow like the Nile at high-silt.

"Some wine, sir? Madam?" A tinkling caught Billy's attention.

"Alexandra!"

Alexandra curtsied and poured wine for them both. "Too many dogs and cats in this room to flit about as a bird. But I did flit enough to hear what

Chaucer was telling Mr. Snelling, who Chaucer keeps calling 'Your Highness.' "

A nearby lady tugged at Alexandra's gown then pointed to her own goblet. After Alexandra filled the goblet the lady nodded, then blew her nose onto her sleeve, leaving it glistening with mucus. A gentleman pecked the lady on her cheek, leaving a shining grease spot visible even in the firelight and smoke. Alexandra turned and finished pouring wine for Soapy and Billy.

"Chaucer's reciting a poem about the four of us. I think that he and the one called Honest John are having some contest to get the king's attention. Chaucer's going to win because he keeps winking at the woman next to the king, that Lady Perrers."

"Lord," Soapy exclaimed. "You don't suppose old Mr. Snelling could have really been King Edward of England in a previous life, do you? And Mrs. Snelling could have been that tart Lady Alice?"

A mucus-free lady dressed in green overheard Soapy and nodded pertly at the combination of "tart" and "Lady Alice." Soapy bowed, then spoke lower: "Bogus, do you think you can stop eating long enough to give this room a look-sniff?"

Bogus shook the wicker and whistled on seeing a hound. The dog trotted over, but skidded on seeing a snake coiling from the basket. Bogus slung the rabbit's ribcage at the dog, which sniffed cautiously, finally deciding to take the gift, despite the giver.

"Good thing I'm not Greek and he's not Trojan," Bogus commented. He then tested the air with his forked tongue, hacking as he did. "Good golly Ms. Molly. This room could use some old-fashioned oxygen. But besides the carbon mono- and dioxide levels I don't sense anything dangerous.—Hand me another slab of meat, would you? How about a whole chicken before that bewhiskered creature next to you eats them all?" Once Bogus got his chicken he disappeared back into his basket.

They sat for nearly an hour, listening to intermittent belches and tall tales. Then Chaucer approached and told them that the "king" wanted to see Sir Uh Billy.

"He has a message for *us*?" Soapy asked. The woman sitting across from them, the one who'd smiled at Soapy's remark about Lady Perrers, slitted her eyes and nodded slyly. Underneath the table, Bogus rocked the basket.

"Be careful, Billy. I never have trusted the old coot," Soapy whispered.

Chaucer tugged at Billy's shoulder. "The king . . . hurry."

When Billy and Chaucer reached the king, Billy was no longer so sure that it was Mr. Snelling. The king was old, certainly, but taller and much more portly than Mr. Snelling. And what Billy had thought was a cat was a ferret. Mr. Snelling would never be anywhere without his cat, would he? Even an hour's conversation had told Billy that. And the woman, Lady Alice . . . though a hint of cinnamon clung about her, that could come from the mulled wine. And her breasts and shoulders certainly weren't over a century old! Billy saw a ring glint on her hand, its ruby so large that it qualified as conspicuous consumption, right up with 24-karat Monopoly boards. This Perrers woman would have done well in America.

"We have heard of your bravery, Sir Uh Billy," the king said, offering his hand. From the little dramas Billy'd been watching from the end of the table he knew he was expected to kneel and bow. He did so, and Lady Perrers rose.

"For your bravery against the sorcerer, I give you this token." She took off the ruby ring and placed it on his pinkie. Billy blushed, remembering his uncharitable thoughts of only a minute before.

"And I knight thee truly as Sir Uh Billy the Dauntless."

Billy looked into the king's wine-red eyes and saw him raise, with some struggle, a large sword and flatten it in the air. But then the eyes turned sober and mean and the sword whistled with its sharp side down. Billy felt frantically for Frazzle. No use, for he'd left his machete at the table.

KLUNK!

Billy saw his body, decapitated, kneeling stupidly in the smoky room, he heard the king and Lady Alice laughing, he felt a dog sniffing blood around his ear. His head, he realized, his head was lying on the floor. That same head watched his body fall forward, that same head lost contact with its body as a dog slung that same head into the air. *What a ridiculous way to end my life*, Billy thought while his head spun upward, open-eyed and watching the sooty ceiling, then downward, gazing into the open jaws of a waiting mastiff.

Third Leg: Know Thyself

Chapter 14

Billy awoke facedown, staring into a weave of leaves and pine needles, their resin overpowering. He twisted to see thickly tangled grape vines draping smooth-barked trees. The vines swayed overhead like endless clusters of mating snakes. He realized he was lying flat on a musty forest floor. *I wasn't decapitated, just knocked out.* That helped, since he was fond of his skull, but it left another problem: he had no idea where he was. Plus, since so little light filtered through the trees and the vines, it was impossible to tell the time of day.

"Ugh!" He slapped at his face. In return, something pinched his cheek. He yelped and slapped again, knocking a black beetle onto the ground. It was the size of a silver dollar and clutched a piece of white Billy-flesh between two huge pincers. Billy hopped up to stomp it, but the ground was soft to the point of foam, so his stomp was fruitless—a glance at the beetle heedlessly crawling out from under his boot, still clutching the white piece of cheek, affirmed that. Nonetheless, Billy stomped again, with the same squishy non-result, with the beetle once more crawling out with even less of a struggle than previously. What the hell was on the beetle's so persistent back? Billy leaned to see an emblazoned white skull and crossbones. More house humor, no doubt.

"Get a life!" he shouted, shaking his fist at the air. Not a vine swayed, so he kicked the beetle away. As far as he could tell, the porous land was dry, not disguised swamp that might suck him into an early grave. To be dry and this spongy, the forest must have laid a foot-thick carpet. How old would that make it? Older than any forest in America outside the California

Redwoods—certainly older than any in harvested and re-harvested and re-re-harvested Alabama. Billy gazed at the towering trees and vines. *Tarzan?* That ridiculous thought pounded the nail in the proverbial coffin: *I'm still inside the house, all right. As if the graveyard beetle's trademark didn't clue me in to that already.*

The beetle or its twin chose that moment to crawl up Billy's boot and bite his calf. "Bad Form!" Billy yowled, kicking the bug loose. It scurried off then turned to click its black pincers obnoxiously, so Billy ran through the trees, bouncing trampoline-like on humus all the way.

All the way to where?

When he stopped for breath, he couldn't be sure how far he'd come, since what lay behind looked the same as what lay before. For that matter, behind and before looked the same as left or right or where he stood: more tree trunks and vines and spongy ground. *Bad Form*, he told himself. *You just left the spot that most likely held a passageway to take you back to Soapy.* He tried to retrace his footsteps, but no use, the forest floor was entirely too springy; his footsteps had disappeared as if he'd never been there. What was that cornball saying? Leave nothing but footprints? He wasn't even leaving those. That was food for thought. He rubbed his cheek, feeling an indentation and blood where the beetle had taken a chunk.

"Bogus! Soapy! Alexandra!"

No answer, so he walked—forward, backward, or sideways didn't seem to have meaning: he just walked. After an hour? two hours? three? there was no appreciable dimming or intensifying of natural light. The only hint to time's passing was his hoarseness from yelling for Bogus and Soapy, that plus the tiredness of his calf muscles. Another thing: no wildlife, besides the biting black graveyard beetles, though he never encountered more than one at a time, and of course he did everything he could to avoid the pincers then. He almost came to view the beetle in the singular, capable of angelic teleportation, as a personal bodyguard, or at least companion, since nothing else showed itself. Did this void of life in the forest indicate a siesta, or maybe an off moon-cycle? Or simply that he was making too much noise? But his voice had grown hoarse. And he left no footprints. It was as if he didn't exist.

In mocking echo of this last thought, a graveyard beetle loudly scraped shiny black pincers to break a twig from a sycamore sapling.

"Do I know you?" Billy asked, squinting. The beetle scurried down the sapling to toss leaves and pine needles to form a rectangular plot. The broken twig was transformed into a miniature cross. The beetle kept twisting its jointed neck and re-shaping the plot as if taking Billy's measurements. None of this struck Billy as particularly funny, though he was sure the house was holding a regular masquer's ball of laughter. He shook his fist again, but the sky retained its lambency, the scenery its sameness.

He tiptoed onward. It seemed foolish, but he thought he could still hear the beetle digging. Then he encountered another beetle scattering leaves and pine needles to dig another grave plot. A larger plot with an accompanying larger twig, though the beetle was the same size.

He walked on. Another beetle, another gravesite, another roughly hewn cross. Another, then another. By the ninth one the twig had become a branch and the gravesite one by two feet. It was as if a troupe of beetles were working ahead of wherever he walked.

Miraculously—or what felt so after maybe fifty grave-digging beetles and graves—ochre touched the trees. This ochre slipped to gray, dropping evening into his lap. The last grave he'd seen could have accompanied a preteen male. Billy sighed, and that hurt his throat, reminding him of his near decapitation. He realized how tired his legs were, so while there was still light he found a large tree trunk that could envelop him in its Y-like indentation, enthroning and protecting his sides and his rear from the beetles or whatever else might roam at night. Wrapping his arms about himself to ward off the chill, he gave one last croak for Soapy! Alexandra! Bogus! then settled in to stare out toward the quiet.

And listen.

Shouldn't an evening forest be filled with sounds? He heard nothing. Blackness descended like a weighted velvet curtain, though in the distance he spotted what he imagined to be grave gas, which turned out to be a full moon lifting its bony countenance on the horizon. Why wasn't there any sound?

As if in answer, he heard leaves and pine needles being shuffled. Pressing against the tree he listened to a steady scratching, like an intent craftsman at work. One of the damned beetles, he was certain. The sound came from his left but he didn't look, for in this moonlight the white skull he'd seen on the beetles' backs wouldn't seem so damned funny. Neither would an open grave. He stared, at what he couldn't say.

Some time later, an owl hooted, interrupting the insistent scratching. *Woo-who, woo-whooo.* The call was followed by a flapping, then a tiny squeak that shocked the nothingness.

Rest in peace, mouse.

Woo-who, woo-whooo.

A scratching to his right this time. A second beetle? An opossum? Armadillo? Raccoon? Snake? Snakes don't dig, he told himself. But Bogus would be just the kind of snake to dig, for downright contrariness if nothing else. "Bogus?" he whispered. The scratching stopped. "Bogus?" A scurrying through leaves, then silence.

Woo-who, woo-whooo.

More scratching.

"Damn!" Billy slapped at his cheek, pulling off another beetle. Feeling blood trickle he squeezed the beetle as hard as he could; not only did its shell remain impervious but its legs rasped his fingers, so with a scream he flung the bug away.

Who, who? Who, who? Had the owl transformed its call into a human question?

For a while, he lost the moon. His pupils bulged, trying to soak up any rods of light, though few existed. A scratching sounded to his rear now. At least it wasn't the scrape of a metal spade hitting gravel: he'd know for sure his grave was being dug then. But this soft, insistent scratching sounded like . . . *Someone planting pumpkins?*

Graveyard humor didn't help. Rubbing the new gash on his cheek, Billy sniffed his forearm and felt comforted with the smell of a living body, his living body.

Who, who? Who, who?

Owls presage a family death, he'd always heard from his grandmother. Well, with her and his parents and Linda gone there wasn't a hell of a lot of family left, unless the itinerant generations of roaches following him from household to household counted.

Who, who? Who, who?

Maybe he was dying, finishing what he'd started—how long ago?—back in the farm pond. Maybe Snelling's sword really had cut through, maybe he really was dead and this was the big sleep, the day of doom, the day of anger and wrath, the tiny private judgment followed by …

Who, who? Who, who?

Something brushed his nose so he gave a slap, hitting it so hard that he went into a sneezing fit. When he could focus, the moon had reappeared through the trees. His nose throbbed, along with his sinuses and his brain cells. Seconds later, he jumped as a graveyard beetle bit his rear. With a curse he tossed it, then looked at the moon and closed his eyes to concentrate on its bony afterimage.

Who, who? Who, who?

Eyes still closed, he concentrated until the afterimage of the man in the moon became his own Billy Wise face. He worked on giving it a smile, heavier eyebrows, sort of a Billy-as-Mr.-Potato-Head look. The teeth became Bogus's goofy teeth. Then he gave the mouth Soapy's smile. How about jingling bells like Alexandra's? He worked for a hot-pink hue. Then he plopped on an R.N. cap like his mother wore, put a pen in his pocket—just visible under the afterimage's moony glow—a pen like his dad used as an accountant. But when he opened his eyes all he saw was the same old bozo man in the moon.

Who, who? Who, who?

Was that the moon or him?

Sir Wilfred's dagger pricked his stomach. Nothing dumber than accidentally gutting himself. That'd suit old Wilfred just fine, give him leave to comfort Soapy with his grimy shirtsleeve. Grabbing the ruby hilt, Billy moved the dagger to a safer spot, then closed his eyes to again concentrate on changing the moon's afterimage, but that bozo smile wouldn't leave. *Who,*

who? Who, who? Great. Comic-book psychoanalysis: Billy F. Wise, this is your Smiley-face life.

He opened his eyes to see the moon stranded on the horizon. He blinked. Yes, on the horizon—once more—though it had been seated over that oddly crooked tree an hour before. It was as if time had reversed, or ...

Who, who? Who, who?

Scratching sounded somewhere before him now. He felt queasy. Could he have passed out for twenty-four hours? That was the only explanation, other than two moons in some sci-fi fantasy. He felt the two punctures on his cheek, the bite on his butt. The blood was still wet and fresh, not scabbed. He narrowed his eyes to see that the moon was . . .

"No! No! No!" He slapped ferociously at his forearm, knocking a beetle onto the dark ground and randomly stomping, trying to kill it. But he only twisted his ankle on a root. Panting, he looked at the moon, still on the horizon. Time hadn't budged. The dagger bit into his back and he experienced a premonition. In the moon's glow, he could see his forearms sheening in red; his clothes torn and his body covered with gashes. His face felt stiff, as if someone had dumped tubes of super glue on it. Drying blood.

Once more, the moon was rising. Hearing a rustling he expected a bite, but none came. Would he remain in this one spot watching the moon rise and re-rise until he bled to death from stupid bug bites? There, behind him now the patient scratching had made a full circle. The moon once more lay on the horizon. Once more.

Who, who? Who, who?

The worst job he'd ever had was in a pizza joint. As the sole waiter he covered the entire pink and white palace, slopping out syrupy soft drinks, greasy pepperoni, and gooey mozzarella to drunks, snot-nosed kids, angry parents, and smart-ass teenagers. In recurring nightmares he skidded from table to table, trying to appease angry faces, holding nothing in his open palms but a plea. A plea, when what they wanted was around-the-world pizza.

But tonight wasn't a damned dream. He looked at the man in the moon, whose lips curled in a fiendish onion grin, whose pepperoni eyes glared under eyebrows arched in mushroom-capped insanity. *Why did I call in sick today—or whenever? What possessed me?* Then Billy thought: *Better, why didn't I call in and quit? How much different from the pizza parlor is my university job? Schroeder in, Schroeder out. Half-baked either way. Has my whole life been like tonight? Have I ever left a track anywhere?*

Hearing the scratching again, he screamed. "Soapy!"

Why don't you just walk away?

Who said that? Who?

Slumping, Billy heard the beetle's clicking drone. "Help!" He tried to shout this, but tremors ran through his body and he retched instead.

Who, who? Who, who?

The moon was once more on the horizon. *Why don't you just walk away?*

Better, why not run? Billy jumped, scattering clicking beetles to run toward the sound of the owl. He stumbled, smelling rotted wood. He heard a very un-Bogus like slithering. Nothing, though, would send him back to the tree, back to the boredom of hearing his life being scratched away, stuffed in a pizza oven as the moon forever rose.

Who, who? Who, who?

Twice, the owl flew off, but Billy persisted, looking back to see that the moon, silvery white now, had risen past the crooked oak, the azimuth it previously had retreated from several times.

Who, who? Who, who?

This time, Billy stayed quiet ... There it sat, twenty feet above, regal on a limb, its strictly-business talons holding the remains of a rat. Billy thought the owl was pure white, though he couldn't be sure since the moon was half-hidden by leaves.

Descending! The moon was descending! *Daylight*! This brought a rush of adrenaline whose only effect was to make Billy realize how tired he was. He watched the owl rip at the rat.

"My name is Billy Francis Wise," he said after the owl finished its meal.

"*Woo-who, woo-whooo,*" the owl replied.

"Can't you talk?"

The owl rotated its head oddly in acknowledgement of the foreign sound below.

Billy sighed. "Maybe you think it's dumb of me to expect you to talk, but I've recently met a snake and a macaw who carried on intelligent conversations, so it's only reasonable I'd think that you, with your reputation for wisdom and all, could talk too."

The owl gave no response. Feeling blood trickling from a beetle bite, Billy glanced to the ground before stepping forward. "Do you ever go out in the day, just to see what you're missing? Humans do. Go out in the night, I mean. Looking for something they missed during the day. At night they take on wings and gather in roosts to become birds ... You know, night owls and night hawks..."

The owl remained impervious to Billy's babbling, though Billy continued for half an hour. Once, he saw the owl's stomach feathers ripple. Indigestion from listening to Billy-babble?

"I know who you are." Billy pointed an accusing finger. "You're Wisdom, aren't you? I mean capital W Wisdom. And I'm supposed to learn from tonight, this being the House, after all. A moral at the end of every story, I mean every room. How about that for Good Form?"

The owl stared at some distant desire, maybe a rat raised on whole grains. Noticing something drop, Billy leaned, expecting a Rosetta Stone, or at least a Zen koan on brown rice paper. The owl lifted its tail feathers and more scat plopped onto rotting leaves.

"Wisdom—see?" Billy shivered, not from the cold, but from a wired and tired energy.

Fourth Leg: Lady Wisdom Banished

Chapter 15

Daybreak came. With it he remembered a particularly odd rotting log he spotted yesterday—whatever yesterday meant with the interminable moonrises. The log had odd, tan mushrooms growing underneath, mushrooms that today he realized resembled knobs to another dresser. *A plan. Have a plan. The man with a plan, that's who I am.* Repeating that ditty like a Bogus dictum he searched for the log in hard-edged and boring incremental squares, first counting off ten steps to a side, then fourteen, then eighteen, then twenty-two, then twenty-six, then thirty, then thirty-four...

Dizzying, he remembered that when he'd been promoted to "chef," at the pizza joint, his boss explained how expensive pepperoni was and told him to count the slices. Ten for a small pizza, Billy, seventeen for a medium, twenty-six for a large. Thirty-eight steps, forty-two steps, forty-six ... he'd never find the rotting log at this rate, at least not any faster than those fabled monkeys who, given the right Smith-Corona and the right amount of infinity, would eventually type out Shakespeare's *Hamlet*. Fifty steps, fifty-four—

Billy bolted. He ran, ran, ran until he tripped over a peculiar sycamore whose roots enveloped a large black boulder. *Wait. Not a boulder, it's a potbelly stove.* From his heart rate he had the oddball feeling that his head was going to drop off, as if Mr. Snelling really had decapitated him instead of pounding him with the flat of the sword. Squatting, Billy felt his blood pressure calm, so he tentatively touched the stove's door, fearing the house's humor might render the iron fiery. But it was "room temperature." He laughed at how meaningless that phrase was in this house. In fact, the door, which was quite large, was cool in relation to his hands. He judged its size: he could just fit in. But on grasping the black iron handle, he hesitated. After all, the hell he didn't know could be a *lot* worse than this one, the one he did know. Here, he wasn't particularly hungry, here he wasn't under any particular stress, other than fighting off a few beetles. All he'd done for the last few nights was … images of the moon rising, re-rising and re-re-rising sent a shiver through him. *Seventeen pepperonis for the medium, Billy boy. Always count 'em out.*

He twisted the iron handle. True, it could be worse, but it could also be better—the other side could hold Soapy. Setting his teeth and pulling out the dagger Sir Wilfred had given him, he crawled into the opened door …

… to tumble into a small, comfortable room paneled with pure knotty pine. "Damn!" he shouted, holding his neck in pain. Was he ever going to learn to jump into the key passageways? He'd have to get the form down right, or sooner or later he'd pop a vertebra.

He stood and scanned his new surroundings: a weathered roll top desk and an inviting chair faced the room's only window, which had collected more than its share of cobwebs. By the desk, a floor-length, brass lamp cast in the form of a nude woman balancing an amber globe atop her head blinked on. The nude woman was staring winsomely toward some imaginary star in the ceiling. Behind the lamp, outside light filtered through the window's cobwebs.

Attracted to any hint of sunshine after the dismal forest, Billy walked to wipe away the cobwebs, but drew back, for the window overlooked the graveyard he'd seen days earlier, and two stooped figures in black were walking among the graves. It was foggy out there, early morning he guessed. He watched the figures idly stooping toward each headstone, as if they'd by chance stumbled onto the graveyard and were curious. Placing Sir Wilfred's dagger to the window, he considered tapping a signal … but no, in this house it was wise to let sleeping cats lie and androgynous mysteries walk, especially if they walked in a graveyard. A time to be brave and jump, a time to be calm and lurk. Not quite *Ecclesiastes*, but close enough. Billy backed from the window to open the roll top desk. Inside, a note lay in plain view:

MEMORANDUM
TO: BILLY F. WISE
FROM: VICE PRESIDENT OF BUSINESS AFFAIRS
DATE: TODAY

IT HAS COME TO MY ATTENTION THAT YOUR WORK ABSENCES HAVE TOTALED EIGHT DAYS. PLEASE BE ADVISED THAT UNIVERSITY POLICY REQUIRES A DOCTOR'S WRITTEN EXCUSE FOR ANY EMPLOYEE MISSING OVER TEN DAYS. OTHERWISE, SAID EMPLOYEE WILL BE TERMINATED WITH THE UTMOST DISCRETION.

How could anyone be "terminated with the utmost discretion"? Would the university assign a tenure-track professor in chemistry to gas him? Would an English professor make him read Jane Austen backwards, starting with a marriage and ending with a meddlesome spat? He felt a note attached to the back of the memorandum and flipped it over to read, on an institutional green sticky Post-it:

Wise up, Wise. If you want your soft Soapy back in any form besides what you see, you'd better paly our way.

That's how it was written, "paly our way." *Play*, no doubt, was what some boob of a dyslexic house Mafioso had wanted to write. But what did the note mean, "Besides what you see"?

Looking to the lamp Billy gasped. The globe atop the cast-bronze nude's head was amber, and that amber encased a doll-sized Soapy, floating on her back to face the same stupid no-star ceiling. Was it really Soapy? Who could tell in this crazy house? He touched the amber.

Cold, cold. And then—

Jingling. Despite the sound's familiarity, Billy tightened his grip on Sir Wilfred's dagger. On turning, he saw a smallish unicorn he knew must be Alexandra shifting hooves in the doorway. This unicorn was pure white, as you'd expect, unlike the tawny color she'd worn when licking the salt block behind his house. She stood about the size of a Great Dane, and draped about her gold horn and over her back was Bogus, fangs to the fore and looking glum, even for a rattlesnake.

"It was Snelling who did it," Bogus said. "Right after he knocked you out as a party favor."

"No!" Alexandra shook her horn as if to toss the snake from her back. "That was a phantom, it wasn't really Mr. Snelling."

Bogus wrapped tighter about Alexandra's single horn and spoke, "She thinks that in all that smoke and firelight we couldn't see the usual tale-tell signs of phantoms, the glowing red eyes and shimmering outlines. But it was Snelling—or Snellings. Both of them. He walloped you and she kidnapped Soapy. One minute Soapy was gabbing with some knight, the next minute, the Perrers dame—a.k.a. Mrs. Snelling—walks by. Poof, a cloud of dirty smoke floats where Soapy stood. The knight's hand was still raised to where her bare shoulder had been. Hell, I've been telling the council all along that there are entirely too many coincidences involving Snelling and his cinnamon-y Mrs. And guess what? No one can find either of them, now that Soapy's gone. Neither one's in the throne room where they belong."

Billy tucked his dagger into his pants and caressed the standing amber lamp. "Come here and look. Is this her? Is she trapped inside this lamp?"

"No," Alexandra answered, without even walking over. "That's only a likeness. I touched it with my horn the minute we came in here to wait for you. We've been outside searching while you made up your mind."

"Made up my—" Billy remembered the pizza parlor dream and his hesitation about the pot-bellied stove. He blushed to think his indecision might have slowed finding Soapy.

"A unicorn's horn possesses magical empathy, you know," Alexandra said. "That's why I became one, so I can use it to find her."

Billy nodded and moved back to the window. The two veiled figures still lurked outside, bent over a tombstone. He motioned to Bogus and Alexandra.

"It's-s them," Bogus hissed on coming to the window.

"It can't be. They're outside the house! They can't go outside anymore than we can," Alexandra protested.

"Uh ..." Billy started to ask how she'd gotten out to walk behind his house and entice him into sleepwalking along the floor of the scummy pond, but he stopped, figuring that would somehow—no doubt—be a Bad Form question. Or maybe the pond and island were part of the house?

"It's them," Bogus insisted. "Tap the window and see."

They didn't need to tap, for a skeletal hand stretched from under one black cloak to trace a name on a headstone. Billy leaned to see that the hand and forearm were literally white bone—held together by who knew what. The face accompanying the hand turned toward its companion; then both of them looked up toward the window with fierce grins. Instinctively, Billy, Alexandra, and Bogus backed from the skulls' gazes. The taller cloaked figure withdrew its hand from the tombstone; then it and its companion hobbled out of view. A morbid thought occurred to Billy: if skulls had eyes, they wouldn't be as frightening.

"Can you read what they were pointing at?" he asked.

"My guess is that we'd rather not," Bogus said.

But Billy insisted, so with a sigh Alexandra gave a great shaking of her single horn, which slowly transformed into a flapping of wings until she was a sharp-eyed hawk. Settling on Billy's shoulder she peered out the window.

"What's it say?" Both Bogus and Billy asked.

"I still can't read it."

But Billy had felt a shudder pass through Alexandra's two hawk claws. He knew she was lying.

Chapter 16

After an angry peck at the window, Alexandra hopped from Billy's shoulder and changed back to a unicorn, reminding him that as a unicorn she could best sense the presence of Soapy. But he noticed that her empathetic gold horn first pointed toward Bogus before scanning the room to search for her sister Soapy. Had the headstone held some message about Aristotle Bogus, charter member of * + * The Society Of * + *? Billy had no time to pursue the question, for a muffled ringing sounded from the desk. Opening a drawer, he spotted an old-fashioned phone, the type that cradled a receiver on a hook and had its mouthpiece attached to the stand.

"Hello?" Billy answered.

"This wasn't your ring."

"Pardon me?"

"I said it wasn't your ring! It rang twice, that's my ring, not yours! Get off the damned line!" The voice was that of a cantankerous old man. Billy wanted to reach through the receiver and wrap the stiff, cloth-covered phone cord about the jerk's neck, but another voice interrupted:

"Billy? Billy Wise? This is Janet Gateman. Billy, I've got to tell you this: last night someone broke into the office and stole ten computers, including the one from your desk. Billy, Schroeder suspects you. Supposedly some frat boys parking in the lot gave a description of the thief that he swears fits you."

Janet Gateman, calling here? He glanced from Alexandra's golden horn to Bogus, who had his head stuck in a mouse hole. *Well hell. Why not?* Billy looked out the window and caught sight of the tombstone.

"Billy, did you hear me? They gave a description that fits you."

Billy looked at the phone. "Uh, Janet, it's not like I'm exactly a Wolfman freak or an Adonis. Plenty of guys on campus could look like me at night, as much as that, uh, fact hurts my feelings. Anyway, why the hell would I want to steal those damned computers? I work with them everyday; most high school hackers have faster machines in their bedrooms."

"I know, but I just thought I'd call and tell you. Are you any better?"

"Uh, no I'm still—you know—uh, sick at the stomach."

"Have you seen a doctor?"

"Yeah, and she said I need to stay home and rest." Always good to throw a female pronoun in to help verify your lie. Billy instinctively felt his nose.

"Okay, Billy. Drink lots of juice, okay?"

"Thanks. Uh, Janet, uh how did you find out—how did you reach me here?"

"I picked up the phone and called, how do you think? Billy, are you all right? I mean really all right? Who was that old guy who answered—"

"Come over here, youngster, and I'll show you old! I've got a pecker bone that—"

"Uh fine, Janet. I'm fine. I don't know who he is—some loony redneck whose line has crossed mine."

"Well teach him some manners, I told you moving to the country was a mistake. Okay, Billy, remember what I told you about Schroeder. He's become a real maniac now that those machines have disappeared."

"Thanks, Janet." Billy hung up and turned to Bogus and Alexandra, but the room was empty and its door stood open. He ran out into an unbelievably long hallway with Persian carpet and taupe walls—the house up to more of its tricks.

"Wait up!" he shouted, seeing Bogus atop Alexandra, who was trotting fifty yards away down the palatial hall. Alexandra turned, pawing the carpet impatiently. Upon realizing that she was even farther away than he first thought, Billy also realized that she'd changed into a larger unicorn, one the size of a thoroughbred stallion.

"Hop on!" Bogus said when Billy caught up.

Once Billy did, they rode at a goodly pace down the hall for ten minutes, occasionally passing a regally stuffed chair or a barren pew outside one or another of the many doors. It seemed as if they were traversing a huge Five Star hotel, except there were no room numbers. They passed another pew, over which was hung a glass case holding an antique fire hose whose weathered fabric would burst with even a trickle of water. Alexandra touched her horn to the glass then cantered onwards.

Beside a farther door hung the painting "Blue Boy." Billy did a double take to see the kid leaning on a red BMW.

When Alexandra slowed with a wheeze, they seemed no nearer the end of the hall and its source of light than before. She bent to touch a door on their right and her horn glowed crimson.

"Soapy's in there!" Bogus said.

Alexandra reared to smash at the door. In doing so, her horn sprung a series of wood panels in the ceiling and they were inundated in a flurry of old-style greenish-white computer paper, fanfolds and fanfolds of it, enough to knock Billy and Bogus off Alexandra. The avalanche continued as paper drifted down from ceiling panels that kept springing in a chain-reaction. When Billy dodged one fanfold of paper he was hit with another, getting knocked down three times. Then came a muffled closing, like trap doors being shut. Billy was aware of the sound, but he saw nothing other than paper above, under, and around him. He was trying to shove it away from his eyes and nose when Alexandra's thrashing hoof slammed into his shoulder. He screamed for her to be careful. In answer, he heard a heavy thud: evidently entangled in the paper she'd slipped. Her thrashing increased, and Billy pushed away from her panic.

"Alex-sandra, Alex-sandra, Alex-sandra..." Bogus chanted until the unicorn slowed to listen. "Change into a gnat and fly up. Your horn left a scuff on the roof. Look for it, then change into a macaw and call us over. We'll get to your sister that way. It's the quickest way."

There was a rustling and Billy presumed Alexandra was doing as Bogus had suggested.

"Bogus, are you okay?"

"Yes-s," the snake answered.

Though that hiss left no doubt what the snake's teeth looked like, Billy felt reasonably safe: even as a gnat, Alexandra must be having trouble getting through this morass of paper, so how could anything dangerous get to him? Logic, no? Except what the hell was computer paper doing in the house anyway? Didn't old geezer Snelling say they'd decided against computers because the house didn't have electricity? Logic, yes? But then maybe he and his old lady had put the cart before the horse, or maybe the security crew at the university had discovered the house too and dumped old test scores here. Billy looked at a sheet, but any reading light was blocked by so many other sheets.

He felt something tug his sock. Bogus. He bent down, grimacing at the crackling roar of shifting paper. Being surrounded by the stuff had a way of magnifying its intensity. It was worse than carrying six round-the-world pizzas at once.

"Clackers are on their way," Bogus said when Billy stopped moving.

"How do you know?"

"I can hear them."

"How—" Billy bit off the question. He'd always understood that snakes couldn't hear, that they had to use their tongues to sense heat. More of the house's magic, no doubt.

"Vibrations, Billy, that's how. You'd be surprised what you can learn crawling around on your belly. A little humility towards your brethren and sistren species, for one."

"Over here, over here!"

"Alexandra," Billy answered. Yes, now he heard clacking too, or rather a scissor-like cutting mixed with clacking, and it was coming from the same direction as Alexandra's voice.

"On thy belly, homo s-sapiens-s." Billy felt a tug at his blue jeans until he tumbled through the slippery paper. "It's easier to pass through this mess-s by crawling," Bogus explained.

Billy got on his hands and knees and crawled—his movement was noisy so they had to stop and listen as Alexandra kept calling in her incarnation as a myna bird. Whenever they paused, the clacking and scissor-like cutting seemed nearer. At last Billy found the doorjamb and worked his way up to the doorknob. A scissor-like snip closed near his head and tingled his scalp. Though he'd dodged, blood flowed down his temple. He'd managed, however, to keep a crouching hold on the door.

At his feet he could hear thrashing. He pulled Sir Wilfred's dagger from his belt as the scissor-arms of a clacker opened for another try. "Frazzle Two!" he shouted, sweeping the dagger in a wide arc until it contacted and cut through the brittle clacker, who gave a tinny death cry.

The noise of the clackers increased in a flurry.

"Open the door, Peanut-head!" Bogus yelled.

Billy's hand gripped the doorknob and turned . . . locked? No, he was turning the wrong way. Another turn in another direction and the door opened. He spilled into what looked like a tan living room; he spilled in along with computer paper and who knew what else?

"Close it, close it!"

Billy felt a stinging on his leg then heard a brittle snap, then another. Finding traction on a carpet he shoved the door, leaning into it at a nearly horizontal angle. With his newly christened Frazzle Two in hand he managed to clear away enough computer paper to see several wiry black bamboo arms and legs working their way inside.

"Alexandra! Change into a unicorn and help me push!"

No sooner said than Billy was shoved aside by a bulky flank and the door was moved to within a few inches of closing. Shaking off computer paper he saw spidery black bamboo arms, more like razor-honed coat hangers than anything organic, writhing about the door's seams. He hacked at them and pulled at paper, trying to avoid the razor-tentacles.

"Frazzle Two! Frazzle Two!" he shouted...

Chapter 17

Even if Billy had been a Civil War buff and had mapped and plotted every battle from Harper's Ferry to Appomattox, he couldn't have predicted how long it would take to close the door. Forty minutes later they were still fighting, for every time he pulled paper from between the doorjamb and the door, a clacker's black tentacle would slice out, preventing him from closing it. How could the clackers be so strong yet so thin? Was it because they piled outside the door like lemmings at a cliff? They seemed as careless of their lives as lemmings, very unlike his first encounter with them. With all those black bamboo tentacles slashing under and around her, Alexandra was nearly hamstrung and finally had to slump her withers against the door while Bogus and Billy cut, pulled, and hacked.

Billy's voice became hoarse from shouting "Frazzle Two" without effect. He shortened his more-cough-than-yell to "Frazzle!" Within a minute, all the clackers were gone after shouts of "Sfword! Sfword!"

It took him and Bogus two more minutes of thrashing to realize the fact.

"What happened?" Billy asked, his head against the door listening to the silence from the hallway outside.

"Frazzle. You yelled 'Frazzle!' "

"I've been yelling that all along!"

"You've been yelling 'Frazzle Two!' all along. I guess they didn't know what you meant."

"Nobody's that stupid, not even Florida voters."

But the undeniable fact was that the clackers were gone. So Billy and Bogus shoved the computer paper out and closed the door. It had a safety latch, which Billy latched. Alexandra hadn't moved. She had several bad slices on her legs, and Billy worried she really might be hamstrung. Pulling off his belt for a tourniquet, he convinced Bogus to squeeze his snake body like a boa constrictor about the gash on her other foreleg. Doing so, they both became slick with her blood.

In the stillness, they sat assuring Alexandra and apprising the room they were in. If you carted away the huge pile of bloody computer paper littered about, it would be the living room to a typical middle-class American house from the 50s: couch, La-Z-Boy, coffee table, even a TV set that was for some reason turned on and showing Lawrence Welk lifting a tiny conductor's baton. As bubbles floated stupidly on the screen, Billy thanked all the stars in heaven that the television's sound was off or broken. He sniffed: something somewhere was cooking, maybe corned beef and cabbage. He leaned against the door, feeling glumly elated.

Glumly elated? Oxymorons, he realized, were part and parcel to the house. "Frazzle," he intoned again, lifting the dagger Sir Wilfred had given him. Two rubies were in the hilt. Wait, hadn't there been only one before? And the ruby ring Lady Perrers had given him: it was missing. He was too tired to think.

"Frazzle," he said again after breathing. "All I had to do was say 'Frazzle' and not 'Frazzle Two.' I don't believe it."

"Believe it," Bogus said. "The clackers would make great fodder for your American school system."

Billy ignored the insult, for Alexandra moaned. He leaned to wipe her brow and idly read a piece of computer paper:

House Rules

1. Don't cuss.
2. Always sit up straight.
3. Remember your Mom and Dad on Valentine's Day.
4. Obey all signs.
5. Don't chew gum in the halls.

5a. Don't stick chewed gum under carpets.

  6. No cut-offs or tube socks.

  7. Observe Good Form: never leave a room in the house before spending the night.

  8. No horseplay. Ever.

  9. Smile: it uses fewer muscles.

  10. Be happy.

"This is the most ridiculous thing I've ever seen." Billy handed the rules to Bogus, who barely lifted his head.

"Oh yeah, House Rules. We had to memorize those when I was a kid."

Billy gave the snake a frown, doubting that he'd ever been a kid; then he looked through the computer paper surrounding them. The same rules were printed on every sheet. "Stupid, stupid, stupid." He was too tired to delve into more analytical detail, so he checked the door's lock and fell asleep. He dreamed a modern art canvas of white, crisscrossed with shiny threatening black wisps. The image made him twitch, but then modern art always did that to him.

Chapter 18

It was his nose that woke him. Corned beef and cabbage *was* cooking. "Ow!" he intoned with his first movement. Tiny cuts he hadn't felt all night now made themselves known. Gashes made themselves even more known. He blinked away tears of pain. Gazing over a three-foot mound of computer paper beyond his sprawled feet, he saw an archway leading into another room. That second room's ugly green wallpaper, a tall cherry cupboard, and drawn blinds peeped back. Taking several deep breaths, Billy stood as quietly as he could since Alexandra was asleep. He winced on looking at her legs. She needed to sleep. The wounds had stopped bleeding, but the floor and much of the scattered paper was dark maroon. Bogus was still coiled around her leg, though he was no longer squeezing.

Billy smiled. Always smile, no matter what. Uses fewer muscles. At least he was obeying a house rule. Hearing something drop in the next room he pulled Frazzle's replacement from his belt and tiptoed through strewn and bloodied paper.

Besides the furniture he'd seen, the second room held only a wooden dining table and chairs. Adjoining to its right was a short hallway with two, three closed doors; adjoining to its left, a small open kitchen. On the stove in the kitchen a large soup pot steamed—the corned beef and cabbage? On the kitchen's dirty green tile floor lay a paperback. Billy bent for it. *Thus Spoke Zarathustra*, with a picture of a mustachioed Nietzsche. As he lifted the book a rose petal fell. He touched the petal to his nose and smelled. Soapy, he was sure of it, though he couldn't say why. He didn't even need Alexandra's unicorn horn to tell him. He rubbed the dark, velvety petal: still fresh and soft.

"Soapy!" he called, lunging for the kitchen's back door. But it was dead-bolted and its curtain—ridiculously—was on the other side of the glass, leaving him in effect blind as to anything outside. Giving a last jerk at the door, he ran to check the rest of the house, briefly peeping over the mound of computer paper at Bogus and Alexandra, who were still sleeping.

The other side of the house consisted of the three doors in the almost non-existent hallway. He opened one to a bedroom with a four-poster bed, a baby crib, a dresser and two closets packed with musty clothes. The windows were also closed to any outside view, with curtains again placed ridiculously on the unreachable side, the outside. Billy tried to raise one window, but it was locked. Emerging from that room, he saw Bogus, who was blinking hard to clear sleep from his eyes.

"I found this," Billy said, showing Bogus the book.

"So?"

"So I'm sure it belongs to Soapy."

"*Thus Spoke Zarathustra?* Why would she read a translation when she could read the original German?"

Billy looked at the book doubtfully. Then he showed Bogus the rose petal. Bogus forked his tongue out at the petal in an exploratory manner.

"Maybe," he said.

Billy nodded toward the two remaining doors. The one straight ahead was a bathroom that stank like it belonged in a gas station, the one to their right was another bedroom, smaller, and as before the locked windows were curtained on the outside. They opened a closet, empty, except for mothballs scattered on the floor. Turning from the closet, Billy noticed bookshelves hidden behind the door. The top shelves held mostly paperbacks on philosophy, the bottom shelves held Uncle Scrooge and Donald Duck comic books.

"See," he said to Bogus. "She didn't have any choice in her reading matter."

Bogus weaved his head noncommittally then gave the books a once-over flicker of his tongue. "Maybe," he said, coiling back and slithering out the door.

Billy mouthed a "damn," then started out too, but turned back to pick up an Uncle Scrooge comic. His father had always mocked him for reading them. Maybe Uncle Scrooge and his money-hungry ways struck too close to home for Dad's taste.

From the hallway, Billy saw Bogus in the kitchen, coiled and flicking his tongue frantically. He also caught sight of a broom being waved. Bogus struck out and the broom countered. A woman stepped forward.

"Janet!" Billy shouted. "Bogus, it's okay. I know her."

The broom sent Bogus sprawling into the dining room. "Tell *her*, tell *her*!" Bogus shouted.

"Janet! It's okay. I mean, it doesn't look okay, but it is: he's friendly. Change your teeth, Bogus. Show her."

Bogus traded his fangs for his Jimmy Carter-Teddy Roosevelt campaign smile. Janet laughed, a bit hysterically, so Billy walked to reassure her. Janet was a mid-sized but wiry woman in her late twenties, with freckles that came out every time she returned from a ballgame or vacation, or hunting. She was an avid hunter, having learned that from her father—or so she told everyone in the office. She had a pleasant way of tossing her coal black hair every time she smiled, and that had always intrigued Billy. Before his divorce, they'd talked at office parties. He'd toyed with the idea of asking her out since then, but hadn't got up his nerve.

"How in the world did you get here?" he asked, stepping between her and Bogus.

"What's a rattlesnake doing in your house, Billy? Are you nuts?"

"My—" He saw that the window to the kitchen door behind Janet was open now. He could see what looked like his back yard, deck, gate, field and all.

"Who's she?" The voice was edgy. It came from Alexandra, who stood midway in the dining room, under its arch.

"A pony, Billy? You keep a pony and a snake in your house? What's the horn on its head? Is it some African animal?"

"Janet, this is Bogus and that's Alexandra. They're uh friends of mine. And this is Janet: she works with me in Purchasing at the University."

The three stared. Not particularly a mutual admiration society.

"Well?" Billy asked.

"Pleased to meet you, I'm sure," Alexandra said, giving a mock curtsy. Billy noted that she wobbled as she did.

Janet completely ignored Alexandra and kept talking to Billy: "What's going on, Billy? Are these real or—"

"Mmmph," Bogus said, his coiling upward effectively cutting off Janet.

Billy could swear he heard a hiss buried in that "Mmmph." Was this really Janet or just another phantom like the one in the cave that pretended to be Soapy?

"She's real enough," Alexandra said, as if reading Billy's mind. "And if she's from your office, the question becomes, just as you asked, how'd she get here?"

"And why?" Bogus added.

"Billy? Why aren't you answering me? Why is this menagerie in your house?"

Billy gave Janet a look. She made no indication of having heard either Bogus or Alexandra speak. "You can't hear them, can you? You can't hear the snake and the unicorn talking."

"Unicorn?" Janet leaned to peer at Alexandra, keeping her eye on the snake. Then she looked at Billy: "Talking, Billy? Talking?" She nodded toward the stove. "I put on some chicken soup for you. Eat it; then go see a doctor, Billy. You don't look well at all."

Janet backed toward the door. When Billy stepped forward she made a slight motion with the broom.

"Eat the soup, Billy. Schroeder's sending some cop out here to your house this afternoon: he's sure you stole the computers. Billy, don't tell the policeman that your friends can talk, okay? Campus cops don't have any sense of humor; they get it from dealing with drunken students and alumni during football season."

Janet dropped the broom and stepped out the kitchen door. Billy rushed forward, but it was dead-bolted by the time he reached it. And once more, the curtain was on the outside.

"Bullshit!" he shouted, taking the broom handle and breaking the window. Wind sucked the broken glass outside and even pressed him to the door.

Bogus was being slid along the floor and Billy could hear Alexandra neighing. Billy's nose and face chaffed where the wind blasted past. Suddenly his hand was sucked against the broken pane. It stuck there, as if to dry ice. He jerked away with a yell as the wind stopped. Filling the pane was a thick layer of solid white ice. His hand had a patch of skin torn off and throbbed like it had been burned.

On the stove, the soup pot bubbled.

Chapter 19

"It's not corned beef and cabbage," Billy said, lifting the lid. "I thought it smelled like corned beef and cabbage."

"She said she was cooking you chicken soup, so that's what it is. Proof that not all humans speak with forked tongues."

Billy picked up a ladle and glanced at Bogus, who was resting his triangular head in the seat of a yellow vinyl chair whose chrome legs came straight from the 50's, just as the Lawrence Welk on the TV had. Most of the snake's body, however, coiled fatly on the dirty green linoleum floor. It really didn't look comfortable at all, more like some weird yoga pose. "Bogus, when I first woke up, corned beef and cabbage was cooking, I'm sure."

Alexandra, remaining a unicorn, was limping through the hall touching her horn to the doors and the hardwood floor, an act she'd been repeating obsessively since Janet Gateman had left. She clip-clopped to plop her haunches spraddle-legged on the floor near the dining room table, and her stare turned immediately blank. Billy noted thick patches of ugly black gore blood clotting her back inner legs, too, not just her forelegs.

"Uh, can't you change into a new, healthy body?" As soon as he asked he figured he'd get the usual "Bad Form" answer.

"The magic of transforming won't cure physical ailments," Bogus replied, as Alexandra seemed too preoccupied or too sick to answer.

"Corned beef and cabbage was Soapy's favorite," Alexandra said, stirring from her lethargy, though her delivery stayed flat.

"You see, I told you she'd been here, Bogus," Billy stopped stirring the soup. Without taking his eyes off Alexandra, he lifted the philosophy book from the counter and walked to her. "Look at what's inside." He opened the book to the rose petal. Alexandra touched it with her horn then stirred nervously, unwilling to sit longer, though she had trouble standing and slipped once.

"This rose has been with my sister. We need to go, we need to find her."

"Bad Form, Alexandra, you know that. Stay in each room at least a day to learn something. And always eat what the house provides." Bogus nodded toward the stove and the chicken soup. "You need rest and you need nourishment." Bogus, who'd finally oozed up to settle on the yellow vinyl chair, slouched his head over its back.

"I'm not going to eat *that*," Alexandra said, throwing her mane haughtily at the soup Billy was stirring. "*She* made it, not my sister; she made it and threw out what Soapy made. It's probably poisoned."

Billy nervously sniffed the broth. It smelled great, not poisoned. "You both said that Janet wasn't a phantom. If she wasn't a phantom and was really Janet Gateman, then this isn't poisoned. Janet's a friend."

"Why's *she* visiting you anyway? What's *she* doing *here* anyway? A friend? She'd have to be awfully interested in you for the house to bring her here."

"Alexandra's right about that, Billy. The house doesn't pick up strangers willy-nilly."

Billy poured the soup into three bowls. He wasn't so sure about the house's motives and said so. After all, it had picked him up willy-nilly. But then … could Janet Gateman have a romantic inclination toward him? Why else would she have troubled to drive out to his house and warn him about Schroeder? Drive out, evidently, with a pot of chicken soup. Maybe she was just being nice. Maybe, he told himself, you shouldn't get your hormones roaring so quickly. Just because Alexandra's in a tiff doesn't mean you need to follow her fourteen-year-old lead. He placed a bowl before Bogus and the snake immediately began slurping. Alexandra, on the other hand, moped and turned her head when Billy placed a bowl on the floor near her.

"Better eat, Alexie baby. Shhhhhllluuup. You know the house rules: Always eat what the house gives, when it gives."

Billy sat at the kitchen table before his soup. "I didn't see that printed on those ridiculous rules that fell on us."

"An unwritten rule, sort of like your golden one, 'Love thy neighbor as thyself.' "

Raising an eyebrow, Billy wondered if the unwritten house rule about eating was obeyed as poorly as the golden one about loving. Dipping his spoon into the soup, he closed his eyes against Bogus's slurps. But after only one spoonful, Billy realized how hungry he was and began to slurp himself. Within minutes, he'd served himself and Bogus a second helping. Regardless of whether Janet had concocted this with love in mind or not, she cooked a mean potion. Alexandra, though, still pouted in front of her untouched bowl. A spraddle-legged unicorn is not a pretty sight, Billy decided. And she looked pale, with all the blood she'd lost from pushing the door closed.

"Alexandra," he said between spoonfuls, "this soup's great. You really should eat some before we go looking for your sister."

With a wallop of her hoof, Alexandra sent the bowl skidding across the kitchen floor to splatter against Billy's chair.

"Alexandra!" Bogus shouted, his eyes bulging and his snake tail quivering. Chicken soup dripped from his mouth as he shouted "Alexie, don't!"

The snake was showing more concern than Billy could comprehend. After all, she was fourteen and had lost her sister. She was entitled to a tantrum.

"Alexie, do something. Pick it up, say you're sorry. Eat it. Do something!"

Alexandra hobbled from the dining room toward the smaller bedroom where Billy had found the philosophy books. The door slammed. Bogus looked as pale as a fat tan and brown rattlesnake can look. He sullenly turned to finish his soup, mumbling "Bad Form, Bad Form."

"How can a house care about form? Just what is this house, anyway, some type of creature?" Billy asked suddenly.

"What's your earth?" Bogus answered with a shrug that rumbled along his neck. "Give me a lever long enough and I'll move it. Doesn't mean I'll explain it, though." After a slurp, the snake continued, "You want to know what I've thought the house is for maybe a hundred years or more? Being as this is my latest theory, I'll tell you whether you want to know or not, since I need a sounding board. I think it's the center of the universe, like maybe a computer on a spaceship or a gyroscope on a nautical ship or maybe a nucleotide in a cell. More than a center, maybe a testing ground like you Americans had in the Nevada and New Mexico deserts."

"Then why was I called here?"

"A test for the testing ground? You got me. Maybe you're the lever."

"But Soapy said some council or other brought me here."

"Soapy," Bogus sighed, looking toward the direction where Alexandria ran off. "Soapy's a beautiful girl, but I bet her corned beef and cabbage isn't nearly as good as this chicken soup because, you know, Soapy just might occasionally toss a few cut-up tarantulas from that Nietzsche book into her corned beef. I'd keep that in mind in case you ever do get to taste it."

Billy crossed his eyes. "Tarantulas, like Gila monsters?"

"Metaphorical tarantulas. Like, you know, 'God is dead; yay God!' That one strikes me as a pretty thick-haired tarantula."

Billy absently ran his spoon through his soup. "What about this council?"

"Council, shmouncil. A bunch of frightened bureaucrats. The Snellings send them directives like your man Schroeder drops you memorandums." Bogus lifted his head from the soup bowl; a noodle stuck out of his mouth like a bleached Snidely Whiplash moustache. "Billy, you're not the first person to be brought here, you know—"

"Edison."

"No, Edison was a fluke. Most people who are brought here are just like you: workadays with no special qualifications other than a lot of heart." As Billy crinkled his brow, Bogus added, "That's a compliment, by the way."

"Compliment, shmompliment."

Billy relented, and at Bogus's insistence they finished the pot of soup except for one bowl. Bogus said their show of hunger might appease the house for Alexandra's intransigence then added that maybe they could entice her to eat the last bowl after she'd slept or cried her fill. "This kidnapping of Soapy," the snake added as an afterthought when he flipped his bowl up to the sink for Billy to wash. "This isn't the first time something like this has happened. Alexandra is extremely idealistic, which goes with the territory of her youth." Bogus paused to study something on the wall and smack his lips, but let out a snake belch instead of pursuing whatever he'd seen. "But then again, if

Alexie had been around for the other kidnappings maybe she'd be even more upset."

"What happened then?"

"Soapy almost died." The snake looked oddly at Billy, as if weighing him for a recipe. Hmm, let's see: one hundred sixty pounds of Billy meat, forty-five pounds of potato, fifty pounds of garlic ... "Maybe that Chaucer fellow we met had it right when he called her Lady Wisdom. What would you think if that were true?"

Billy shrugged.

"I can tell you this much: when disorder moves the house out of balance, that's always when Soapy disappears. And it's always when the council elects Mrs. Snelling to take over and run affairs..."

Bogus became lost in his own thoughts while Billy ran water over their empty bowls, figuring what good form it would be to clean the dishes. He glanced to the back door: the ice on the broken pane was still throwing off vapor, but something odd was attached beneath. "Damn," he said, walking over to pull off another Xeroxed note.

MEMORANDUM

TO: BILLY WISE, ET. AL.

FROM: ERNEST SCHROEDER, M.S., B.S.

DATE: TODAY

RE: IT HAS COME TO MY ATTENTION THAT YOU ARE RECEIVING NON-DEPARTMENTAL MAIL THROUGH THE MAIL (SEE ATTACHED XEROX). MOREOVER, THE MATERIAL IS SEXUALLY OFFENSIVE. THIS PRACTICE MUST CEASE. SEE ME WHEN YOU RETURN TO WORK WITH YOUR DOCTOR'S EXCUSE IN HAND.

Billy flipped the memo over to see a Xeroxed cover to *Hustler*. Circled in red were his name and the address of the purchasing department. He certainly hadn't ordered the magazine. Did it still exist? More of Linda's bad taste, no doubt. He'd hoped that her one joke with the *Playboy* centerfold was enough. Evidently not. Well, *she* knew plenty well how to take advantage of stupid rules. She always had. Talk about Bad Form, she was its queen.

"Something to do with Soapy?" Bogus asked.

Billy shook his head. "How are you at biting ex-wives?"

"Not too good," Bogus admitted. "They usually chip my fangs."

Billy slid the memorandum on the table and the snake laughed.

"Flip it over," Billy said. "My ex-wife sent it. Her idea of a joke. All I need is one English professor to find that in my campus mail and I'd be hauled before a major politically correct ethics committee filled with New Age Dominicans."

"Hell hath no horn like a woman's scorn."

Billy stared at the noodle still sticking out of Bogus's mouth, wishing the snake would at least get his corny dictums right. Or wipe his mouth, one.

Bogus flipped to the Xerox of the bimbo beauty from *Hustler* and rollicked, swaying the chair. "Whew! Hard to tell whether this gal spent more money on breast or lip implants. With lips like hers she could swallow two Gila monsters at once." Bogus finally slurped in the noodle. "This ex-wife of yours ... how'd a nice guy like you ever tangle with a bear-baiter like her? Oh never mind—stupid question—snakes have hormones too, you know."

"Shouldn't we go check on Alexandra?" Billy snatched the memorandum and the *Hustler* cover, crumpling both.

"Touchy, touchy. Dry the dishes first then we'll go. And bring along the bowl of soup. She'll need it."

When they reached the small bedroom, Billy smelled a rot hanging in the air, like liquid iron, a rot that completely blotted out the soup he carried. He shifted uneasily before the door.

"Go ahead," Bogus said, but his voice cracked and his Presidential smile was missing. *So he smells it too.* The light from the kitchen and dining room behind reflected sickly yellow in the hall.

Alexandra groaned as they opened the door; at least Billy thought she did. She lay sprawled on the bed in a most unnatural manner. A gash on her right leg had evidently reopened, for blood had puddled on the bed sheet. Her mouth was working slowly, her chest barely heaving. Billy rushed to touch her forehead: clammy. He looked at the leg, but since the blood had congealed once more, he was afraid to shift her. Not knowing what else to do, he stuck the soup by her mouth. Her tongue fell out once to lap it, but drew back in, letting the soup trickle onto the bed.

"Alexie, you have to take some soup." Bogus had crawled up the foot of the bed and was pleading, nudging one of her hooves with his nose. Billy moved the bowl closer but there was no further response. Her eyes were open and fixed on the wall—no, on a rose petal in the bed. Seeing it, Billy bit his lips and placed his hand on her neck.

"She's dead."

No response.

"Bogus, she's dead."

Bogus coiled and struck viciously at a wooden window frame by the foot of the bed. Glass shattered and he flew through. Just as in the kitchen, Billy felt air being sucked from the room and his lungs. He started toward the broken window to follow Bogus, but gasped and passed out, crumpling against the frame and broken glass instead.

Fifth Leg: Bad Form, Good Form

Chapter 20

Billy awoke slumped against a persimmon tree. Bogus, either asleep or in a daze, lay stretched atop a fallen pine. They were at the edge of a field, with a couple dozen cows grazing nearby. It was mid-morning, judging by the heat and light and smell of manure. A single ripe persimmon lay orangely by Billy's side. He reached out and ate it, its pulp incredibly sweet for so early in the season.

"You're awake." Bogus lifted his head. His voice had lost its liveliness; in fact it droned, while his two rattles lay as listless as un-popped kernels of corn.

"Why'd you strike at the window?" Billy asked, rubbing his growling stomach.

"I was so upset about Alexandra that I wanted to hit at something—no, I wanted to hit at the house. Like a kid kicking the earth." Bogus dropped off the rotting pine and crawled up the stump that once had been the pine's home, coiling to search the area. "Bad Form, you know—striking out at the house like that, I mean." He twisted about, still intent. "I think, Sir Uh Billy, that by doing that I've landed both of us in a jam jar with a sealed lid."

"We're alive anyway," Billy said.

Bogus stared at him dully.

Remembering Alexandra lying dead on the bed, Billy bit his lip and gazed off at the cows, which had moved closer. They looked tawny and familiar. "Damn," he whispered. "Bogus, let me up on that stump."

Once there, Billy saw a familiar grey roof. "I can see my house in Tuscaloosa, right over that rise. So we really aren't there anymore, are we? In the real—in

The House, I mean. Can we even get to Soapy? Or back to Alexandra to bury her?"

Bogus shook his head morosely. Billy sat on the stump, but jumped up quickly when he was stung by fire ants. Dancing around, he slapped at the seat of his pants, cursing and kicking the stump. This action only bruised his toe. "Damn it, Bogus, why didn't they bite you?"

Bogus just rippled his skin.

Billy frowned. "Look, Bogus, we'll just go back to the pond and the bath tub. We can do that, can't we?" Billy wasn't even sure the snake had heard him. "Bogus?"

"I just can't shake the image of Alexandra lying dead in that bed," Bogus sighed.

Billy flinched, worrying that he'd never see that room or Alexandra again. Would someone bury her? He hated to think of her body in that bed, her open and glazed eyes staring at that single rose petal, rotting. It was then that he spotted the Nietzsche book under some leaves; he must have grabbed it before lunging through the window after Bogus. Lunging, yes—but he hadn't really made it through, he was sure. He felt gashes on his stomach, deeper than the cuts from the fight at the door. Pulling a piece of glass out, he realized how tired he was, and stiff.

"Bogus, did you pull me out that window, out of The House?" Billy recalled his last conscious thought, one of pain as glass ripped through his shirt to do its damage.

Though Bogus let out a snake hiss, it didn't sound ominous, just tired. "It was more like you were blown out by the wind. Then the window iced over; then the damned House disappeared. Poof! Its outside was an ugly purple brick—good riddance to bad architecture."

"Brick? I thought it was cedar."

"What's it matter? Accidental form is the very worst type of Bad Form."

"Uh, I'm not sure what you—"

"Philosophy. Aristotle, my namesake."

"Oh."

They were silent for several minutes.

"I guess we should at least walk on back to my house."

Bogus didn't respond, other than to slither into a patch of sunlight, away from the shade that was edging toward his tail. *It's not morning, it's late afternoon*, Billy thought dully. With inspiration, he hopped back on the stump and looked toward the woods, quickly jumping off before the fire ants had another chance at inter-species intolerance.

"Bogus! Listen to me! We're close, really close. Why can't we simply dive into the pond, then into the bathtub again, then walk back to The House? That's how we got there in the first place, after all."

Lifting his head, Bogus displayed his Presidential teeth. "Defy the House Rules! I like the ring of that. I've always figured that maybe it was Bad Form to worry too much about Bad Form." The snake's tongue darted to flick at a fire ant on his skin. "Not today, though. It's late, and you remember how long it took to walk to The House after the bathtub, don't you? We can't be caught in those fields of tall grass at night."

"We could at least go to the pond and sleep."

"No way. There's snakes!"

Billy laughed, arching his eyebrows.

"I'm serious. Blacksnakes prowl at night and there's nothing they'd like better than a yummy rattlesnake. Normally, I wouldn't go there at all, but it's the one relaxing place where I can talk with Soapy or Alex—" Bogus cut himself off and stared at a distant treeline.

"Easy enough, then," Billy said, changing the subject from Alexandra. "We can stay the night at my house."

He really didn't think it was easy, though, for Alexandra's death and the fight at the door had taken their tolls. He was tired and wasn't up to any more dealings with The House or magic that evening. They'd probably do Soapy more harm than good, even if they could find her. And too, he wondered about Bad Form, in spite of Bogus's enthusiasm to defy it. Were they obliged to stay out of The House for a night, treat the outside just like a room?

Chapter 21

A note from Janet Gateman was taped on the screen door when they reached Billy's home:

Wise—

What the hell's going on? I come here again after worrying about how weird you acted today, with the "unicorn" and pet snake and all, and I go into the house since there's no answer, thinking you might be passed out or something and guess what I find? Yeah, I'm sure you know. The ten computers from work. Why, Billy? Don't bother answering. And don't worry either, I'm not going to snitch. But do us both a favor and quit work, so I'm not tempted to, okay? Great knowing you.

Janet

"Ten computers? What the—" Billy ran inside to his bedroom, bashing his hip on the dining room table as he did. There they perched in all their get-fired-from-your-job-grand-larceny-glory: ten computers recognizably from the purchasing department because of their metal inventory tags. Atop each computer sat a color monitor with its own metal inventory tag. Billy's heart thumped and he looked wildly out the window, fearing the entire campus police force would barge in with riot guns, shock wands, and attack dogs.

"Bogus!"

Bogus slithered into the bedroom. "Starting a collection?" the snake asked.

"Very funny. Someone's using my home for storage of items that could not only get me fired, but get me some prison time, too. These computers came from the office where I work."

"I thought you were working for Snelling and Snelling now."

Billy did a double take, then remembered Mr. and Mrs. Snelling. "Yeah, well I haven't seen a paycheck yet, so I'll not burn any bridges. Bogus, you don't suppose that someone in The House—or someone at work?" Billy threw up his hands. "I'm just an ordinary jerk, it's not like I've made any big Mafia enemies."

"What about that loving wife of yours?"

"Not even Linda would—"

"Shouldn't you at least hide them while you're debating their origin?"

"No, what I should do is call the university police and ... hell, I don't know, plead insanity, tell them I've been kidnapped to a magical House by a mysterious woman and her sidekick snake and unic—" he stopped at the mention of Alexandra—"no joking matter, sorry. Why don't I fix us some coffee?"

"How about a Maker's Mark instead?" Bogus pulled out one of his miracle half-pints, claiming it was his last until they got back to the house. Billy doubted it, from the bulges remaining in the snake's skin.

"No need to squirrel your bottles away from me. You're in civilization now, remember. There's liquor stores peppered all over Tuscaloosa."

They went to the kitchen. At first Billy himself refused any Maker's Mark, percolating coffee instead, but with Bogus's third saucer, the sweet mash smell drifted up and Billy gave in, dolloping a jigger into his coffee.

"Why's my life been so tangled lately?" he asked, taking a large dose.

Bogus slurped. He was resting his triangular head over a breadbasket atop Billy's small wooden kitchen table. They sat by a window, watching the sun setting through treetops. A crow flew by, black against the roseate sky.

"Maybe it's always been that way, Billy. Maybe you're just now growing up and realizing it."

"Great answer. You ever thought of a career in counseling? Your clientele's suicide rate would save America millions in psychiatric fees."

"Life's hard, and then you turn to grave-mush. What do you want me to say? I just lost Alexandra because of some stupid rule or her hardheadedness—I mean, maybe that damned soup would have given her enough energy to fight off the wounds. On top of that, Soapy's lost, and if I ever find her I'll have to tell her that her sister's dead. You, you're worried about computers. I gave you the only advice I knew: hide them. Why don't you take them to that woman who made us the soup, the one who left you that note?"

Billy felt his shirt pocket, surprised that he was still carrying Janet's note. *Where's Soapy's book?* The thought panicked him and he rushed from the kitchen without a word.

There. Under the dining room table. He must have dropped it when he hit his hip running in to see what Janet's note meant.

"Don't say I didn't warn you about her," Bogus said from the doorway as Billy assured himself that the rose petal was still between its pages. "Come on, Romeo, we can at least put those computers by the door. If nothing else, we can tote them to the lake and drop them in."

"We?" Bill asked. "Would you be pulling the wagon load in your incarnation as a nearly rattle-less rattlesnake?"

"I'm the moral support crew. A moral without support is like a morning without dew."

But when they walked to the bedroom, the computers were no longer there. All that remained were their imprints on Billy's bed and pillows.

"It's The House, isn't it, Bogus?" Billy said, placing his hand on one of the imprints and looking around his empty bedroom. "The damned House. It's not Linda; it's the Snellings. Mrs. Snelling said she wanted computers, so she just took some." He smacked the flat of his hand against the bedroom's door. "Why didn't she steal them from Office Depot? Why from my department? Why, Bogus?"

But Aristotle Bogus was no longer behind him.

"Bogus?"

"In the kitchen!"

Billy felt for Soapy's book, gave one last glance to the imprints on his bed then walked to the kitchen. Bogus was back on the table. He'd somehow poured himself and Billy a drink.

"Welcome to Why-World, sports fan," he said. "Let's toast it."

Billy picked up his glass and nudged Bogus's saucer.

"Cheers," they both intoned glumly.

The sun set and the crows hushed, to be replaced with the lonely hoot of an owl. "Bogus, just how magical is The House?" Billy asked, noticing that the half pint had barely been dented on their fourth drink. "I mean is Alexandra, can she—"

"She's dead, Billy, and there's no cure for it. Nothing's that magical."

After finding a computer cable tucked under a pillow and tossing it into the bedside trash, Billy went to sleep and had a dream: he was carrying a suitcase full of computers to a train station, and on his shoulder was strapped a bag of computer cables. Since he'd never been on a train in his life, the train he dreamed was a TV train, complete with smokestack and steam. At the station, a crowd of sullen people saw him off. Among them was Janet Gateman. When he waved, she frowned, pointing to his bag, which was nearly pulling his shoulder from its socket. The ticket master, an old man with a terribly long moustache, took his ticket, which was a fuchsia calling card (one of only two colors in his dream). As Billy walked through the cars, he heard a loud clacking and was afraid people would want to look in his suitcase since it kept thudding against their seats. Sometimes a computer cable would slip out from his shoulder bag and sometimes one of Alexandra's bloody hoofs would slip out from the suitcase. When he finally got to his berth, it was like a hotel room. On a roseate bed, Soapy lay waiting with her heart-shaped smile. He didn't want to tell her that computers were in his heavy suitcase, but mostly he didn't want to tell her about Alexandra...

Chapter 22

illy awoke slumped against a persimmon tree. Bogus, either asleep or in a daze, lay stretched on a fallen pine. They were at the edge of a field, with a couple dozen cows grazing nearby. It was mid-morning, judging by the heat and light and the smell of manure. A single ripe persimmon lay orangely by Billy's side. He reached out and ate it, its pulp incredibly sweet for so early in the season.

Wait a minute. I've done this before. Watching Bogus, he knew the snake was going to turn and say, "You're awake."

"You're awake," Bogus said.

Billy shook his head and spit out the persimmon seed, trying to stop himself from asking "Why'd you strike at the window?" But he asked anyway and Bogus answered, as Billy knew he would, "I was so upset about Alexandra that I wanted to hit at something—no, I wanted to hit at The House. Like a kid kicking at the earth."

And things proceeded from there, just as they had before, with Billy discovering that they were once more on his rented farm after he stood on the ant-infested stump and saw his gray rooftop, once more discussing going back to the pond to try to re-enter The House where Soapy was kept. Had they gotten caught in another time loop that would condemn them to forever repeat this part of the day? Billy tried to rush things along: it was his worst nightmare taking on real life once more, just as it had in the forest with the ever-rising moon.

Maybe rushing matters was why he caught Janet Gateman at his back door, directly before she would have entered his kitchen. He checked her expression and her hands to make sure: a smile, not a frown; a set of car keys, not a nasty note. So some things were different. Oh yeah, and he hadn't sat down on the ant–infested stump this time, proving no doubt, that his brain was working nearly as well as his prehensile thumb.

"Aha. You *are* playing hooky," Janet said, giving a dimpled, freckled grin.

Billy motioned with his hand for Bogus to stay back in the grass or behind a shed, hoping the snake caught his signal. "I uh thought the walk would do me some good."

"And did it? You looked like hell this morning, which is why I'm out here now. Did you eat the soup I left?"

Billy stepped up on the deck and patted his stomach, inhaling deeply to bulge it out with air, though he didn't need as nearly much air as he hoped to make his paunch look like a beer gut.

"I feel like I should take you by the hand and tuck you in bed," Janet said.

Billy blanched at the probability of ten computers lying on that bed, and his pale face made her take to the idea even more. He glanced around to make sure Bogus hadn't followed. Seeing he hadn't, Billy said, "Uh thanks, but Bogus, my pet snake, is loose somewhere in the bedroom and I can't find him. His poison sac's been removed but not his fangs."

"God, Billy. What are you? Some type of masochist?" Janet peered in the door to the house then stepped away from it. "Hey, speaking of that, Shirley told me that she overheard your loving ex bragging down at Storyville about how she'd ferreted a bunch of girlie magazines and mailed them to purchasing. I told your and my friend Schroeder the same, and Shirley backed me up. You're at least off the hook on that one."

Billy leaned against a rail on the deck. The drooping sun was turning roseate. Janet's hair took on a burnt red tint he'd never noticed before and he had an urge to caress her cheek, but Soapy's Nietzsche book, still in his hip pocket, stiffened as his arm moved. *Damn, another place, another time ...* He blinked at that thought. "No thanks," he muttered.

"Pardon me? 'No thanks,' for what?"

"I meant 'Thanks,' Janet. And thank Shirley too. You're both pals, really. Between Schroeder and Linda and this damned stomach flu I'll be lucky to have a job when I can come back and really thank both of you. Especially you." Again thinking of the ten computers no doubt piled on his bed, Billy held his stomach in fake pain and tried to suppress a fake grimace with fake bravado. Fake on fake on fake—a dramatic concept worthy of Sir Laurence Olivier. Billy was proud of his acting.

Janet gracefully took the hint to leave, especially as Billy added, "I've got a real problem thinking of food right now, but maybe we could go out to dinner at Cypress Inn once I'm better. My way of thanking you." As Janet gave him a peck on his cheek Billy swore he could feel the book in his pocket burn, or at least the rose petal in the book. Tugging at his cheek to rub off any lipstick as she got into her car, he told himself, *Janet Gateman's fine, but she's not Soapy.*

He watched her drive away then looked down at Bogus, who'd slithered nearby. The sun was still setting, and they were standing in front of the house just as they had before. Only this time there was no note from an angry Janet Gateman.

"What the hell's going on, Bogus?"

"I'm tired, Billy. I feel like I've lived two days in one."

"Oh yeah? Funny, that's precisely the way I feel. What's going on?" But try as he might, Billy couldn't get Bogus to, um, bite, even with the temptation of a drink of Maker's Mark. Bogus did, however, suggest they check out Billy's bedroom, the closest the snake would come to admitting they'd just been through a repeat of what should have been the previous gone day.

Surprise. The computers weren't there. Surprise. The ten indentations *were* there, as was the cable that had accidentally worked its way under the bedspread's pillow fold.

"I wonder if my ex-wife and the Snellings are somehow related?" Billy asked, once more tossing the cable into the wastebasket.

"Enough's enough," Bogus said. "I'm going to belly around and look for some mice—a pigsty like this ought to have plenty. Oh yeah, don't you think you should do something a little more inspired with that cable? Evidence is evidence, you know."

Billy took it from the garbage and tossed it at the snake: "See if you can get one of your mouse friends to carry it into a hole."

Bogus took the cable in his teeth and grinned broadly as he slithered away.

Billy sat down on his bed, thumbing the Nietzsche book. He glanced through its table of contents: "On the Three Metamorphoses," "On the Pale Criminal," "On the Tarantulas," "Night Song," "Dancing Song," "The Soothsayer," "The Wanderer," "The Honey Sacrifice," "The Magician," "The Ugliest Man," "The Ass Festival," "The Drunken Song"—*Great bedtime reading, Soapy.* Then he sniffed the still fresh rose petal and closed his eyes.

This day though, these two days almost the same—what were they about? "Welcome to Why World, sports fan." Billy chuckled remembering Bogus's toast of the previous(?) night. *The hell with it.* He didn't even care if he had the same stupid dream about carrying ten computers on a train—Soapy was worth it. He fell asleep with that thought.

Chapter 23

"It ended the same either way. That's the whole point."

Billy voiced this inspiration when he got up at 3 a.m. to pee. When he searched the house to tell Bogus, he couldn't find him, so he went back to sleep, leaving a low light on in his room for the snake. The second time Billy awoke was at 4:30 a.m. when Bogus crawled into bed and draped over his legs.

"Just me, don't get out the baseball bat," Bogus announced. Still, Billy jumped; then he turned his bedside light on to tell the snake about his inspiration.

"Huh?" Bogus asked, tossing off a sheet.

"That's the whole point of the two repeated days. Some things will work their way out, no matter what you do or don't do. I guess I'm thinking of Alexandra too, Bogus."

The light lit Bogus's face and Billy caught a grimace.

"It's like a moral, Bogus, see? There are some things you can control in life and some things you can't."

"Bad Form," Bogus said. "Very Bad Form. Any time you think you have The House figured out, you're getting ready to be thrown from your horse, Poncho. Besides, things ended differently: on the first day the Gateman broad hated you, on the second she adored you." The snake looked away. "But it's a good thought you had about Alexandra."

"Sure thing." Billy noticed tears in both of Bogus's eyes. Well, Alexandra's death *was* enough to make even a snake cry. He looked away with embarrassment.

"Hey, it's nothing," Bogus said, forcing a laugh that jiggled Billy's leg. "Each and every animal is sad after sex."

"Sad? After sex?"

"*Omne animal post copulum sunt triste.* It sounds more exotic in Latin. Too bad my namesake only spoke Greek."

"Latin. Greek. Sex. Sure thing." Billy paused and looked directly at Bogus. "She was a fine friend. Don't worry about the tears."

"Friend? She was my daughter."

Billy stared. "How?"

"A long story, for another night. I'm really not up to it."

"But—"

"Really, I'll tell you soon. *Post copulum* and all, you know ... Good night, Poncho."

"Good night, Cisco." Billy answered automatically. Before turning out the light, he thought he spotted a moustache on Bogus then realized it was the tail of a mouse sticking from the snake's mouth. His stomach fluttered and he wiped his own mouth and lay back, curling his toes nervously as Bogus's weight shifted onto his right foot. Hadn't Soapy said she and Alexandra were sisters? Did that mean that Bogus was Soapy's father too? Thoughts of Bogus as a father-in-law flickered like a mouse's tail in Billy's mind.

Chapter 24

Billy woke when he heard a belch. Bogus was lying on the pillow opposite his own head.

"Bogus, were you really eating a mouse in bed last night?" Eyeing a series of lumps in the snake's body, Billy quickly added, "No, please. Forget I even asked."

Bogus complied by belching again.

After coffee and pancakes, the latter striking Bogus as so revoltingly fluffy and carb-filled that quivers passed through his thick skin, they walked—or crawled as preference and Darwin dictated—in silence to the pond. Though curious, Billy let the topic of Alexandra and Soapy's parentage go, seeing Bogus so glum that his very viper sacs drooped. When they came upon the barbed wire, Billy mentioned having seen his ex-wife, or maybe a phantom mimicking her on that first morning he'd come out.

"Mm," Bogus said, assenting to the possibility.

Though Billy presumed that Bogus was too preoccupied with Alexandra's death to respond, a niggle made him wonder whether or not Bogus was responsible for his ex-wife's appearing—a sort of pretest. He let that thought go and held Frazzle Two up to climb over the barbed wire, remembering the weird Linda phantom in that creepy black funeral dress. The wire twanged, reminding him of Alexandra's bells, and he sighed, quickly hoping Bogus wouldn't hear him. But then, how couldn't she be on their minds?

When they reached the pond it was once more enveloped in a creamy mist. Despite this, a Day-Glo pink note stood out, tied with fishing line onto a sassafras sapling at the water's edge.

MEMORANDUM
   TO: EMPLOYEES
   FROM: SNELLING
   RE: NEW EQUIPMENT

THERE WILL BE A MEETING AT ONE-FIFTEEN TODAY CONCERNING THE TEN NEW COMPUTERS OUR DEPARTMENT HAS ACQUIRED. PLEASE MAKE EVERY EFFORT TO ATTEND.

"Another one?" Bogus asked as Billy tore down the note.

"Yeah. Old Schroeder never misses a chance to get his name in print. Want to see it?"

"Why not? Maybe it'll cheer me up." Bogus read, his triangular head bobbing as Billy held the memorandum. "Hey, it's not from your Schroeder; it's from one of the Snellings."

Billy pulled the paper back and saw that Bogus was right; He'd misread *Schroeder* for *Snelling*.

"Ten new computers, eh? Well, Poncho," Bogus said, giving a heave of what passed for a chest, then terwilliping a three-note rendition of *Three Blind Mice*, "one of them wants your blood bad. Try whistling a happy tune when they get you cornered; that's my advice. It may put off their aim."

As Bogus again whistled *Three Blind Mice* in an oddly distracted manner, Billy added the pink memorandum to the collection growing in his pocket, glad he'd changed to looser pants, even though he and Bogus presently stood ankle-deep in mud. It had obviously rained since he'd been away. Bending, he stuck Frazzle Two into the water and couldn't see its point. "The pond's too murky from the rain; we won't be able to find the bathtub."

Bogus stopped whistling. "Damn, I hate to do this." Bogus extend his forked tongue into the water then pulled it back. "Yug, tastes worse than I remembered." He forced his tongue out again, then spoke, with its two forks dangling like fish bait, "Thum on, thput your hands around my neck and hold thon. I thknow the smell of that rotting tub like a mamma thknows the thmell of her baby's thair."

When Billy hesitated Bogus spoke in urgent gasps.

"Thum on! Thgrab my neck and clothe your eyes. And be shture thoo thold your breath—no magical Soapy or Alexandra thoo help."

Billy got on his knees, keeping his hand low on Bogus's neck as they entered the pond. This time the water was cold as he lay alongside Bogus and gulped one last breath of air. After a few seconds of swimming, he partly opened his right eye and was immediately sorry, for a sliver of silt lodged in it, which in turn made him cough. He gripped Bogus tighter, feeling near panic until the sides of the tub hit his hips. Too late, he worried about Soapy's book in his pants pocket getting soaked.

Billy tumbled from the tub onto the meadow's grass, in a sputter. He'd landed on his butt, an improvement in that department, at least. But a wash of water followed, unlike his previous trip. It was as if the pond were vomiting him. Writhing and sputtering, Bogus lay ten feet away. Unlike the cool morning weather at the pond and his rental house, the sun blistered this field, so hot that Billy was glad of his drenching. He rubbed his right eye, clearing it enough to tiptoe and look for the house. As in capital T, capital H, The House.

"It's there," he told Bogus, coughing to spew water. "We did it."

"We?"

"Moral support team," Billy admitted, slinging water from his arm.

So they headed toward the cedar house, Billy correcting their movement at the rise of each hill, sweat soon rolling down his brow instead of water. Panting, he glanced at Bogus crawling through the grass. He remembered Bogus tossing off the sheet last night in bed.

"Uh, since you're cold-blooded, what do snakes do to get rid of heat?"

"Suffer."

Bogus's voice was thick, so Billy didn't talk anymore until they neared the house. Somehow, its wood siding looked darker, and when they closed in, it seemed that streaks of tar had dribbled from the roof's shingles to stain the siding. The weather wasn't *that* hot. He couldn't make sense of it until Bogus told him to fetch and throw a large rock. When it hit, the lines on the cedar transformed into shiny scissoring black clackers, frantically nudging one another aside to attack the rock. The entire front porch looked like a dry cleaner's convention, with upstart coat hangers revolting for better wages. Jumping back, Billy grabbed Frazzle Two.

"Come on, Let's go around back and see what it's like."

Billy stood still. "Are you sure they can't come off the porch?"

"Bad Form to be sure about anything, even the rising of the sun."

"You sound like my college philosophy professor."

Bogus grunted and slithered around the house, snapping up a bumblebee along the way. To keep in practice, Billy guessed, since the snake spit the bee out and it buzzed away.

The back near side was like the front—that is, packed with the ominous dark stripes. Near the kitchen they came upon the same graveyard, but now there were two freshly turned graves: one open, one filled, with several low grassy mounds intervening between. Billy and Bogus headed toward the fresh graves. The headstone of the filled one was for Alexandra. Billy's heart skipped, looking down at the black loam. He read Alexandra's full name on the headstone: *Alexandra Innocenza Riddle*. This was the first time he knew it. The inscription underneath read, "Lest we forget, angels watch." He knew Soapy hadn't had anything to do with that sappy line and guessed she still didn't know. Bogus was at the other stone, hissing out a snicker. After three steps, Billy could see that Aristotle Bogus's own name was on it, though no death date had been inscribed. Billy stood quietly then glanced to the second floor window, remembering when Alexandra had changed into a hawk in that room. Had she seen her own name inscribed then?

"Don't be so somber, my bi-pedal friend. Look closely at the inscription. It's a joke, a sick joke from Ma and Pa Snelling."

Billy bent and read: "*Even on his belly he stood tall.*"

"A joke. A real knee-slapper."

From the way the snake shifted in the mounded dirt, Billy could see that Bogus was trying to convince himself of the humor. Leaning, Billy peered into the fresh snake grave to see six feet of yawning black earth; then he did a double-take at the last name on the stone: *Riddle*, Aristotle Bogus Riddle. It wasn't as if he'd disbelieved Bogus last night when he claimed to be Alexandra's father; it was just that it hadn't seemed real.

Billy whistled lowly. "Riddle. So you meant that you two were literally father and daughter. I'm sorry, I—"

"Why? I'm glad. But thanks, and I understand your doubts. Her birth wasn't along the lines of your standard biological operating procedure, probably would give that Watson fellow DNA fits if he ever found out about her or Soapy either one." Bogus turned toward the house. "Let's hie us inside and find my living daughter," he said. "I'll explain it all later, I promise. We need to hurry, though. I don't want to lose both of them."

"Lose Soapy? I don't want to do that either."

"Well said."

They circled the house three times, looking for some way inside. By the third time, the rock Billy had thrown onto the front porch had disappeared, replaced with a tangle of dead clackers who'd evidently killed one another in their rush toward the rock's movement.

"As frenzied as they get, what about another diversionary tactic on the far side of the front porch?"

"You mean another rock?" Bogus tried to whistle but it came out like a tire deflating. "Davy may have handled Goliath with a stone, but there was only one giant. Before we commit to rocks let's look in that shed we passed. Maybe the ninth cavalry's hiding there, just waiting for someone to save."

But no cavalry stood at the ready. The only things they found in the shed were digging tools and ten blank gravestones. "Can you lift one?" Bogus asked.

Billy chose a small, rosy granite one and gave it a heft. It weighed around a hundred pounds, but with an effort he thought he could get it on his belly and from there tumble it onto the porch. With a laugh Bogus commented it would be poetic justice if they tossed *his* gravestone instead.

So they did.

The plan worked better than they expected, for Bogus's stone crashed through rotten timbering, swallowing many of the clackers. He and Billy immediately ran to the door, where they encountered a small group of clackers that Frazzle Two and Bogus's lightning-fast strikes dispensed. Still, once inside with the double doors safely locked, Billy had a gash on his leg. Remembering Alexandra, he sat on the stairs and used one of Bogus's miracle half-pints to cleanse the wound. And since Bogus had lost his last two rattles out on the porch, Billy dabbed his tail too.

Bogus gave a grin and a sniff. "Just as well. Rattling first and striking second always seemed a waste of momentum."

Billy studied the room: nearly empty as before, with minor changes: a blue couch and three wooden rockers before the huge fireplace; a braided blue rug hung over the railing of the second floor. Outside the front door, he could hear clackers still worrying over the tombstone.

"Where do we go from here, Poncho?"

As Bogus asked this, Billy eyed a yellow Sticky note hung on the front door's knob. He walked to read its minuscule script: *Coming or going? Don't forget: meeting at 1.* He glanced at his watch, whose battery had chosen this as a working day. 12:28 a.m. "Looks like we'll go to a meeting with the rest of the bureaucrats, Cisco." Billy pulled the Sticky from the doorknob and dangled it on his thumb before Bogus, who nodded and replaced the Post-it with one of his fuchsia calling cards for *+ * The Society Of *+ *.

Now that Billy looked around more closely, he spied yellow notes pasted abundantly: one on the banister's knob, one halfway up the stairs on the wall, one on a riser at the head of the stairs. It was as if a short fourth grader had been told to leave notes wherever people would be sure to see them. What's more, Bogus was duplicating the mindless planning by sticking his own fuchsia calling cards under each yellow Sticky. Billy shook his head, then re-read the yellow note and realized it didn't tell where the meeting would be.

"Can tell you're new here, Sir Uh Billy. There's only one place we ever meet, and that's in the Snelling's reception room, at the end of the hall, where you had your job interview."

Billy gave a snort at the phrase *job interview*. His laugh stirred the clackers outside on the porch. "Uh, maybe it would uh be smart to check things out before we walk on blindly." Billy jerked his head toward the closed double doors and the noise at the end of the hall—not such a long distance today—thanks no doubt to more House magic.

"Good idea, Sir Uh Billy."

Despite occasional candles ensconced on the walls, the hallway leading to the Snelling's reception room was much darker than Billy remembered. Bogus only shrugged and said Billy would get used to changes like that in The House. Still, Billy pulled Frazzle Two from his waist. There was a third ruby in the hilt now, and the blade seemed a trifle longer, like he was being rewarded for good conduct. He started to say something, but only got out an "Uh," on seeing the snake tape another fuchsia calling card on the seat of a wooden chair set against the wall. The card dangled under another yellow Sticky note about the meeting. Sometimes Bogus didn't inspire much confidence.

As they walked farther, Billy could hear his footsteps echo. Then, smack in the middle of the floor, a set of steep stairs cut of stone opened downward. Billy teetered, feeling his breakfast pancakes toss. The stairs descended at least a hundred steps. Somehow, light showed at the bottom.

"Look!" Billy pointed, still teetering. "Isn't that Soapy?"

At the bottom, a cloaked woman sat on a flat stone. Behind her, waves lapped, tossing froth on gray, dismal sand, though no sound drifted up. The woman was dressed in blue, though at this distance her blue barely differed from the sand's gray hue. But she was reading and her head tilted a way that both of them recognized.

"Soapy!" they yelled.

She didn't move.

Billy started down in a run, but his foot thudded sternly against a solid, perfectly clear barrier, jolting his spine. He kicked at the barrier and yelled again, joined by Bogus, but the woman kept her attention on the book in her hands. Billy ran back for the thick wooden chair where Bogus had pasted a calling card, hoping to use it to smash the barrier. Instead, the chair's legs gave way with his first bash, and he was left huffing as both the yellow Sticky and the fuchsia calling card floated down to rest atop the clear barrier.

"If it's Plexiglas, it's at least three feet thick," he said, tossing the remainder of the chair aside.

"She didn't even look up once, with all that noise the chair made," Bogus said. "It's no use."

"Excuse me. Is this the way to the 1 o'clock meeting?"

They'd been so intent on the invisible barrier that they hadn't heard footsteps. They turned to stare at a matronly woman coifed like Marie Antoinette or maybe pre-liberation Dolly Parton, wearing what in polite society is known as fire-red fuck-me heels. A blue rhinestone heart was pinned halfway up her stacked silver hair. She, in turn, stared at the broken chair seat and the four legs lying on the stone floor.

"Uh," Billy started, hoping to offer some explanation; then he noticed that the Plexiglas revealing Soapy had disappeared and that the chair's legs now lay scattered over stones matching the rest of the hallway's floor. The woman no doubt thought he was mad.

"Straight ahead, I believe, ma'am," Bogus intoned in a Southern drawl Billy hadn't heard before. Billy hoped the snake hadn't picked it up from him: it sounded like boiled simple syrup. With fiendish pearl nails that rivaled her extravagant hair, the woman tapped a note pad and thanked them, careful not to nod her towering head and the blue rhinestone heart, lest she tumble off-balance.

Glancing down at the fuchsia calling card face-up on the stone, she hissed, "I see *they've* been here."

From the intonation of that *they*, Billy and Bogus knew to keep quiet and let her pass. When she was out of hearing, they knelt to pick up the card and search the stones for a lever or a crack. They soon had to abandon their search as the passage filled with foot travel from people and animals, all heading toward the meeting, each carrying a note pad either in its hand or somehow attached to its body—twine, tape, and rainbow colored paper clips being the most used implements. One or two times, Billy thought he heard Soapy's name mentioned as he and Bogus backed against the wall, foolishly pretending the broken chair wasn't there. During a spate of passing rainbow paper clips Billy worried that the Snellings had raided his office desk at Alabama.

At the end of the hall, the regal doors to Ma and Pa Snelling's reception room were thrust open, accompanied by what could only be described as a chorus of tomcats in heat. Over the crowd's heads, Billy could see Ma Snelling walking on a platform that hadn't been in the room before, pacing faster than he'd ever imagined possible for the old gal. He could almost sniff the cinnamon ball wake she left behind.

"There's nothing we can do here, Poncho," Bogus said quietly. "Unless, *amigo*, we rob thee two o'clock train and steal dynamite and blow thees floor all high into thee sky, no?"

Billy rolled his eyes at the fake Mexican accent. "You should stick to hissing," he hissed under his breath.

"I heard that," Bogus replied.

Sixth Leg: Omne Gatherum

Chapter 25

In the throne room, a serving line formed on the right. Joining the line, Billy tiptoed to spot two coffee urns and several mounds of white-bread finger food delicacies stuffed with pink and green cream cheese. He noticed the woman with the blue rhinestone heart in her hair: she held a mini-sandwich between her thumb and her first finger. Her other fingers waved like pennants. A thin line of something mint green and gooey separated the two pieces of white bread, and all the bread's crust had been carefully pared away, as if its dusky brown were too vulgar to endure her manicure. Billy sighed. University Catering served this same delicacy at all official functions. What happened to the crust, he always wondered. Did they use it to slop hogs or football players?

Bogus tugged at his jeans and Billy glanced down to see a Siamese cat in a frilly white skirt prancing past, turning her nose at both of them. On her skirt a pinned hot pink button read, "Wisdom Will Win."

"Lunchtime," Bogus leered, forking his tongue at the cat's head. Nonchalantly shaking her tail as if spraying deodorizer, the feline walked ahead, in effect cutting into the serving line.

Billy eyed a man with incredibly thin white fingers coast a pasty mini-sandwich toward his mincing lips, where the sandwich wedged momentarily, like a sun-bleached cotton bole. Billy leaned to whisper, "Do they actually expect us to eat—" Bogus hissed sharply and Billy straightened—"I know, I know," he continued, "Bad Form."

So they stood in the winding line awaiting coffee and tasteless, nutrition-less sandwiches that must have originated in the fairy-food fantasy of some long-molding, Deep South debutante. "Dahhhling, have an emerald mint fluff from King Arthur's own fairy dell." But not to worry about food, for the line had stopped moving. If the coffee was lukewarm by the time they reached it, the sandwiches would be congealed like Elmer's Schooltime Glue. Billy shifted from foot to foot, waiting in the non-moving line, keeping ultimate Good Form. Five minutes, and the line had moved not as many inches.

There was no doubt about it: Soapy's name was being mentioned in many conversations, along with occasional whispers about Alexandra. Billy looked at Bogus, whose eyelids had drooped. Was the snake pretending to ignore the comments?

A purplish gentleman whom Billy took to be a Bahamian Black joined the line. When Billy turned to smile, he noticed that purple-black whiskers covered the man's entire face. The man was dressed in tight-fitting jeans that had been dyed the same purple color. His hands, his shoes—everything about him cast that same purplish hue. Even his eyes, which were set deeply in his whiskery pad, looked purple, though Billy guessed they were surely brown. Billy's stomach pooched nervously against Frazzle Two.

"You seen my daughter, Ricco?" It was Bogus who spoke.

"Soapy? No mon. We all so sorry about your Alexandra baby. What happen?"

Bogus glanced around. "You know: things."

Billy had been sure Bogus was going to say 'Bad Form,' and was relieved he didn't. The snake's eyelids lifted, and he coiled to whisper and arrange a meeting with Ricco after this "hoo-der-all," as the two of them called it. Another cat pranced by; Bogus and Ricco stopped talking and nodded; the cat ignored them.

Billy remembered the large orange cat on Mr. Snelling's bed; this was some close, fat relation, wearing the same hot pink button about Wisdom Winning that the Siamese had worn minutes ago.

The line lurched, maybe a foot. Twenty more feet and Billy would just be able to touch the table. He was actually beginning to hunger, even for mint-green fairy food.

"Billy, pay attention. I want you to meet a friend."

Billy turned to look at the purplish man.

"Ricco, this is Billy. Billy's our latest star, fallen from Alabama."

"Ah. Alabama. KKK and Roll-ll Tide." The purplish man gave a purplish salute.

"Cut it out, Ricco. Billy's good blood."

"Sorry, mon. It been in the air here for hundred years. Not your fault, not nobody's fault, I know."

The orange cat pranced by again, joined by another, even larger orange tom who was licking the last of a finger sandwich. Everyone in the line nodded. Everyone also, Billy noted, quit talking as long as the two cats were near.

"Ricco used to have an island. Then, after a hurricane, all the islanders were brought here, so he became employed as head janitor."

"Domestic engineer," Ricco corrected, giving his chest a thump and grinning. Billy could see his teeth for the first time: a beautiful white, like the sands of some virgin beach. Ricco gave a shimmy. "In our hips, mon. We was made for humping thee brooms and thee mops from time of Creation. Praise heaven for Columbus and thee slave trade."

"The house, as you may have gathered, reflects the world," Bogus said to Billy, arching a brow over one golden eye.

"Too damn well, mon," Ricco added.

The line lurched again. Billy was reaching for a coffee cup when a server indicated with a sharp tap on the metal that the urn was empty. He assured Billy and those remaining that another was on the way.

"On thee way," Ricco repeated the phrase twice, as if tasting it. He thought the phrase immensely funny for some reason. Bogus crawled by Billy and coiled to drop several fuchsia calling cards near the empty cups when the server wasn't looking. Billy glanced to the line behind him, which stretched out the door. Most of those standing in it now were purplish-black, like Ricco.

"But The House is, uh, magic, isn't it?" Billy asked. "Why would it need janitors? And why can't it just wave the coffee urn full?"

Ricco let air slip out the side of his lips. Bogus leaned to speak, but a large gong and a loud voice interrupted.

"Close the door, close the door. Come on in and close the door, please." The voice was feminine and grating, inflecting her 'please' with an implied 'Hurry-up, children.'

Peering between shoulders, tails, and manes, Billy could see Mrs. Snelling speaking through a megaphone. No wonder her voice sounded so squeaky.

"Close the door, please. Close the door. I know we all want to get back to our duties, so close the door and we'll have our meeting."

On a long table next to Mrs. Snelling were the ten computers from the University's purchasing department. Billy couldn't see the identification plates, but he was sure: same color, size, same dinky monitors. And the second computer from the end was missing the cable that he hoped was lying in some mouse hole.

Mrs. Snelling moved the megaphone from her lips and said something. As people near her laughed in response, the laugh pressed nervously through the crowd like an obligation. She took up the megaphone once more: "Most of you already know that, as previously agreed, Mr. Snelling and I soon will be changing positions, and I am grateful for the many, many supportive comments I've received." She paused, swelling her breasts with an intake of air. What Billy had taken for a matronly figure upon his first meeting, now took sharp features, features that magnified as she continued to breathe in—would she ever stop? It was as if she were being inflated for a Macy's Parade ... a reverse Macy's parade, say All Hallow's Eve, for he couldn't shake the idea that her breasts were gun turrets. They continued to swell for a full minute; then she exhaled into the megaphone with a gush. "WISDOM WILL WIN! Yes, my friends, wisdom *will* win ..." She paused to let the phrase gather lather. "Friends, I would like my coming directorship to offer the mildest transition we in the house have ever had. I would like my directorship to go down in history as a period of intellectual advancement and opportunity for all. I would like my directorship to be known as a time when peace prospered and understanding was the most urgent word. And I myself would like to be known as the first Wisdom Director ...

"... As a kickoff gesture in accomplishing these goals I have recommended the institution of a new department, the Department of New Education. This department will give the House new motivation, new goals. I foresee it providing the guiding light to rocket us from the insecurities of the past twentieth century into the steadfastness of the twenty-first. And to head this department of Wisdom and carry out these sacred plans, this sacred trust, this guiding light, I'm going to recommend a feline who has been among us many years, a feline who has worked closely with both Mr. Snelling and me, a feline who has seen both lean and fat times, a feline who has proven himself time and again in this great hall to be a conscientious and caring servant of the House, a feline who has worked so carefully in the past with you all. In short, I am going to ask that the Board unanimously approve Mr. Tom C. Powder to serve as the Department of New Education's first head."

Yowls of approval arose from the cat contingent. This started a wave of applause and foot-stomping. A large orange cat wearing an equally large hot pink "Wisdom Will Win" button stared his way, so Billy clapped politely. Narrowing its eyes, the cat strutted behind the temporary platform. Sitting next to Mrs. Snelling, on what looked like a barstool, was the large orange cat Billy had seen in bed with Mr. Snelling. Evidently this was Powder, the new department head. It licked its jowls as the audience applauded, then groomed an eyebrow with a quick brush.

"Thank you, thank you," Mrs. Snelling intoned through the megaphone. "One of the first tasks that Mr. Powder and the Department of New Education will tackle will be dissemination of The House Rules. These rules will once more be open to public discussion, and I might add that any of you who wish to be on sub-panels to discuss them should give your name to one of the felines in the hall."

Billy noticed Bogus chewing on his lower lip and the purple man named Ricco heavily gathering his brows.

"Remember: House Rules are made for you. In my heart I carry 110% trust that Mr. Powder will gather a new momentum for an intelligent understanding of our House Rules, and that some recent, unfortunate incidents can be put behind us." Mrs. Snelling dropped the megaphone from her lips and glanced briefly at Bogus, who swayed slightly. She spoke again: "We all know how confusing our modern house is, we all know how things can change drastically within seconds." She stepped aside and motioned with her hand. "With these computers, Mr. Powder and his Department of New Education will be able to track your movements more closely to prevent just such tragedies as we've recently witnessed." Mr. Snelling appeared on the stage, evidently having climbed steps to the right. He stood next to his wife, smiling grandly and holding a brown paper bag. She nodded then turned to the audience. "Of course I want to thank Mr. Snelling for the wonderful years we've had. I know that all of you will give him a grand round of applause now."

Billy started to clap, but Mrs. Snelling continued without missing a beat, even raising her voice, if that were possible.

"By the way, you can expect new copies of House Rules within 24 hours—many of you, in fact, will have received them when you return to your work stations today. Read them, think, and be ready for the upcoming room-by-room panel discussions. Well, that's all. I know you're anxious to get back to work. Remember, Working for The House is Working for You. Wisdom Will Win!"

A flurry of cheers arose from felines. Mrs. Snelling turned to Mr. Snelling. He opened the brown bag and handed her something that she popped into her mouth. A cinnamon ball. As Billy watched, Mrs. Snelling edged her husband aside and walked down the steps with the orange cat named Powder.

The double doors behind Billy were opened, and the cats were ushering people out. Billy gave a look to the stand where the coffee had been, but no servers had ever returned and the empty urn still had its lid off. The five silver platters didn't even hold crumbs. He did notice that all of Bogus's cards had been taken. Looking about, he saw one man's brows crinkle at the fuchsia card then furtively slip it into a pocket. Could it be that Bogus was practicing subversive Bad Form?

Chapter 26

Billy, Bogus, and Ricco stood in the hall by the broken chair, ostensibly discussing it and similar housekeeping problems as the crowd passed by. Two yellow cats whose parents had likely interbred with Florida panthers posted themselves by the great doors to urge the staff not to mill, occasionally flexing incredibly long claws when anyone dared meet their green eyes. Finally traffic in the hall thinned; with a last sharp look at Billy, the cats heaved the doors to. Just before they did, Billy saw workers dismantling the computers by simply yanking the cords and flinging them around the machines. A fact dawned on him so strongly that he interrupted Bogus and Ricco:

"Uh, there's no electricity! What good are computers going to be here without electricity?"

"The right people got electricity, you bet," Ricco said.

At the other far end of the hallway, almost to the stairs and the doors leading outside, three young Blacks were shouting angrily. A door opened and two very large cats stepped out, and close behind them tottered fifty or so clackers. The young men ran off at the sight. Both cats and clackers followed in a steady, unhurried pace, the clacking of the latter echoing menacingly along the stone hallway to reach Billy's ears.

"We've got to find her, Ricco. You've got to get us as much help as you can."

Ricco only shook his head at Bogus's plea.

Billy presumed they were talking about Soapy.

"Why not?"

"Look there. You see what I'm dealing with, mon?" Ricco pointed to the receding Black teenagers just as they disappeared around the stairs toward the kitchen. "These kids so stupid they push-shove their anger on one another instead of where it belong." To indicate where he thought it belonged, Ricco gave a small jerk of his head back toward the hall they'd just exited. "And the old people, instead of being wise old people and leading like they should, they draw into themselves like dead tarantulas, waiting for venom to take effect. And look last!" He pointed to the two cats, followed by the clackers as they sauntered around the stairs, toward the teenagers and the kitchen. "Them cats training them clackers with stun guns just add to the bad."

Bogus forked his tongue. "Training them? With stun guns? How long has that been going on?"

"One month. Them cats use their magic electric wand on them dumb clackers. First, we all thought it funny-funny to watch through keyholes. No one don't laugh funny-funny now." Glancing back to make sure the grand hall doors were still closed, Ricco bent and placed a skeleton key in Bogus's mouth. "You forget where you got this, eh, mon?" Ricco straightened and turned to Billy. "Bogus say you good blood. Also he say you and Soapy turtledoving, so the magic must be strong. I ask: you have enough magic to free the words in those computers, mon?"

Billy shook his head, not understanding.

"Give the knowledge back to the people, mon. To the people. Snelling and her cats locking it up, bit by bit, until we too stupid to do anything but wash dirty dishes and eat leftover foods. Maybe on sunshiny days we foot race in hot dust to entertain muckity-mucks with our high hipbones and big lips. We all becoming that stupid, no mistake. Soon we be thanking Snelling for throw-out, moldy hog ears to boil in soup. 'Ah, Mrs. Snelling your majesty, you too kind, even left bristle on so we poor nigras get roughage in our primitive stomachs.' "

Behind came a clanking of bolts from the meeting hall doors. Ricco jumped, quickly promising Bogus and Billy that he'd see them later, then with his own skeleton key he opened a nearby door and disappeared behind it.

"I thought all the doors were unlocked in the house," Billy said, as Bogus stuck the key Ricco had given him into another door and gave it a twist.

"They are, but with this key, you aren't required to spend a night in the room. Housekeeping keeps them for cleanup."

"Sort of a Bad Form eliminator, huh?" Billy said.

The doors at the end were screaking open and Bogus urged Billy inside a small library of sorts—of sorts because its furniture was more suitable to a parlor than a library or study. There was even a pool table to the side. But the room's main function must have once been as a library, for books reached from the floor to the ceiling of each wall, no small height since four wooden ladders on rollers were spaced around the room. Diagonal from the pool table was an equally large oaken reading table with several flowing blueprints scattered on it, and very utilitarian bare wood chairs scattered about it.

"Someone's had the same idea I have," Bogus commented, going to the table and fingering the blueprints.

To Billy, the blueprints were close to indecipherable. Just as some people automatically turn off numbers or graphs, he automatically turned off any form of schematics or maps. Nonetheless, he leaned, pretending interest. One thing for certain that he could make out: the house held literally hundreds of thousands of rooms, for Bogus was using his teeth to peal back layer after layer of blueprint, each layer displaying twenty to fifty rooms.

"Some rooms key into different layers, if you're wondering," Bogus said, not looking up from the page he was reading, but swaying over it in a hypnotic fashion.

"Like the Panama Canal keying into two oceans?"

"Um."

Billy couldn't be sure whether Bogus was answering his question or had found something interesting, so he took out Soapy's book and gave the rose a sniff. He looked at the passage marked by the rose; it was called "On the Blessed Isles." It would be too good to be true that she'd left the rose as a clue. Too good ... But when they'd seen her an hour ago—through that barrier—she *was* by a shoreline of some sort.

"Uh," and he found himself telling Bogus about the marked chapter in the

Nietzsche book.

"Too good to be true," Bogus agreed. "But ..."

"But?"

"But over there you'll find an index of the different names that all the rooms have acquired over the centuries. In that walnut file by the iron candle stand."

Billy walked over and thumbed through. "Nothing," he said after a moment.

Bogus looked up from the blueprints. "What are you looking under?"

"Blessed, the B's."

"Try island or isle."

Billy made a face, then shifted to another drawer. Nothing under isle, but under island were quite a few entries: *Death, Dog, Devil's, Evil, Fingerless, Harried, Murderer's, Narcoleptic, Pincer, Sacred, Silly, Spider, Worry, Wilted, and Zealot's.*

"Lovely," Billy whispered to himself. "A regular tourist paradise, each one."

Bogus must have heard him, for he looked up from the blueprints to ask if Billy'd found anything. "I can tell you one thing," Billy answered. "No travel agent named these places." He read them off and Bogus laughed.

"The only one close is 'Sacred,'" Billy said. "That's pretty close to 'Blessed.' Maybe it was simply mis-named. Do clerks make mistakes in the House?"

"Do they ever! But you're pushing for a long shot," Bogus answered. "Still, I don't have a better suggestion. Look Sacred Isle up and find the blueprint key's number—it'll be in the right-hand corner of the card."

Billy looked up the card. A large, red M-172 was in the right corner. And the card itself read "Blessed," not "Sacred." He told Bogus this and the number, then studied the rest of the card while Bogus shuffled through the blueprints.

M - 172

ISLAND, THE BLESSED

Good: Sub-Spaniel Stream, sweetfruit, oranges, bananas,
wild pears, mangoes, peaches and plentiful other fruit

Bad: Mosquitoes, yellow flies

History: The Blessed Isle was discovered in M 77456 by
Captain Sophia Riddle and subsequently charted.
Passage to the Blessed Isle is reputed to be
treacherous, especially as one must enter through
either The Horn of Fear or Hardship Mountain.
Rumors also persist about historical ghosts such as
Bluebeard, Casey Jones, and Thomas Edison,
leading some to claim the island contains a
wormhole to earth-time.

Earth-time? "Bogus! A Captain Sophia Riddle is mentioned on this card—uh, is she any relation to Soapy?" Spotting a pencil and some scratch paper atop the file, Billy began copying the information.

"She *is* Soapy."

Billy's notes disintegrated into doodles—a pear and a banana. He was glad no one was watching over his shoulder, for they looked lewd.

"Uh, what does M 77456 translate to in Tuscaloosa, Alabama, time?"

"That's easy. Just subtract 76,000 if the date's over 75,000; but if it's under 75,000 you have to derive the square root then add 12,011. That's because of the hurricane that blew through."

"A hurricane blew through The House?"

"No one knows what else to call it. Maybe it was a big atomic war, maybe it was the Black Death mixed with a plague of locusts. I was on vacation, so I don't know—and Ma and Pa S. won't talk about it."

Billy stared at his doodling. He'd written down a minus 76,000 and was looking at that figure and the 77456 on the card. That left 1,456. 1456 A.D.? Some thirty years before Columbus? Soapy? His Soapy?

He confirmed the date with Bogus. "Uh, that means that Soapy is nearly six hundred years old, Bogus."

"Six hundred, huh? Jeez," Bogus said in a mocking tone that Billy didn't like at all, not at all. "*Nearly* six hundred is just close, Sir Uh Billy. Didn't I warn you that the Janet dish with the noodles and the noodle soup might be more your speed?"

What the hell, Billy thought with a frown. *Maybe she's immature for her age and needs a man to guide her.* He finished copying the card's information and walked over to Bogus, who was still shuffling through blueprints. Billy watched the snake tug more pages.

"Come on, Bogus. Is she really that old?"

"Yep." Bogus stared at a page, then flipped to another. The snake had somehow sneaked on a pair of reading glasses.

"Uh, then how old are you? No, let me guess: you ran around the cobblestones of Athens with Socrates and barely missed catching a social disease from the old pederast."

There was a commotion outside the door that sounded as if someone were wheeling something extremely heavy. Billy and Bogus listened as it passed, then heard the large doors to the reception hall creak open. Then a voice cried out angrily and the doors creaked closed and the heavy wheels were reversed to head back through the hall, back toward them.

"Odd, hearing noises from the house like that," Bogus said, rippling his skin. "It's the skeleton key, you know. You don't remember hearing sounds when we were in the desert, do you? Or when you were in the forest?"

"But the kitchen, the living room ..."

"Oh sure, some rooms and halls remain communal. The house couldn't very well function if people disappeared every time they walked into a different doorway, could it?"

The sound was nearing the library. Bogus looked at the blueprint he'd turned to and exclaimed quietly, keeping an ear out for the door.

"Help me tear this out," he said.

"Tear it out? This is a library."

"You see a copying machine around?"

"No but . . ."

"Look, I agree that it's extremely Bad Form, but I've got a badder than bad feeling about the noise out there. Come on, hurry—if you ever want to see Soapy again in your lifetime."

Billy certainly didn't like the phrase "in your lifetime," being associated with Soapy, and he didn't like the murmur of voices gathering outside the door, either. The rolling groaned so heavily that he could feel it in his feet. So he used the opportunity to mask tearing the blueprint, then folded it into Bogus's secret pouch. While stuffing it alongside the reading glasses, Billy felt a half pint.

"Go ahead and pull that out," Bogus said.

"In here?"

"Yeah, in here. And shut those walnut files you left open, then hurry over to the pool table and follow my cue—no pun intended. Hurry, Billy." When Billy hesitated, Bogus said, "Something bad's getting ready to happen. Something that's happened only a couple of times before. Hurry!" Bogus was flipping the blueprint pages back to pretty much the way they were when they entered the room. "Hurry," he insisted, dropping off the study table and slithering toward the pool table.

Billy shut the drawers he'd opened then rushed to where Bogus had set up the pool table to look as if they were in the middle of a game. The snake nodded and coiled over one side of the table, holding a short cue in his mouth, steadying it by looping his body. He made a shot, knocking in the three-ball with a loud crack. "Grab a stick and look interested."

No sooner had Billy taken a stick from the rack than the door opened. A large yellow cat with faint tiger-striping swaggered in. "Game room and library are closed for renovation for the coming exhibition, gentlemen."

"But we're in for the night. Bad Form to leave, you know."

The cat, which weighed fifty pounds if an ounce—a real pin-up for Purina Cat Chow—licked a paw and hopped atop the walnut filing cabinet to pace. Satisfied with whatever he saw or didn't see, he commented, "Not Bad Form if Mrs. Snelling gives her okay. And she does. Just have the clerk outside give you a blue slip."

"Okay, if you're sure," Bogus said.

The cat didn't reply, but kept pacing and swishing its tail, studying the room. "You two weren't reading or anything like that, were you?"

"There some law been passed against reading?" Billy asked.

The cat stopped abruptly to lick its paw.

"Hey, screw reading," Bogus said. "We got twenty bucks on this game.

Can't we at least finish?"

"Sure," the cat replied, "as long as you don't mind spending a year or so in here without food while the walls and doors are being repaired."

The walls and doors looked plenty solid to Billy. Still, several workmen in chalky jeans walked in, tugging at a portable cement mixer, which they placed before a black potbelly stove. Opening the stove's door, they began shoveling in concrete. Billy realized they were sealing off the room's magical access to the rest of the house.

"I've got only three solids left and you've got six stripes. I'm willing to call it a game if you give me five."

"Huh?" Billy said, looking to Bogus, then the cat, then the table. "Uh sure." He handed over five dollars from his pocket. As he did, Soapy's book fell out.

"What's that?" The cat jumped from the cabinet to patter along the floor, stopping before the book and nervously twitching his tail. The workmen stopped shoveling cement to watch.

"Nitskee?" the cat asked.

"An American football player," Billy said. "It's my book, not the library's. I'm reading about his life in the pros."

The cat's eyes narrowed as he pawed the book, looking at the mustachioed face on the cover. "Ugly enough to play football. Okay, I suppose something on sports won't do any harm. But go on and get out of here. Don't you two have work to attend?"

Billy, noticing Bogus dropping fuschia * + * The Society Of *+ * cards where the workmen were sure to see them, coughed and asked the cat how long the game room would be closed.

"I just told you. At least a year. More, maybe. Get on out. We've got things to do."

Billy and Bogus left, picking up their blue exemption tickets from clerk waiting outside. This clerk was a thin, nervous type whose hands shook as he entered their names into one of the stolen computers.

Billy saw a long orange electrical cord leading back to the reception room. A veritable boulder weighing at least half-a-ton rested on a handcart parked near the library's door. That must have been what was making the squeaky rolling noise. He stepped back to take in its size. Its face was inscribed with the ten house rules. Behind him, workers were removing the knob from the library's door; it looked like they were planning on blockading the same with the boulder and its rules. Billy eyed the last rule: *Smile; it uses fewer muscles.*

Chapter 27

"That's exactly what they're going to do," Bogus said once they were clear of the hall. "It happened ninety years ago, two hundred and ten years ago, and four hundred years before that. Mrs. Snelling took over the directorship all three times."

They turned past the stairway into the short hallway and were once more sitting at the round oak table in the kitchen. Bogus had swaggered out of the library with the half pint, past the guards and the clerk, and now Billy couldn't dissuade him from opening it. To tell the truth, Billy only half-heartedly tried, for the window to the kitchen door had been cleaned and it looked directly upon those two fresh graves, the one holding Alexandra, the other awaiting Bogus.

While outside in the graveyard the sun shone late afternoon, the room itself emitted an unseasonable early chill. Billy drank his Maker's Mark neat, which sent a whiff of emotion to his head, a tremor of nausea to his stomach. He concentrated on the emotion, thinking of Soapy as he'd first seen her by the lake, reading with that lovely heart-shaped smile of hers, those huge blue eyes. He took another sip.

"Is she really that old, Bogus?" His voice cracked as he stared into the windowpane, refusing to see beyond its Windex gleam and smell.

"Mrs. Snelling? You bet. And that mean too, but everybody forgets and—"

"Soapy, not Mrs. Snelling."

"Ah, Soapy. Of course." Bogus sniffed at the bowl Billy had put out and lapped its whiskey. "Time's different here for some of us. It's different for Soapy and me, though I think it would have been the same for Alexandra as for you. Alexandra really was only fourteen years old, you know. Her mother—well, her mother's another story, a surprise jolt for this old man, so to speak. But Soapy ... listen, let's say you do succeed in doing what she wants, what the council wants. Let's say you take her back and hide her in Tuscaloosa, America, football and pig-fry capitol of the world."

Billy's brows wrinkled on hearing his hometown maligned. He was about to say people don't fry pig when he remembered bacon, and though he'd grown up with the Bear Bryant legacy, he had partially reacted against it after seeing his high school classmates drooling onto their chins every time they drove by the stadium. Still, not everyone in Tuscaloosa slipped into dumbo gear the minute someone waved a dirty jock strap. Not everyone in America watched Monday Nite Football, either, did they?

"If you succeed," Bogus continued before Billy had a chance to ponder his question, "—and I'm giving that only a glimmer of a chance—if you succeed, then Soapy will be a lovely, intelligent—" Bogus gave a brief laugh—"vivacious, twenty-nine year old Alabama woman called Soapy Riddle Wise. Since I presume you two would get married."

Was there a paternal threat in that? *Don't plan on co-habitating with my little girl, buster!* Billy leaned against the sink. A normal-sized yellow tabby tiptoed up to the hall door that led into the kitchen. It looked at Billy, Bogus, and the nearly empty half pint and smiled. Billy wasn't sure, but instinct told him that anything which made these cats smile should make him frown. He did so. Bogus wasn't facing the door and hadn't noticed the cat at all, or at least he didn't acknowledge it, for he continued talking:

"You asked how old she is. She's as old as me, give or take a day or so. Sprung right out of this thick skull of mine when I courted her mother, an owl I took a fancy to since we were competing for pretty much the same food chain. My, I thought, if I could only fly like that white-winged beauty can. I suppose the pretty lady owl thought how wonderful it would be to edge along the warm earth and more or less stalk food at her leisure like I could. You know, opposites attract, who can tell the ways of love, and all that poetic B.S."

The cat left, giving a cat yawn that revealed lots of sharp, yellow teeth. Billy walked to the door leading to the hall and looked out: empty. The door that had sprung the clackers what seemed like weeks ago when he first walked down this hall was ominously cracked, though, and his stomach tightened.

"What are you looking for?"

"There was a cat here."

"There's cats everywhere." Bogus began whistling his favorite tune, "Three Blind Mice."

"It's gone now—who's the council?" Billy asked, turning back to face Bogus. "Why are they so concerned about Soapy and me?"

"The council's a secret organization composed of concerned members of * + * The Society Of * + *. As concerned members, it's their job to be concerned." Bogus grinned and grabbed the bottle in his teeth to pour more Maker's Mark.

Billy, however, grimaced, walking to the table and grabbing the bottle. "Cynicism and drinking aren't going to help Soapy. Do you want the same thing to happen to her that happened to Alexandra?"

Tail twitching slightly, Bogus stared at Billy, then relented. "All right, all right. The council is just what I said it is: a secret society, like Knights Templar in the Middle Ages. We're so paranoid that our votes are cast blindly and our meetings are held in a tripartite structure, dividing up the twenty-seven members into nines so that members only know a third of the membership at any time. The council's been around over three millennia now, despite efforts to destroy or disband it."

"Mr. and Mrs. Snelling? Are they in the council, or are they trying to destroy it?" Billy asked.

"People say that they're in the council, though I've never personally seen them at any tripartite meeting."

Leaning against the sink, Billy remembered that Soapy had thought they were in the council too. He also remembered that she seemed to place implicit trust in whatever decision the council made concerning himself and The House—and herself?

"Soapy thinks they are. But you think differently?"

Bogus twisted to eye the door to the hallway. Billy, in turn, twisted to eye the clean glass in the door leading outside. He could see that the snake had been staring at his proposed tombstone and open grave all the time they'd talked. The mound of Alexandra's fresh grave was just visible.

"Uh, wouldn't you rather drink somewhere else, instead of staring at those graves?"

Bogus straightened. "There's a village in Mexico where the people, on their fortieth birthday, go to the undertaker and purchase their coffin, which they carry to their house and display in a well-used room. That open coffin puts everyday worries like spilled tequila, barking dogs, broken pottery, and burned burritos into perspective." Bogus clinked a tooth against Billy's glass. "But you're not three thousand years old, you're not even thirty. You didn't have any trouble at all in ignoring that obituary notice that I arranged to blow out from the house when you first came. And that stupid vulture doing a back flip on your fence: you didn't even see that. And your ex-wife, lovely Linda in mourning clothes. They were all legitimate enough warnings, mind you, not just a game. But you went right on. So yes, let's forget the graveyard and go somewhere else to drink."

Bogus slurped the last of the whiskey from his saucer and dropped to the floor, a bit slovenly, Billy noticed. But then on feeling his own cheeks flush from the whiskey he remembered he hadn't eaten since that morning in his own home. Late afternoon was coming on.

Bogus crawled toward the fireplace and raised himself to peek at the black kettle that had been re-hung. He swayed momentarily like a fabled fakir's snake, hypnotized by some distant music—Maker's Mark Symphony #3 in A#? When he bit at the kettle, it tipped and he fell backward, laughing. He tried again, with the same results.

"Sir Uh-Billy, I think I'm going to need your help. Drop me in there, would you, then jump on in yourself. That way we'll be able to talk in private."

Billy stepped toward Bogus, then stopped. He thought he was used to the snake, but how do you get used to something like that? "Uh, your teeth, do you mind?"

Bogus grinned. "See? Even not-yet-thirty-year-olds aren't immune to an occasional fret about death." He closed his mouth, belched, then grinned to show his Roosevelt-Carter choppers.

Billy took the lid off the pot and eased Bogus in. Curious as to what would happen, he stared, but was rewarded with a sooty, inky fog, though he did think he heard a whiskey bottle clank on the receiving end, wherever that was. A door opened or closed out in the hallway; Billy could hear its lock click. That was as good a signal as any, so he picked up the lid to cover his tracks and stepped into the pot. The last thing he heard before landing on his head, was the iron lid clanging down.

Seventh Leg: Choo-Choo Express

Chapter 28

Bogus laughed as Billy dropped onto the plushly carpeted floor. "You just never learn, do you? Jump in headfirst. The House appreciates enthusiasm, you know."

Billy shook like a mishandled chicken. The thin room they were in vibrated, and occasional metallic thuds and steady clacks resounded through the royal red carpet. Leather hand straps swayed from the ceiling, which had a foot-wide translucent skylight running its length. He felt himself sway slightly with the straps. Was this a room in motion? Hell, why not?

A brass bed stood at the far end, a small couch and coffee table nearby, and two writing desks in the middle, one against each wall. The room itself was three times as long as wide, and reminded Billy of Deep South shotgun shacks, except that these walls might very well be made of sheet metal. The windows were curtained with red silk, but through a split in one he could see the panes were blacked out anyway. At a loud clack the floor shifted; at the same time, a locomotive's horn blasted. Were they on a train?

Bogus was sorting through a fat black trunk by one of the desks, gathering half pints and tucking them into his skin. Well, at least the mystery of that source was cleared up, though it was no clearer how the snake managed to get around with all those bottles bulking him.

"The rooms provideth," Bogus said. "Straight from Kentucky. I always wanted to go to Loretto and thank someone before I died, maybe shake a grand distiller's hand or something. A one snake hand shake, for auld lang syne's sake."

Billy didn't quite see how a handshake would be possible, given Bogus's fanged state in life, but let it go. A whistle blew again and the room or railway car lurched, again like it was part of a slowing train.

"Not our stop," Bogus said, noting Billy's questioning look.

"Then we *are* on a train?"

"As near as anyone's ever been able to tell. When you get off, you just arrive in another room, same as if you'd opened a door. There's always a sealed, rubberized passage leading from your compartment to the new room: it's not like you can see tracks or anything. Some people swear they've heard that same whistle and those same vibrations through different walls of different rooms, though, which feeds the conjecture that it is a train connecting key parts of the house." Bogus turned to fetch another half pint.

Billy sat down at the desk, just as the whistle sounded and the car gave a forward lurch. He eyed a flickering gaslight lamp on the metal wall near where he'd landed. Under it a red exit sign's old-fashioned painted finger pointed out a narrow hallway. He hoped a bathroom would be back there. That was about all that would fit. Other than an exit, that is.

"How long do we ride?"

"As long as we want, within reason. It'd be Bad Form to ride too long, be presumptuous of The House's hospitality. This train's a good place to talk privately, which I thought might be a smart idea, considering that cat snooping around the kitchen."

"Have the cats been in power before? Do they report to the council?"

"Wrong, wrong," Bogus said, moving from the trunk with a half pint in his mouth and his skin bulging. He grinned, evidently satisfied with his stocking measures. "Come to think of it, cats were in power quite some time ago, around the period you would think of as dynastic Egypt, and they had trained the clackers then too. Ricco's not anywhere near that old, or he might have remembered." Reaching the red velour couch Bogus slithered up, motioning Billy over with the obvious intent of drinking the Maker's Mark. A glass and a shallow bowl lay on the table—where the hell had they come from, Bogus's skin?

"What about Soapy?" Billy obstinately kept his seat at the desk.

"Soapy's fine. There's nothing we can do now, anyway; it's almost dark, you know." Bogus jerked his head toward the skylight and Billy could see that its gray had deepened in the few minutes they'd been in the room. He walked over and sat on the couch as Bogus did his trick of unscrewing the cap.

"But as her father I'm thankful you're worried about her. I hope you'll keep it up when the two of you return to Alabama."

"What makes you so sure that's what will happen? I thought you said you didn't believe it would. Or was that all for the benefit of that prowling cat?"

Pouring the Maker's Mark, Bogus grinned. Billy was grateful to see that his own glass had water in it. Whiskey neat wasn't his idea of a sweet, neat, treat, despite Bogus's constant homily to that effect.

"I'm sure it will happen because they—" Bogus's intonation, though heavy, still left Billy unsure who *they* were—"want her out of The House. Why do you think she's trapped where she is? You don't think those cats and Mrs. Snelling will let her roam around when they're boarding up all the libraries, do you? Soapy? No way. She'd cause mucho trouble."

Ah. Mrs. Snelling again. Billy fretted: "Why would they care more about Soapy than anyone else?"

Bogus took a slurp of Maker's Mark just as the car again lurched. "That poet fellow Chaucer told you the answer: she's Lady Wisdom. He recognized her. If your hormones weren't working overtime looking at her lips and other attributes, you'd recognize her too."

Billy swirled his water. Not much had made sense since he'd picked up the newspaper days ago and read that ridiculous headline about rattlesnakes. Walking underwater and breathing; fighting a slew of animated coat hangers; seeing a girl turn into a doe, a bird, a gnat, and a unicorn before she was killed; reading his own obituary notice; finding and then as quickly losing the computers stolen from his office—none of this fit a typical rational, we-can-make-sense-of-this pattern. But being chosen to be a protecting soulmate of Lady Wisdom? Why? His I. Q. might be 120, give or take the standard deviation of twenty points. Normal, not genius. He was a "really nice, but a little bit lumpy guy." That, he later found out, was exactly how one of his co-workers had described him when she agreed to set Billy up with a blind date. Lumpy. Not Adonis, not Arnold Schwartzenegger. And certainly not Nietzsche, Plato, or Aristotle. So why?

As the gray from the skylight dimmed to black, six gas lamps about the room went on with a poof. Billy could just make out his reflection in the water as he swirled it. He needed a shave, he looked like he'd been hunting wild turkey with the boys. Bogus said Soapy would become another Alabama girl once she got to Tuscaloosa. Did that mean Lady Wisdom would speak with a Southern drawl, chew pig's feet, and swill beer? Would she tease her hair until it caught in Wal-Mart's ceiling fans? Would she eat those awful finger sandwiches made of mint cream cheese?

Billy coughed. "Uh, I think you were right, Bogus. I think the council's made a mistake about me ... Do you mind?" He reached for the Maker's Mark and poured some, after finishing the water.

"The council knew exactly what it was doing. You're a computer expert, right?"

Billy nodded, taking a sip of whiskey.

"Then you can link into those ten computers that Ma Snelling stole and enter in everything Soapy knows."

Billy's shoulders fell. "A typist, then. A glorified typist is what the council chose me for."

Bogus's chunky teeth smiled. "And heart, Sir Uh-Billy. And heart. That's the most important House Rule there is: have heart."

Clack-clack, clack-clack.

Billy listened to the wheels underneath their car and looked to the snake, but Bogus just sipped Maker's Mark and grinned.

Clack-clack, clack-clack.

Chapter 29

Was it the Tin Man who got a heart or the Cowardly Lion, Billy wondered. Bogus was asleep—passed-out would be an unkind phrase, considering everything that had happened. It was just as well, because the more Bogus told him about where they'd have to go if Soapy really were captive on The Blessed Isle, the more Billy's heart had turned to chicken feed—or better, pig slop—or even better yet, those gooey donuts puffed with air and coated with slick grease that university students sold at fund-raisers. But what mostly troubled Billy on listening to Bogus's warnings was the fear that he might never see Soapy again. This possibility was his reward for doing exactly what the marriage counselor had suggested, "Follow your instinct." His instinct had told him to fall flat out in mad love with Soapy and look what had happened.

Clack-clack, clack-clack.

Instead of putting him to sleep, the sound of steel wheels on a steel track agitated him as he considered his and Bogus's recent conversation: *Before the Blessed Isle, there'll be a cliff, Bogus had said. On the cliff live angry rocks with razor-claws.* "Live?" Billy'd asked. *Live, Bogus had iterated, you can hear them breathing collective boulderish gasps.* "Ugh," Billy replied. *You mean Uh, don't you? And that's not all. Before that cliff, there'll be a cave, Bogus said. And in the cave lurk murky creatures whose ignorant babble entices any passerby into their muck until that person can no longer breathe.* "My Lord," Billy had said, thinking of weekday afternoon soaps on TV. *And after the cliff, lies a boiling blood sea, Bogus continued, the shouts and anger of all the dead swimming therein can rip and scald a swimmer's flesh or a boat's bark.* "Natch," Billy'd replied.

And then Bogus, damn his snake hide, leaving those delightful thoughts to buzz Billy's skull, had crawled over the room's floor, half-pint bottles bulging his skin and clanking, to hog the entire king-size bed and its red satin sheets, where he still lay, in precise, hog-heaven diagonal. A protractor couldn't have divided the sheets better. As Bogus snored, Billy scowled and scrunched on the small couch. He contemplated tossing an empty Maker's Mark bottle from the coffee table, and this made him realize he could no longer discern the lumps in Bogus's skin where the other half-pints were stored. He supposed the snake's stomach muscles eventually indented to accommodate the load, which explained why he'd never seen the lumps or heard the clanking until tonight.

His own stomach burned here, there, and everywhere, like a sad Beatles' tune. Stretching on the tiny couch to give his gut breathing room only spread gastric gas, so he sat up and pulled the Nietzsche book from his pocket. Placing Soapy's pressed rose petal to his lips, he read the marked passage about the Blessed Isles, which started out describing figs, autumn, seas, and a northern breeze, in a sort of a fantastical travelogue. But then he read, "God is a conjecture." Again and again the book insisted on that proposition as the railroad car click-clacked through what Billy supposed were the hidden tunnels of the house. "*God is a conjecture ... And what you have named World should first have come from your imagination ...*"

Did Nietzsche mean that the world isn't real on its own, that he, Old Herr Fred Nietzsche, and I, young Billy Wise, create it? Billy plucked at the cushion's red velour. *If so I would've picked a more sedate color, even velveteen Roquefort green would have done. And I hardly would have chosen either clackers or Mr. and Mrs. Snelling to inhabit this house's world. And the cats would have been a lot more friendly, their purrs wouldn't quite so resemble conspiratorial whispers.*

He glanced around for other things he would and wouldn't have placed in the traveling railway car, since it too was part of his world. He would have put a bathroom in it, for instance, right by the exit. And a shower stall. And a telephone, a happy, bright pink one since he'd use it to call Soapy. And while he might have put in a trunk of Maker's Mark, some walnut brownies, milk, and cold Heinekens sounded pretty good too. *Sorry, Nietzsche,* Billy decided, *but trying to make humans into gods is like trying to make sulphured molasses taste good. Neither has the pizzazz.*

Sticking Soapy's rose petal in his wallet he tossed Nietzsche onto the coffee table, deciding he needed more realistic bedtime reading. With a glance toward Bogus, whose selfish position hadn't veered, Billy forsook the cramped couch and walked the short corridor marked 'EXIT.' A tiny closet was recessed into its left wall, empty except for four coat hangers and a fire extinguisher. A bathroom with a shower stall opened directly beside the closet ... and a hot pink phone sat pretty as you please on the counter top.

Billy shivered. Had the house read his mind and decided on some practical joke, or had this been here all along and he'd subconsciously picked up on it? Or was he truly creating the world, as Nietzsche suggested? More like the world was creating him, king of the jerk-arounds, since that same world now insisted he relieve both bladder and bowels. Which was probably why he'd thought of a bathroom in the first place.

Through the floor, he felt the train's click-clacking slowing to a halt, so he checked the exit door to ensure it was locked, then closed the privacy curtain that separated hall from bathroom. He sat on the toilet staring at the pink phone. The more he stared, the more it spooked him. Was it all just chance? No, surely he'd subliminally seen it on walking in. But then again, he hadn't walked in, he and Bogus just found themselves dumped in the living room. "Damn this House anyway," he muttered, half expecting the pink phone to ring and some screechy operator to chide him about Bad Form.

But it didn't, so while completing the duty that even kings and queens must complete—*Remember creature, that thou art compost and to compost thou shalt return*—Billy lifted the phone: no dial tone. *Figures,* he thought, eyeing the two flickering gas lamps on either side of the shower curtain—*no electricity, right?* The train lurched to pick up speed, so he tried peeking out the small window, but it was curtained and blackened, though some determined passenger had chipped a triangular hole in a corner. Billy could feel icy air rushing in as he leaned indecorously from the toilet seat to stick his eye to the same hole. Doing so, he spotted a * + * The Society Of *+ * card on the window sill. Not Bogus's, because Bogus had stayed in sight the entire time. Anyway, this card had lain untouched for years, since it was covered with dust and spotted with water stains. When Billy tried to pick it up, he found that its glue had seeped out and molded it to the metal sill. He picked at it with a fingernail, then gave up and placed his eye to the crack in the window: a platform ran alongside the track, as far as he could see, with doors spaced every thirty or so yards. The whole platform was dimly lit with—aha, not gas but electric lights. So Bogus's friend Ricco was right. And one more thing, each door they passed was inscribed with a name in foot-high neon lettering. *Wind Room, Desert Room, Flower Room, Tiki Room.* The doors helped Billy gauge the train's speed at about forty miles per hour. Several click-clacking minutes passed, repeating the same scenario, only different names. *Dandelion Room, Lake Room, Meadow Room.* The doors continued with maddening regularity, despite what Billy guessed: that their interiors ranged from minuscule to National Park. Had they been passing these rooms with this same regularity since boarding the train? If so, there must be thousands upon thousands of them in the house. Well, that's what Bogus said; that's what the blueprints indicated, wasn't it?

Billy took a break to rub his eye, which was sore from the cold. Then he leaned to peep until the train slowed to one more halt. He backed from the window in case any cats or clackers were waiting on the platform, though he could still see out. All the doors in sight opened automatically, and rubberized corridors like the commercial airlines use accordioned toward each car. So it seemed from his vantage on a toilet seat.

The phone rang, nearly sending him through the tiny crack.

It rang again. When he answered, the connection was poor—some wonder deal Ma Snelling had worked out with a fly-by-night phone company, no doubt. Billy could barely make out that the voice on the other end belonged to a woman.

"Soapy?"

Whoever had called kept on talking, evidently having as much trouble hearing as he was.

"Soapy, I can barely hear you. Your father and I are coming. If you're on the Blessed Isle, rap the phone receiver twice, hard—I can barely hear you. If you're not there, rap it three times."

The voice paused as if listening. Then a crackle popped Billy's eardrum like a drumstick. Then came a woman's voice, clear:

"Mr. Wise. This is Ms. Debra Jackson at the University of Alabama's Development Drive. Mr. Wise, you've no doubt heard just how important this year's United Way Campaign is to the President and to the university's image. Mr. Wise, we're asking employees in your bracket to commit only fifteen dollars a month to the payroll deduction plan. Can we count on your support, Mr. Wise?"

Billy looked straight ahead and saw a floor-length mirror, and reflected in it, his jeans slumping around his ankles like two frogs, tuckered out from galvanic experiments. In the reflection he also noticed a third gas lamp over his head, one he hadn't counted before. So there he sat under its flickering, on a train's toilet with his trousers dropped, his bony knees glowing white, a pink telephone in his hand, and some woman cooing sweetly to him.

"Uh, sure," he said.

"Oh Mr. Wise, we're so grateful! I didn't want to prejudice you ahead of time, but your commitment has just edged the entire university over this year's goal. Isn't it wonderful what a single candle can do? Isn't it just wonderful?"

The train started with a lurch, throwing Billy's back against cold porcelain. He inhaled deeply. Meanwhile, the woman asked him to confirm his department, his supervisor, and his social security number. Leaning to look through the crack in the window as she talked, Billy made out blinking neon signs, as if a strip of bars and fancy restaurants were stuck here in the bowels of the house. If so, no one was taking advantage. The train was traveling slowly, and thumps sounded along the rooftops as if bundles were being tossed onto each car. The woman spoke through all this; he could even hear her pen scritching as she wrote his social security number.

"No, that's 7-7-ZERO-1," Billy told her.

"Zero-1?"

"That's right."

"Zero-1. Thank you, Mr. Wise."

"Uh, thank you."

Hanging up, he glanced at the floor and saw a puddle of blood. *Blood? It can't be, I don't feel—*. Then he kicked on seeing black movement. It came from a clacker using its coat hanger hands to slice Billy's bleeding left leg.

"Bogus!" he yelled as the clacker clattered across the floor. He reached for Frazzle Two, but didn't find it. Twisting he saw the jeweled knife lying in a second puddle of blood by the toilet. Tripping in his Fruit-of-the-Looms, he picked up the knife, and though it and the clacker met in mid-air, the clacker still managed to slice a two-inch gash in Billy's left arm before being cut in half itself. This pain Billy definitely felt. This wound he definitely recognized as his own.

"Bogus!"

The two pieces of the clacker noisily twitched on the bathroom's tile. *The coat hangers*, Billy realized. The coat hangers in the closet were clackers. And there had been four of them.

"Bogus!" he shouted again, pulling up his pants and limping out.

Three coat hangers still hung in the closet. He sliced at all three—to no effect, for they were metal, the real thing. With a last glance at the now-dead clacker, its empty black head twisted toward the toilet, Billy limped into the bedroom to see Bogus on the bed. Fearing the worst, Billy shouted. Bogus twitched slightly. There was no blood—or whatever the snake would spill: mud, blood, grape juice, or whiskey. Billy heard a raspy snore working from the snake's rattle-less tail to its mouth.

"You sonofabitch!" he screamed, not knowing whether to be ecstatic or furious. Then he fell and realized he had to stop the bleeding before it stopped him. Ripping a sheet to form a tourniquet, he repeated his epithets against Bogus, all to no use, other than to raise two long snores. His leg throbbed, so instead of walking Billy crawled back to the chest and pulled out a pint of Maker's Mark, the entirety of which he poured over his wounds. Still sleeping, the snake snorted, no doubt judging Billy's teetotalling waste of whiskey as the epitome of Bad Form. Well, he could at least remedy that...

Chapter 30

"Billy, grab hold of yourself!"

"Soapy!" In Billy's state of semi-shock, he first thought he was hallucinating, even dying; so, going on that presumption, he said several things that would have deeply embarrassed him.

"Great to hear from you. Glad you're here in my hour of need, oh Queen of Knowledge. Did I tell you that I really wanted to ball with you that night in the cave? Since you're not even the pigment of my imagination, I can tell you that—"

"Billy, it is really me. Billy, I am really talking to you."

"By magic, huh?" Billy blinked, almost losing consciousness, then continued as he stared at the railway car's ceiling: "Little blue swirlies, just like in the cave?"

"No Billy. By the phone."

"Phone's in the bathroom, the bathroom, the bathroom." Billy belched, then grabbed his leg and twisted toward the bed and its godawful red satin sheets. "Bogus, you sonofabitch, wake up and help me! Wake up and talk to your daughter on the bathroom phone. You've slept plenty and I'm hurt." He laughed, realizing he was half-delirious and half-drunk, since he'd broken the seal to another bottle of whiskey and downed a triple shot after dousing his wounds a second time. He looked at the blood on the carpet and realized he was also probably half-dead.

"Billy, I need to talk to you. I think that the cats and Mrs. Snelling are trying to—"

"Uh, kill me. I could've told you that when I was sitting on the toilet and the coat hanger thing attached, uh attacked me. Sure wished you'd called me then. Moral support. Would have been hard to talk romance with you, uh, sitting on a toilet and all, but still, that would have been—what, our uh fifth, sixth date? Something to tell the grandkids about, huh?"

"Billy, are you all right? Is Bogus there?"

Billy's head spun. "You mean Dad? How come you didn't tell me? Afraid I'd back out of the big love affair if I knew that fat lummox would be my father-in-law? Hey, listen: I'm tired now. Could you go away and let me sleep? Of course you can, since you're me, my imagination. Come back on our Wedding Day. Hah, that'd cause a stir in Tuscaloosa, having Bogus give you away. I can assure you it'd cause a stir, unless we dressed him up as snake tidbits and uh served him at our reception party."

"Billy Wise! That's not funny! And don't you think you're pressing our 'affair' as you call it, a bit? Are you drunk? Did a clacker really attack you? Is Dad okay?"

The voice was shrill and loud. Blinking, Billy searched the railway car to locate its source. *Good heavens, Billy Boy. There really is a phone on the second desk, and its receiver really is dangling down by a cord.*

"Uh," he said. "Soapy, it's really you?" He closed his eyes, then reopened them and sat up to focus on the phone. It was a speakerphone, and it was red, not pink.

"I've been trying to tell you that," a voice from the red receiver replied.

"Soapy! I thought I was dreaming or hallucinating. My God, the things I said. Yes, I was cut by a clacker, but managed to kill it. You're dad's uh asleep, he uh—Soapy, where are you? Have you heard about Alexandra?"

There was a silence on the phone that hung, vibrating slightly from the train's movement. Billy could hear, through the floor, the wheels of the train beating against the rails, *clack-clack, clack-clack.* He started to stand, but his leg hurt too much, so he simply crawled toward the receiver.

"Soapy?"

"I heard. One of Mrs. Snelling's damned cats told me. I knew from the time Alexandra was two that she wouldn't make it long if Mrs. Snelling ever took over during her life. She was too independent, too defiant."

"Your dad's okay," Billy said, reaching for the phone.

"Of course he is. And so am I. But you won't be if we don't get you out of The House and back to Alabama."

"And will you come with me, back to Tuscaloosa?"

"Of course I will. There's no place for me here now that Mrs. Snelling has taken control."

Though her last statement wasn't particularly reassuring—it made Billy feel like a fifth wheel in some grandly rolling plan—the thought of Soapy's heart-shaped lips and the sound of her voice beat down his pride and he listened as she told him what she knew of Mrs. Snelling's plans. What she knew turned out to be a surprising amount.

Evidently, Mrs. Snelling had gotten control of the supposedly uncontrollable train and had prearranged all the stops that Billy and Bogus would be making. This explained why Billy thought he'd seen clackers hiding in the doorway of *Faraway Places*, the last stop their door led to. This clearly meant that they'd have to stop the train somehow or otherwise get off at an unplanned site. Soapy had good news to mix in with the bad, though: she *was* on the Blessed Isle, but a back way existed through any of the house's libraries, a way that avoided all the traps and pitfalls Bogus had so indelicately described.

"The libraries are all being boarded up," Billy said.

"That bitch. I didn't think she'd have the nerve so soon after kidnapping me."

"Bogus tore out a map of the Blessed Isle. Will that help?"

"Yes and no. It'll help if you get here, because I'm on the northwest tip called Kitty-Kat Cove—no comment necessary, since I named the place when I was young and naive."

Somehow, Billy couldn't imagine her being naive, though the young part gave him no problems. He said so, but she cut his flattery off.

"Look, Billy, the first floor's library has a secret access panel under the kitchen sink. It's one of the few projects I could ever get * + * The Society Of * + * to finish. But you'll need some help in getting to that panel."

"Why? How complicated can the underworks of a sink be?"

"Pretty darned complicated," Soapy said, asking if he'd ever tried to replace a Delta faucet or a sink disposal unit. Well, no he hadn't, but still, he'd put in a new hard drive on his home computer once.

"You're all heart, Billy Wise. That's why I love you."

"Could Ricco help?"

"You've met Ricco? You and Bogus *have* been around in my absence. Yes, I was going to recommend him. Ricco hates the cats, and the cats are halfway afraid of him. They're superstitious, they think he practices voodoo even though he's from the Bahamas, not Haiti. Get him to get you into the library, then look up Hardship Mountain. The rest will be self-explanatory. Got to hang up. A cat's coming down the beach, Alexandra just said. Be careful, Billy. Hardship Mountain, remember. Hardship Mountain. I do love you, and we'll be happy as elves in Tuscaloosa, I know."

The line went dead.

Alexandra? Had she said Alexandra?

He tried to awake Bogus, but only aroused hisses and one half-hearted strike that hit a pillow. He decided to let Maker's Mark and time work their magic. Sleep wasn't a bad idea, after all. He did, however, grip Frazzle Two in his left hand. On doing so he noticed that it had grown longer and had one more jewel. Five now. He placed the knife-sword at his hip. It reached past his knee.

How Freudian, he thought, drifting off to sleep.

Chapter 31

"Breakfast," Bogus said, nudging Billy.

Pain shot through Billy's left leg the moment he awoke. He reached to rub it, but more pain stopped him.

"Looks like you had an interesting night. How in the name of House did you manage to slice yourself like that? Get drunk on your lonesome?" Bogus sniffed at a patty sausage on a nearby breakfast tray and opened his mouth to take a bite.

"Wait, Bogus. Wait. Where'd the two breakfasts come from?"

"Who knows? It's always been this way on the train. You stay overnight and you get served breakfast. I'm surprised the railroad isn't packed."

Remembering the neon lights and the thunk on the car's roof last night, Billy grabbed the patty that Bogus was about to bite and sniffed it. It smelled fine—no tell-tale almond or Clorox smell, but still . . .

Billy found Frazzle Two lying next to him on the floor and leaned toward Bogus to whisper, "Don't eat a thing. Stay here while I check something out." He stood and nearly fell down again from the pain in his leg. Using Frazzle Two as a crutch—it was now just short the length of a sword—he walked toward the closet and leaned against the wall.

Four hangers. With both hands he sliced through the clacker—obviously different from the coat hangers if one was expecting to see it, camouflaged perfectly otherwise.

There was a brief squeal, the first time he'd ever heard a clacker emit a sound of pain. He picked half the clacker up on his sword and checked the bathroom. Then he checked the exit—still locked from the inside, though that was obviously meaningless since this clacker had somehow gotten in. Looking up he saw how: a hatch was cut in the roof. No doubt a rope ladder was attached outside. He peered and …

"Interesting," Bogus said.

Billy jumped and gave a yowl of pain as his leg gave way and he slid into the vanity cabinet in the bathroom.

"Damn it, Bogus! Why are you around when you're not needed and away when you are?"

Bogus only smiled and nudged the dead clacker. "You wouldn't have said that if there'd been more than one of these lovelies, would you?"

Billy tossed the halves of the clacker into a wastebasket, then did the same to its previously demised comrade from the night before. "Bogus, I thought you said these railroad cars were havens."

"Used to be," Bogus said.

"Well what if the breakfast that used to be complimentary is now sedimentary?"

"What do you mean?"

"What if it's poisoned and leads to an early grave?"

"They wouldn't do that. Extremely Bad Form. Extremely."

"Bogus, you're the one who told me that when you think you know what the moral is, that's when you'd better watch out." Billy grimaced at a shot of pain from his leg and motioned toward the main room. Bogus backed off and they left the bathroom.

Billy fell onto the couch and told Bogus what Soapy had said last night. At first Bogus dismissed the conversation as delusion, dream, or drunkenness, just as Billy himself had.

"Alexandra's alive, Bogus. Soapy said so."

Bogus's narrowed eyes snapped alertly open. "Already? That can't be."

"Already? I thought you told me that Alexandra was dead, that even the house couldn't change death. Bogus, why'd—"

"Alexandra *is* dead." Bogus's tail had grown a new rattle and it twitched as he looked over his neck to the two breakfast trays. "Do you think the coffee's okay?"

"Who knows? If one thing's poisoned, it's probably all poisoned, wouldn't you think? If you want some that bad, just make some. I thought that was one of your wishes."

"Ah." Bogus reached into his skin and pulled out two tin cups, then a plastic pouch of water, then two large brown-green tablets.

Bogus, the traveling pouch. No wonder he's so fat, Billy thought as he watched Bogus pour water over the tablets, which commenced to boil furiously.

"Old army trick," Bogus commented, watching the water fizz. "Compliments of your Uncle Sam."

"So how do you get all this stuff, Bogus?"

"Connections. I trade the Maker's Mark for Army goods, I trade the Army goods for Maker's Mark. Connections is the name of the game."

The water stopped its dance, and what looked suspiciously like coffee remained. Billy thought of a quote he'd read from Abraham Lincoln: "If this is your coffee, please bring me tea; if this is your tea, please bring me coffee."

Bogus nudged one tin cup toward Billy and sniffed the other. "Drink up; it's the same concoction you were thankful for in the cave, days ago."

Billy did, making only slightly more of a face than he had the first time. "Okay, what's going on about Alexandra?"

"The name Alexandra is Soapy's peccadillo," Bogus answered, sipping his coffee. "I guess she does it to—to, I don't know, minimize the hurt when another Alexandra dies, to remember all the past Alexandras, to give herself hope, to—I don't know. This Alexandra is number, well the number is meaningless. This Alexandra is one of a line of many."

"One of many? And she's Soapy's sister, the same as the others? With the same father?"

"The same." Bogus sipped his coffee.

Billy swore he saw Bogus's snake chest swell at that.

The train slowed to a stop and they heard the rubberized door press against their own. Billy stood as best he could, his sword ready, and Bogus slithered past the bathroom toward the exit, fangs showing. But nothing happened, and the train chugged away once more.

"You're this one's father too?" Billy asked when they sat down again.

Bogus's viper fangs were replaced with his Carter-Roosevelt choppers and he grinned broadly. "Yeah, and so soon. Remember the night we spent at your house? There was this doll of an owl—I'm nuts over owls, you may have guessed—and we sorta hit it off, as you Americans say, when we both pounced on the same mouse. I ask you: am I a man or what? Was that owl some woman or what? Two days has to be a record. The only better mate I could have picked would be a fruit fly." Bogus took a slurp of coffee, smacking his lips.

"You're not kidding, are you?"

"Too serious to kid about. But in case you're thinking I'm a boor going out so soon after Alexandra's death, it had to be done right away. Propagation, I mean. Soapy, all the Alexandras, and I come in a package or we're no good." Bogus pulled a fuchsia card from his skin and flipped it across the coffee table.

Despite himself, Billy turned it over. The same legend was inscribed:

*+ * The Society Of * + *

He stared, then said, "What's it mean?"

Bogus sputtered his coffee on the table. "Great, great, I love it! Don't ever stop, Sir Uh-Billy." Bogus licked some coffee up then said, "Hell, who knows what it means, but keep asking and maybe, on some hazy someday, some someone will find out." He paused and looked at Billy quite seriously. "*That's* what it means."

Chapter 32

It was Billy's idea to break out the bathroom window, then exit when the train stopped. Breaking out the window was easier planned than accomplished, though, for he'd concentrated so thoroughly on its corner chink that he hadn't noticed the thick wire enmeshed throughout the remaining glass. That wire, his wounds, plus a lack of food extended a simple job into two hours hard work.

During the first hour of traveling and stopping, they saw no one on the platform, which was bathed in increasing daylight. Was there some type of computer-controlled artificial sun or skylight? This question brought another worry: would workers soon appear? Personnel on the platform would hinder their escape. They bashed away at the wire and glass, Bogus spelling Billy occasionally by pulling glass from the frame. As soon as he was able, Billy stuck his head out a small gap to locate the source of daylight, but spotted only an overhanging tin roof running the length of the track.

He again wondered about The House's connection to the world he knew in Tuscaloosa, Alabama, USA, Terra, Solar System, Milky Way. Was there a connection? Did The House have a function in that sense? Well, for that matter, did the earth have a function? Dust flew up from the tracks into his face and he sneezed.

"Back to work," Bogus insisted, tugging Billy's pants by the seat. "This window's so small that you're going to need to clear every bit of wire out."

Billy worked another thirty minutes in silence. The end of the wire was in sight when an idea from a college philosophy course struck him: "This house," he asked, "could it be the location of what your, uh, mentor Socrates called The Cave? Could it be where all ideas and forms reside, could—"

"My *mentor* Socrates?" Bogus twisted his lips as if spitting chewing tobacco. "If you only knew how many times I had to prod that torpedo-headed twerp into using his brain. He spent his time dazzled by his wife Xantippe's beauty and wealth."

"I thought she was ugly and that he liked little boys."

"Only when he was in his cups and when he'd been booted from her bedroom. Ugly? Woof, that's bad male press; Xantippe was a beauty. See, his marriage was arranged from age five, and her family was no small beans in Athens, while his family—well, they were stonecutters, though I suppose that mediocre occupation was important enough in those times, like compu—"

Bogus bit off his tongue to stop himself—Billy actually saw him do it, or at least thought he saw a pink sliver wriggling between the snake's thin lips. But Billy was too irritated to be empathetic: "Like computer programmers in our time? Important but mediocre? Is that what you were going to say?"

"Uh, no offense, Sir Billy, but that *is* what I was going to say. But, hey, look what happened to Socrates. No small potatoes in the world of ideas. He's kept poor Soapy's axons and neurons on a fly for over 2400 years now. So the moral is—"

Turning from Bogus with a yell of anger, Billy gave a kick at more wire, then cleared out jagged glass near the bottom. One strand remained, dividing the small window in two unequal sections, just enough to prevent him from climbing out. Leaning against the metal wall for breath he shivered, looking at last night's dried blood still on the floor, complementing Bogus's hourglass tan and ivory pattern in a most unpleasant manner. The throbbing in his leg was nearly as intense as the throbbing in his ear from listening to Bogus.

"So the moral is that even a poor slob of a computer programmer can rise above his or her squalid station in life, if only the muse—or the mouse, in the programmer's case—allows. Thanks for the moral support, Bogus." Billy turned to push and pull at the remaining wire. No result—what was it made of, Titanium XIII? He twisted Frazzle II around it, using the blade as a sort of lever, grunting as he twisted. "Philosophy, my favorite subject.

Of course it's all the more enjoyable when discussing it with a rattlesnake who's known Plato and Socrates personally and even has as his namesake the great Aristotle."

With the blade angled Billy gave a heave to finally snap the wire, the force throwing his face against the compartment's wall and causing him to drop the sword. He shook off the pain in his nose and looked at Bogus: "Tell me something. I thought rattlesnakes only lived in North America, so how come you were in Athens?"

"Aristotle Bogus," Bogus replied cryptically, hitching Frazzle II's hilt in the toilet paper dispenser and unwrapping the wire from the blade. Billy sat on the closed toilet to catch his breath and prop his throbbing leg in the now empty window frame. Along with his nose, his leg had started bleeding again.

"What I mean is," Bogus continued, spitting out the wire, "don't forget the second half of my name."

"A Bogus Aristotle," Billy said, not unkindly, but with an ironic short laugh. "So you're telling me that Socrates was really a dumbo in lovelust with some rich chick. So what then, did you, uh, do: keep dropping your * + * The Society Of *+ * cards in his stonecutting toolbox until he gave in and took the philosopher's pledge?"

"Something like that." Bogus spat more wire into the wastebasket. "How about another cup of java while we wait for the train to slow again?"

"That'd be great. Do you have any cream or sugar? Lots of both since I really need something to eat and I suppose they'll have to do for now, to make sure I don't get poisoned."

"Your wish is my command, O mighty one."

While Bogus went to fetch tin cups from the coffee table, Billy rubbed his leg and stared out the window at the passing rooms. So regular on the outside, so infinitely different on the inside. They were like people. His thoughts wandered to Mr. and Mrs. Snelling, how that old couple had done what old couples are supposed to do—grown to resemble one another like two balls of rising dough. But they certainly didn't resemble one another internally; in fact, they were complete opposites: he, seemingly all good; she, seemingly all evil. The word *seemingly* caught in Billy's craw. He edged his leg up more and its throbbing eased. He figured that he looked like a check-mark leaning against a toilet.

The train approached then passed two men sweeping the platform, purple black like Ricco. Billy jerked his leg down in time to avoid them. The platform and the doors returned to their usual monotony, so after a moment he put his leg back up.

He picked at a stray sliver of glass on the window's sill. The Snellings. Odd, how total opposites sometimes resemble one another in their fanaticism. Hitler, bad guy, slaughtered and tortured Jews, Blacks, and gypsies. How many good-guy religions had done the same? So, just how ideal is the ideal? Sure, in an ideal world—the world that he, Billy Wise, would gladly create if only Nietzsche and God could get their acts together to inspire him with the right computer program—in that utopian world—Billy peripherally spotted a fuchsia card that must have accidentally dropped on the floor and shook his head. *Now Bogus has me doing it. Billy Wise, common computer analyst by day, endowed chair at Harvard's philosophy department by night. Faster than cache-assisted binary math, able to leap gulfing syllogisms...*

Billy felt his body lean forward. Was the train slowing? He heard the squeal of brakes. Yes. "Bogus!" he shouted. "Forget the coffee! Come on! Bogus!" With difficulty Billy removed his leg from the window frame and used Frazzle Two as a crutch to help him into the railcar's main room.

No Bogus. On the coffee table sat a tin cup of steaming coffee mixed to the muddy consistency that only Billy loved. Next to it lay a *+ * The Society Of * + * card, its fuchsia clashing wildly with the couch's red velour. Looking around the empty room he picked up the card, then turned it over. "Good luck, Cisco."

Cisco underlined. No longer Poncho. So he was in charge now.

"Bogus!"

The train's brakes squealed. Tucking the card in his pocket, he searched the obviously deserted room, even peeking under the bed and into the chest of Maker's Mark bottles that rattled as the train slowed. He gave a last shout, then picked up the coffee and walked to the bathroom, checking the closet as he passed. But no Bogus.

Billy looked out the empty window frame and judged that the train was traveling about the speed of a jogger. Waiting for it to stop, he sipped his swampwater mix, thinking he couldn't have made it better himself.

When the train did stop, he saw a rubberized connector extending from a forest green door toward his coach's door, automatically snapping to assure a seal. He then heard their compartment's door click open, as he'd heard it do several times already. He gulped his coffee and eyed the forest green door, a door he and Bogus were obviously meant to enter. That was damn sure one door he *wouldn't* go in.

The tin cup was collapsible, more of Bogus's Army surplus, no doubt. Billy performed his patriotic duty and collapsed it, then turned to call into the coach once more, softly, partially because he was afraid someone or something outside might hear and partially because he knew Bogus had already left. No answer. Giving a salute to the absent Bogus, Billy eased out the broken bathroom window onto the platform next to the rubberized passageway. After a few moments, the seal broke, the passageway began retracting, and the train lurched away.

Billy looked both ways along the seemingly endless platform: nothing, not even fast food litter, for as far as he could see. The green door they were meant to enter closed with a soft hiss, its rubberized corridor shrinking before his eyes. "Skull Town" the violet glitter on the door read. Mrs. Snelling's little joke, no doubt. Billy wondered how many stops she would let the train make before finally boarding and searching the car. Bad Form, Mrs. Snelling. Very, very Bad Form. Like killing the Bishop of Canterbury in church, or siccing attack dogs on Blacks conducting a peaceful Alabama civil rights demonstration.

While the platform was deserted, it did emit the smell of diesel fuel. For some reason, what Bogus pronounced the night they spent in Billy's house flashed back: "All animals are sad after sex." Billy preferred an even shorter dictum: "All animals are sad."

A storage shed sat a hundred yards away. The train's last car was just passing it. Otherwise, nothing but barren concrete, the tin roof, and the mint green wall for company. Who would have imagined the inner workings of a creature as complicated as The House being so bland? But then, wasn't a computer's hard drive a pretty boring-looking affair, considering the information it held?

Billy's heart jumped, for a disappointed clacking—if clacking could ever sound disappointed—came from behind the door marked "Skull Town." He supposed that the clackers awaiting him and Bogus were packing it up and heading for the next destination where the coach's door would happily unlock. Packing up: a good cue. But which way? As long as he stayed behind the train—and he'd certainly do that considering his gimp leg—it really didn't matter, did it? The train was where they thought he was. They. He'd caught something else from Bogus besides philo-so-phi-a. He'd caught para-no-i-a.

Billy opted for the storage shed, curiosity getting the best of him.

Chapter 33

Like the platform's walls, the shed was painted mint green. This color threw perspective off, for the shed wound up being nearly a half-mile away, or so it seemed from the throbbing in his leg. Billy realized he hadn't eaten anything except the swamp water coffee. Stupid, stupid. He should at least have taken a pint of whiskey.

The shed was plywood, secured with a rusty padlock. Billy thought he might be able to bust the lock with Frazzle Two, if he could hold his throbbing leg steady enough to pound in a good swing. He licked his lips, contemplating the possibility.

"Look here, a white mutha out on the 'form."

"Hey man, what the hell you gonna do, break in to steal colored folks' valuable brooms and buckets?"

Three Black teens had evidently come from a nearby room. One held what was likely the key to the shed in his hands. The tallest, a lanky kid in his late teens who must have been raised on string beans, leaned to look at Frazzle Two.

"Back off, Baby. Look at the sticker that man carry."

Billy forced a smile. "I'm looking for Ricco. Can you lead me to Ricco?"

"Shit. Everyone looking for Ricco. We be looking for Mr. Snelling. You lead us to him?"

"I uh—"

"Shit man, go on. We got work to do. Leave us 'lone or cats be out here with them clackers cutting on our ass. We don't carry no truck with Ricco. What he want to see you white self for anyway?"

The one speaking opened the shed. Billy could see that brooms, mops and buckets did indeed fill it. All three young men went inside and slammed the door shut, laughing. So it was just like Ricco said with the teens. Billy stared at the closed door, then glanced left and right. His only option was to re-enter the house, then find his way back to the kitchen and search for Ricco.

The door to the right of the shed was called *Natural Bridge.* That was the door the three teens must have come from. What if cats and clackers were inside? They'd said something about cats coming out and "cutting" on them, hadn't they? Billy walked from that door to check a door on the shed's left. It was labeled *Dark and Bloody Ground.*

Swell. Just swell.

Eighth Leg: Dark & Bloody Ground

Chapter 34

But the more he thought about it, the more he opted to enter the door marked *Dark and Bloody Ground.* The House wasn't the only one with a sick sense of humor, and he might as well go it one better. As soon as he opened its door and stepped in, a young girl with bouncing blonde hair greeted him with a brochure listing, "Spectacular Sales of the Day." Being a good American, he opened the brochure. Another young girl, who must have trotted from the same sorority party as the first, handed him an application for a Shopper's Gala Credit Card, telling him all he had to jot down was his length of time with the company plus his present position and he would be issued his card within five minutes.

"And just for filing the form out," she sang joyously, "you'll receive this brand new, state-of-the-art Teac CD player." The girl shook wisps of blonde hair from her eyes as she pointed out the CD player displayed on a clear plastic stand.

Billy smiled. The CD player was fine, but he couldn't pull his attention from the room itself, which was a huge, as in HUGE, indoor mall, its twinkling, Christmas-light ceiling supported by cathedral pillars, its floor space extending as far as he could see, broken into artificial stations or departments. The floor itself was a highly polished ivory. In the distance a crowded escalator hauled shoppers carrying bags in both arms; above it, another escalator; then another—and more shops lined the mall's three higher floors.

From the room's name, he'd expected isolation; instead he found crowded mania. Under banners, ribbons, and balloons, people of all stations, races, and cultures mingled with the variety of life he'd come to expect from The House. And more than people: dogs, horses, turtles, even the nasty cats appeared intent on handling merchandise or peering into display cases. To his immediate right, six gorgeous women in pastel heels lined up at a counter, trying lipsticks, eye shadows and perfumes. He leaned toward their lank and lovely display of legs, feeling like a microchip about to crash from input overload.

The sorority sister handed him a pen and brought his attention back to the CD player by turning it to a modest roar. One of the six women at the make-up counter noticed the music enough to turn around. Billy glanced from the sheeny black CD player to the ballpoint pen the girl handed him. "I get the CD player free, just for filling out this form?"

"That's right, sir. But even more important, you get your Shopper's Gala Card within five minutes, guaranteed, thanks to our newly installed computer system. And your card will allow a guaranteed minimum and immediate shopping ceiling of 4200 greenies, which you can spend any way you want this very day."

"What are greenies?"

The girl giggled. "Oh, Silly! Greenies are The House's currency. I get paid *nine* greenies an hour."

As the girl seemed especially proud of this fact, Billy offered a congratulatory smile. His stomach roiled hungrily as he did. He realized he'd intuitively associated the girl with donut sales at the University of Alabama.

"Do you have a sister who goes to the university?" he asked, forgetting where he was.

"The university?"

"The University of Alabama."

"Alabama?"

"Uh sorry," he mumbled, taking the pen with a last glance at the CD player. The form asked only four questions: name, job description, length of time with company, and salary. For employer, the words "The House" were stamped in red. A gala red.

He entered "computer analyst" for job description, then paused at the last entry, realizing that while he'd asked Mr. Snelling about his salary, he'd never received an answer. Of course not, for the old man's line about having Soapy being around and Billy not needing to worry about anything else had thrown him. The old buzzard had gotten himself a computer analyst at ditch-digger wages.

Noticing Billy's hesitation, the girl peeked over his shoulder with a silly grin. "Oh, don't worry about that blank, The House will fill it out. Do you want to carry your CD player with you, or would you like to leave it here and pick it up later?"

"I'll uh take it with me."

"That's what everyone says." The girl gave a bright smile and led him to a counter on the other side of the perfume and makeup displays, where young men in ties were helping customers with iPads and Pods, customized cell phones, CD players, flat-screen televisions, and other electronic items. As soon as Billy came into the area, a saleswoman appeared. She must have been lurking behind a row of TVs, for he hadn't noticed her.

"He just filled out a credit application and wants to take his CD player with him," the girl said.

"Won-der-ful!" the woman exclaimed, taking Billy by the arm and leading him toward the wall display stacked with different speakers. A Bob Dylan song named "Dear Landlord" that Billy recognized from an oldies station in Tuscaloosa was playing. The saleswoman tripped switches, and the speakers began sequentially playing, just as if Bob Dylan were a strolling minstrel spreading grace and good will.

"All these speakers are hooked up to the exact same type of CD player you'll receive. Think of your music needs and your living potential, and just g-o go from there. The sky's the limit."

"Uh," Billy said, thinking he'd spotted the catch to the whole deal. "So the CD player doesn't come with speakers?"

"Cer-tain-ly it does, but today we're offering an immediate upgrade trade-in on those speakers for any of these improved systems, Octophonic Sound. And you'll have your Shopper's Gala Card in ..." the saleswoman, a tall brunette, looked questioningly at the sorority girl, who held up two, then three fingers and trotted off.

"... in two or three minutes. Donna's going to see if it's ready now."

The woman eyed Billy seductively and her foot caught the tip of Frazzle Two and pulled it back and forth like a pendulum. "A man like you needs an Octophonic speaker," she said.

They walked to catch up with the sound as one set of speakers went off to be replaced by another. All of them sounded alike, as far as Billy could tell. But he'd always had a tin ear. He felt the woman's foot touching Frazzle Two again and her eyes caught his. She removed her foot with a shy smile.

"Heard a speaker system you'd like to own yet?"

The systems once more changed, and sound blared from an amazingly small set of metal speakers. The woman punched her remote control to ease up the volume even more. Billy could feel his bones resonating, his left leg twitching around its wound.

"Big things come in small packages," the woman said, leaning until he could smell what seemed to be every perfume from the nearby counter coalescing on her brunette hair—or was the aroma rising from her bosom? The sorority girl bounced back with his Shopper's Gala Card. Billy had the feeling that the brunette had just about been ready to tug at Frazzle Two again with her red high heels, so he smiled wan thanks at the sorority girl.

"Do you know how these work?" the woman asked as Billy took the plastic card, which depicted a sunset on a tropical island, his name embossed in gold over the same. The card twisted and Billy thought he saw a naked blonde woman lying on the sand near a red sports car, though he wasn't sure. There was something tingly about just holding the card, as if it incorporated thermoelectric cells that responded to his touch. He shook his head, for the naked blonde had seemed to rub her thigh against the sports car, but when he looked hard all he saw was the barren tropical island, his name, and a long row of numbers.

"Sir? I asked if you knew how these cards worked." The brunette touched his elbow and Billy shook his head, nodding to the sorority girl, who left to greet more customers, the three teens from outside who now stood admiring the CD player. Two of them evidently already had their Shopper's Gala Card, though the tall one was happily filling out a form, pointing to the CD player and laughing at his friends.

"... The House carries your shopping purchases for an unbelievably low monthly payment," the brunette saleswoman said, bringing Billy back. "For instance, if you were to buy these miniaturized Octophonic speakers—" she clicked her sculptured ivory nails against them—"you could own them for only one-and-a-half greenies a month. That's cheaper than you could rent them, if you think about it."

Billy wound up purchasing the two miniature speakers on learning that he'd only have to pay one and a quarter greenies per month because of the trade-in allowance on the standard speakers.

After finalizing the sale, Billy wandered around, deciding that the *Dark and Bloody Ground* was a cross between a huge department store and a mall, for while there were no really separated rooms like in a mall, many merchandising sections sported their own colorful banners and logos. And instead of a food court, vendors carted their wares on motorized carnival stands with recorded hurdy-gurdy music. From one of these, Billy bought four hot dogs with chili and sat at one of the tables peppered throughout the shopping area. He'd used his Shopper's Gala Card for the hot dogs and thought what a convenience that was. When he asked the vendor what the total meal would cost in a monthly payment, the old woman laughed and said, "Honeykins, I can't count that small."

While eating the chili dogs, he noticed a CD music shop on the balcony above. An escalator—one of three sets of triple deckers he'd spotted in the short time he'd been inside the room—was nearby and he decided to visit there after he'd eaten.

But first he stopped at a tie specialty shop, thinking that if he were going to take the new job with the House, he might as well dress for the occasion. Also, he noted, his jeans were torn from last night, so he'd need one or two pairs of polyester slacks from the first men's store he passed.

Halfway up the escalator, clutching his Van Gogh "Starry Nights" neck tie along with his other packages, he spotted a men's shop next to the tie shop and laughed, promising himself he'd return.

This place was certainly packed with surprises.

Another surprise: the CD outlet vibrated—actually, as if it were built on huge mattress springs. He could see racks of CD's shaking whenever a heavy bass note played through the many speakers hanging about. The salesclerks all bobbed their heads, while subtly vibrating customers hunched over racks of CD's. He wondered if some enterprising owner had built the foundation so it would move with the music. If so, they could double the shop as a New Age massage therapy parlor.

Billy stopped at the jazz section, picking up a Wynton Marsalis CD. He decided on two titles, plus an old Herbie Mann reissue called *Stone Flute*. When he looked up, he saw the three young teens across from him, picking out their own music. They seemed amiable enough now; the tall one even grinned on seeing that Billy too had gotten a free CD player. Shopping evidently worked as well as Maker's Mark or football to grease the wheels of fellowship.

Billy purchased the CDs with his Shopper's Gala Card, then took an escalator down toward the pants shop. There, he brought one pair of jeans and two pairs of polyester dress pants and two pairs of corduroys, planning for winter. He wondered vaguely what the seasons were like in the house—well, if they had these and sweaters for sale, it only made sense that the weather would turn cold, didn't it? It wasn't like they'd be selling you something you didn't need. In the fitting room he looked at himself in his new pants and smiled. Stuffing his old jeans in a trash can, he wore the green combed-cotton jeans and paid for them and the other pairs with his Shopper's Gala Card. Pulling that gold plastic out of his wallet also pulled out something maroon, which floated to the floor. Billy glanced absently, thinking lint or a paper scrap had fallen. Light bouncing off a mirror caught in the gold card and he saw himself riding in a maroon sports car with white racing stripes. As the clerk rang up his credit charges Billy fingered a nearby rack of sports jackets, holding a dark red one before him and twisting this way and that, telling himself he could come back later.

He shopped for three more hours, pausing at a wine and cheese stall where a sad-eyed blonde perched thinly on a stool, singing war-protest and animal-rights songs in a sparrow-like voice. Two cows and a small palomino pony sat at a corner table, sniffling over their white wine and cheese. After the song, the palomino applauded politely, though the tearful cows seemed too moved to respond. Billy stayed through a second set of music, but after his third wine he decided he'd better leave. It took over five minutes to organize all his packages. How'd he ever gotten them this far?

Nonetheless, carry them he did, and he even stopped at another stall to buy a black coffee mug with a golden Buddha for a handle. This package was nearly his Waterloo, for when the salesclerk helpfully stuck the boxed mug in one of his larger bags, the box's sharp corners ripped the bag, spilling everything onto the floor. The coffee shop had only bags that were half the size of that original one, so Billy wound up with even more sacks, wrapping his right hand's five fingers tightly and individually around five, while holding the CD player under his left arm and three more bags in that hand. He looked around thinking he'd forgotten or left something on the floor. Frazzle Two. How was he going to carry it? A belt shop across the way gave him an idea, so he had the salesclerk place Frazzle Two in his teeth. Still, as he stepped toward the belt shop, he looked back, still thinking he'd left something. With a shake of his head he carried Frazzle Two and the packages over and bought a large belt for his new combed-cotton jeans. He stuck Frazzle Two inside the belt and was on his way out, but turned to ask the young male clerk:

"Uh, how do you leave this place, I mean this whole place, not just the belt shop?"

"Leave?" The teenager had a red face that Billy hoped wasn't from drinking, at his age. The teen blinked twice, then said, "Well, you could always take the train, I suppose, if you really wanted to leave. But, sir, your Shopper's Gala Card has 1800 greenies of credit still left. I know, because I had to check on the computer. And nothing closes for eight more hours."

"Oh sure, I forgot: I have to spend it all today, don't I? I mean, Bad Form and all?" Billy re-situated one of his fingers, then another, to grip his sacks.

"No, that's not so. This room's an exception, of course. But why not spend all day and all night, too? There's a luxury hotel on the fourth level. If you go over your limit, they'll just up your credit line next time."

"But I haven't even gotten my first check yet. I do have to pay all this back, don't I?" Billy looked about on the floor, fretting even more that he'd dropped something.

"Sure, but the payments are so low ..."

Another customer walked in, and the young man excused himself.

Billy counted his bags—twice—then walked out of the shop, Frazzle Two clanking against the escalator. He counted his bags again. What was it that he'd forgotten?

He passed the men's shop downstairs when he saw two clackers coming toward him. He fumbled for his sword, but they were already near his legs. Instead of slashing, they just leaned toward a display case of gold jewelry, pointing out a chain.

Billy stared in amazement. They were gesturing to the clerk behind the counter; evidently they couldn't talk, but both of them were pinching Shopper's Gala Cards in their thin, razor-y fingers. The clerk pulled out a chain and the clacker on the left tried it on, twisting it about its thin frame so that it wouldn't slip. The second clacker gestured toward another chain, and the clerk fetched it.

Billy walked away, bumping into the sorority girl who'd given him the application. She didn't recognize him, just absently dodged his boxes and bags. Ahead was the door out to the train. A clock above it posted the next arrival in twenty minutes. He saw two tired shoppers sitting on what looked like church pews, both poking their noses about the many bags they carried, like dogs sniffing new ground. Billy himself sniffed some flavored coffee he'd bought and smiled, leaning against another pillar and reluctantly placing several of his bags on the floor.

Nineteen minutes, the train's arrival clock read.

When there were only ten minutes left, the sorority girls rushed back to their posts, checking one another's make-up and their work stations. They smiled at the two sitting customers, who were still sniffing their bags of goodies. Billy shook his head and reached for his billfold. Pulling out the Shopper's Gala Card, he searched for Soapy's pressed bud. It was missing. He felt in his pocket, then checked his wallet again. He pulled everything out of his wallet. No rose. Where was it?

Six minutes, the train's arrival clock read.

He looked through his bags, tossing receipts on the floor. He searched the pockets to his new green pants again. Then he thought of pulling the Shopper's Gala Card out when he'd purchased them. Had he dropped the crushed rose then? Something maroon had fallen, hadn't it?

Five minutes.

He looked from bags piled around him in disarray, to bags similarly piled around the two waiting customers. His hands shook. All these bags reminded him of—what? Ah. The first apartment he and Linda lived in hadn't been cleaned by the previous tenants, it was filthy. When he and Linda finished the task, each room had a pile of trash in its center, a pile that mounted to their knees, just like these bags.

Four minutes.

Wise, you jerk.

He put his wallet into his pocket and kicked at one of his sacks. A tiny figurine of a green and gold elf dropped out. The price tag read 17 greenies. He'd forgotten about buying that. Hadn't there been something like it in the living room pile he and Linda had thrown out? Whether it cost seventeen or seventeen thousand greenies, the same would happen to this worthless elf.

He glanced up to the second floor, where the men's clothing store was, then he glanced to the clock. *Three minutes.* He'd never get up there and back, presuming that the rose petal hadn't already been trampled into the cheap carpet. Somehow, he knew that would be the case.

The pillar he was leaning against had a small sliding door, something he'd noticed on every pillar in the mall. He studied, then opened it. It was a very large dumbwaiter.

Still three minutes, according to the train's arrival clock.

He stared at the dumbwaiter. He'd just broken a window to get off the train hours ago. And now he owned all this junk, but he had lost Soapy's rose petal. The paint on the dumbwaiter's tray was a dull, chipping yellow, worn unlike anything else in this gala, glittery complex. He realized he could climb inside it with Frazzle Two, and hunch over. There wasn't room for anything else, though. The dumbwaiter must be a key passageway to lead him back to the house. He eyed the bags at his feet; he could swear that they'd crept closer, trying to encircle him.

Two minutes, the train's arrival clock read. The sorority girls were glancing at the clock and nervously smiling. One of the customers gathered her sacks, clutching them one by one; Billy could hear her grunt as she leaned for the last three. The other customer, a man with a black beard so meticulously groomed as to be anal-retentive, was eyeing the elf Billy had let fall. Billy kicked it across the room at the man, then he kicked the CD player at the startled sorority girls.

One minute.

He could hear the train's brakes. Holding Frazzle Two between his legs, Billy climbed into the dumbwaiter. The door closed just as the train whistle screamed.

Chapter 35

Billy tumbled along in the dumbwaiter for nearly an hour. Sometimes its walls felt hot, sometimes chilled. Occasionally he heard laughter or voices; once he thought he heard cats and people screeching and screaming as if in a fight. He heard two people talking about the administrative change from Mr. to Mrs. Snelling, how the library on the second floor was closed for major renovations, as well as the one on the first. He heard what he supposed were two maintenance workers coughing and complaining about the lack of air-conditioning. Once, he could swear he heard Mrs. Snelling barking out orders.

He heard everyone except who he wanted to hear. Riding in the dark and listening to the voices, he thought of Soapy's rose petals getting trampled in the Dark and Bloody Ground. That name didn't seem so funny now. It didn't even seem ironic.

Finally the dumbwaiter's door banged open.

"Oh mon! I was going to mark you among the shopping dead. Glad to see you, mon, glad!"

Billy looked into the grin of Ricco, who was extending his hand even as Billy crouched in the dumbwaiter. Billy used the extended bony hand to pull himself out and unfold. He found himself in the kitchen; the dumbwaiter's exit was situated on the wall opposite the fireplace. The door to the dumbwaiter shivered noisily to close and Billy lunged for Frazzle II, pulling it out in time. *Unlike Soapy's rose petal*, he thought sadly. He glanced past Ricco to the sink, where the key to Soapy somehow lay.

While in the dumbwaiter, even though there was no light, Billy had once more gone through his wallet, meticulously fingering everything in search of the pressed rose. He'd discovered that his Shopper's Gala Card glowed in the dark, and he'd flicked its glow against his angry eyebrows for much of the trip. He did this now in the kitchen and caught an image of himself standing on the deck of a cruise boat, surrounded by three naked and very tanned women holding scarlet iPads showing sports and movies. In the background another naked woman dove into a swimming pool.

Ricco jumped away, making a small sign with his thumb over his brow.

"What's with this damned thing, anyway?" Billy said, reflexively faking a motion of tossing the card.

"Oh mon, you still yet not know? *Satanas*. The tool of Satanas." Ricco, turning sharply from the card, strode toward the stove and turned on a burner. Shielding his eyes, he motioned for Billy to touch it to the blue flame.

Thinking of the Dark and Bloody Ground Shopping Mall, Billy was willing enough. But when he placed the card over the flame, it jumped from his hand. He picked it up and put it back. He and Ricco both watched the card again jump from his hand to toss off yellow and green sparks. Fetching a fork to hold the card in the flame, Billy still had to retrieve it from the floor twice when it wriggled free of the fork's tines. The whole time, Billy kept catching glimpses of himself, once entering a Concorde jet carrying brightly colored packages, once skiing down a pristine snowy slope, once sitting on a crushed black velvet couch sipping ruby red wine from the longest stemmed wine glass he'd ever seen...

"*Satanas*," Ricco murmured, backing against the door, as if he'd seen the visions too.

Finally the credit card was consumed. A black cloud bunched ominously, then spread to a thinness that blended with the yellow paint. When Billy put the fork in a cup of water, its tines sizzled.

A thunk sounded in the hall, and Billy looked to see a large Black woman. She was grinning and leaning to balance the weight of a gray tool chest.

"Fan-ny."

Just from the way Ricco sang her name, Billy knew something other than a work relationship was going on. "Fanny, this is Soapy's mon, Uh-Billy."

Bill couldn't tell whether Ricco's "uh" had been an accidental voice inflection or an extenuation of Bogus's joke. "Billy Wise," he said, giving a slight bow and making a half-motion to take the heavy tool chest from the woman. She set it down with a grunt and shook his hand, grinding all four of his knuckles. Obviously she could carry the damned tool chest her own bad self.

"Fanny's my babe, mon. Guess where she'd grew up at?"

Billy looked at the woman, whose skin was maybe a little blacker than usual, though not the island purple-black of Ricco's. "Uh, New York City?"

The woman's brows knitted and Billy knew he'd made a social blunder. "Uh, Alabama," he said, grasping for a quick straw and hoping he wasn't jumping in deeper.

Her face broke into a smile that lifted her brows in joyous wrinkles. A front tooth capped with a golden star glinted. "That's right," she said, shifting her hips and pointing at Billy. Her voice, though playful, encompassed more gravel than a backwoods road leading to a hunting camp. "I was just a little girl in a town called Coatopa—Indian for wounded panther—when I was killed in a house fire from a chimney."

Billy did a double-take at that.

"This is The House, mon, remember?" Ricco added, making a gesture with his light palms, which looked magical against his purple-black skin.

Billy nodded. The House. His throat parched as he glanced out the window toward the damned tombstones. Alexandra's had a lone yellow daisy on it. Bogus's still lay open.

"Then the obituary was right and I really am dead."

"Look alive to me, mon. What you think, Fanny? Bump his shinny with your tool chest to see."

Fanny hawed and grunted to pick up her tool chest, giving a wave of her palm.

"But Ricco, weren't you, uh, killed—"

"No mon, I was taken up in a rape-ture. Thought I was travelling in a purple whirlwind toward streets lined by cannabis, and look what I get—" Ricco gestured at the kitchen then looked at Billy's puzzlement. "Go on, bump him one, Fanny, he still don't believe himself alive."

"Don't pay him no mind. I never do. I ain't gonna bump you, I'm gonna fix it so's you can get to Miss Soapy. We got the word from Bogus you need to get to her bad."

Billy broke into a smile.

"See, Ricco?" Fanny added. "He knowin' he be plenty alive. Ain't no dead man ever smile that way 'cause of a woman." Fanny lugged her tool chest over and squatted before the kitchen sink.

For that matter, Billy thought, *there isn't any dead woman who lugs around a tool chest like you.* But he gave up worrying: it was The House; that seemed explanation enough.

Just as Soapy had foretold over the phone on the train, there was a power outlet under the sink. A bundle of a thousand or so thin color-coded wires fell from inside what had looked like a garbage disposal pipe. The heavy woman's thick fingers moved with a deftness Billy couldn't believe, separating the micro-strands out from one another.

"Fanny here, she want to go to night school and get smart, you know?"

"Night school? In The House?"

"Why not?" Ricco asked. "You have them in Alabama, mon, and who would have that ever thought? Night school? In Alabama? Hey up! When you and Soapy travel back to that great All-America state, why you cannot just ship-to-shore some professors our way? Hey-up, ship-to-shore entire school. As long as you don'na send us no football team, them local crackers be glad to be ridded and applaud with hands and feets both, yes? You take big care of budget problem by dumping teachers. What they calling it? Ed-you-kae-shun ree-form. Them crackers be so happy they elect you governor and buy you a glo-white cotton suit and fried chicken for life. And them professors, you tell them they going somewhere they be appreciated, so no problem there." Ricco lifted his purplish hands to surround his smile, "Everybody be happy. What you call it, windy-win."

Billy chuckled at the thought of the university's professors in regalia wading into the pond then daintily stepping into the bathtub to land on their heads. He rubbed his face and noticed a fuchsia * + * The Society Of

* + * card lying under two screwdrivers in Fanny's toolbox. Her large black fingers were still busily untwisting strands of wire. *Why not?* he thought. At least when she attended college she'd do something other than swill shooters like most American college students.

"That's right," Fanny said, unbending then bending her knee with a pop, giving an accompanying three-note whistle. "Send them geniuses here with them tassel-y hats. I always wanted to go to school and learn me a fancy foreign language."

"Yeah mon, me too," Ricco said. "English."

Fanny punched Ricco's calf then joined two yellow strands together, then two purple, and then two white; then she leaned to reach under the sink to throw a small switch. Billy heard a click. She scooted back on her haunches and looked expectantly around the kitchen. But nothing happened.

"Something wrong?" Ricco asked.

She grunted angrily and came to her knees to look in the tool chest.

"Something wrong?" Billy asked.

But she wouldn't answer; she just pulled out a pair of needle nose pliers, stripped some wire and held it with her fingers, evidently not getting shocked. Her eyebrows bunched and she pulled a large knife from under her loose work jeans. She gave a mean motion with her thumb and a jerk of her head for Billy to move. He did, eyeing the knife, afraid she was going to throw it. But she stood, knife at side, staring at the closed white door directly across the hall, the same one the clackers had rushed from when he first came into the house. Ricco followed her gaze.

"Damn! Them messing with the electric is ultimate Bad Form," Ricco said with pursed lips. He pulled a large wrench from the toolbox. Billy immediately pulled out Frazzle Two, and Fanny nodded. They walked across the hall, which was empty. Billy could see that the front double doors were once more shut. Sunlight flowed in the window on their left.

Fanny tried the doorknob to the white door, but it was locked. Ricco pulled out a set of passkeys, but Billy stopped him, pointing to a wire connection atop the door that looked as if it had been recently installed. Ricco crinkled his brow and Fanny motioned they should wait; she went to her toolbox and returned with a spool of wire, to run a connection from the white door to the next, which also had a protective alarm device over its jamb.

"That quiet that alarm down, sho'," she said.

Ricco then tried his key, but it wouldn't work. He checked the number, tried again, and shook his head.

"The cats changed the lock, mon."

Fanny mumbled something and pulled a sandwich from her smock's pocket, took a bite, offered Billy and Ricco some, then finished it in two bites after they both refused, neither wanting to stand between the woman and her appetite. She motioned for them to move and she walked back into the kitchen. Billy thought she was going for a tool or another sandwich, but the next thing he saw was her running with the toolbox clutched before her chest. There was a splitting and the door gave way.

"Roll Tide," Ricco whispered appreciatively, walking to give Fanny a hug.

Inside the room, she located another control box and flipped a circuit breaker. Immediately a scraping noise came from the kitchen. "The passage, it be open now."

They left the room, closing its busted door as best they could. "Not gonna fool cats too long. We gonna needs make ourselves scarce as angels on Halloween," Fanny said.

Ricco was whistling in agreement. Whatever he was whistling sounded low and slow, like a death dirge.

In the kitchen, Fanny pointed to where a throw rug had folded on itself under the table, and Billy stooped to pull the rug away. Floor tiles slid back to reveal an opening.

"This is it, okay-right," Ricco said, putting his head into the opening and sniffing.

"Here, I got a flashlight." Fanny pulled one from her toolbox and handed it to Billy.

"Once you get inside the library, mon, you gonna be on your own. We gonna close this passage and scram."

"No sir, we ain't neither!" Fanny said. "We got us enough time for you to fetch back a load of books, Ricco. The cats find out about this opening and it be gone, full of enough cement to sink my momma's rose garden. You know that be true."

Ricco opened his mouth, but Fanny shook her finger in front of his teeth. "Look here, Hon. You go for them books, I'm be standing out in the hall and tell anyone that nosy by a leak sprung in the kitchen and dirty toilet water's backing up. Nobody know different." To make her point, Fanny pulled a bowl from a shelf and filled it with water, which she sloshed into the hallway.

Ricco's shoulder gave a nervous twitch: "Okay lady, but you keep that big cat-sticker handy, since I be the one be doing the crawling, work that is nowhere list' in my supervisor of domestic engineering contract."

"What kind of books do you want?" Billy asked Fanny.

"Just grab. You gonna be sending us books and teachers from that university soon anyways, ain't you?" Fanny's gold tooth glinted.

"Right," Billy agreed.

"Right," Fanny said.

"Right," Ricco added.

"Uhm-hmmm," Fanny hummed and threw more water on the floor. Billy clicked the flashlight on and off to test it and swung Frazzle Two thoughtfully at the opening. A rotting smell was rising from it. He and Ricco both grimaced.

"Damn. You tell the Bogus that his ivory and aged rattlesnake self owe me one big favorite for all this," Ricco said, lowering himself into the opening.

"I haven't seen Bogus since the train ride. He disappeared."

Ricco balanced himself in the open with bent elbows. "Not to worry. Your American saying about how bad pennies always be showing up remember me of that snake. He like a green apple, always happy to cause a bellyache." Ricco watched Fanny slosh another bowl of water in the hall. "Enough. Too much just attract attention. Come here and throw this rug over us, woman. We are going down."

Fanny held a half-filled a bowl of water, which she threw at Ricco, getting only his elbow wet. "I told you before don't be *womaning* me, Ricco." Then she bent to give him a hug. "You hurry yourself back."

Chapter 36

"Ugh!" Ricco said.

They descended into a narrow stone passageway and had to crawl single file. When Billy heard Ricco gasp, his nose bumped into Ricco's wet shoes. Soon they emerged into a hollow space the size of a bedroom. Ricco shined his flashlight on two dried corpses leaning against a wall, mouths open. "I always hear this was use' as an underground railway years ago when Mrs. Snelling last took over," he whispered.

"Who were they?" Billy asked, looking at the skeletons.

"Don't know nothing more than what I told you, mon. Come on, let's go, or we wind up the same."

Billy didn't argue. With a last glance, they scurried into the dusty passageway ahead on the far wall. Halfway into it, they had to crawl over fallen rocks, stopping once as the ground shuddered, then scrambling onwards, disregarding the rocks cutting into their knees.

"One thing, Uh Billy." Ricco said with a grunt. "The cool cats cemented the fireplace exit in this floor's library, but the cool cats have cool cement in they head. Every library in this house has as many exits as it has books. Since I be volunteered to go with you, I will show you two exits I know."

Soon they were in the library. It was the same as when Billy'd last seen it—even the balls Bogus had scattered on the pool table were still out. So much for renovations. No, one thing different: the potbelly stove, a key passageway in and out of the room, was bricked up.

Ricco began gathering books to take back to Fanny, and Billy went to look up Hardship Mountain, the back way Soapy had mentioned, in the card filing system. He located the card when he heard a snap, the noise coming from where Ricco stood in the stacks. Billy walked over to see Ricco prying a mousetrap from his finger.

"Them cats. A real barrel of laughs," Ricco said.

The sharpened spring had sliced Ricco's finger. Though the cut was superficial, the trap had also broken a small vial of green liquid, which had seeped into the cut.

Popping the vial to scatter the remaining green fluid, Ricco looked at Billy. "Tell me, why is something called 'a barrel of laughs' in America?"

"We'd better get you back and wash that out," Billy said, ignoring Ricco's question and cautiously sniffing the green liquid.

"You just take care of finding Soapy. I be take care of Ricco Enterprises." Ricco sucked on his finger and spit something that was evidently bitter into a waste can. "Yes. Okay. Uh-huh. Real barrel of laughs. Why not a real trashcan of laughs, a real vatful of laughs?" His cheeks sunk as he sucked deeply; then he spit again, blood spattering the mousetrap. "Myself, I be immune to their barrel of poison humor, though—" he grimaced, looking queasy—"I think, anyway. This not the first time I run into one of their little green mousey traps." He scowled and looked to Billy, who had stood motionless watching. "Go on with you." He waved Billy on to his own work.

Hearing Ricco still sucking at his finger while dropping more books into a satchel, Billy returned to copy information about Hardship Mountain, consulting a slender volume in the stacks, keeping half an eye on Ricco, who was still working on his finger. Hardship Mountain was located on The House's third floor. To get there all one need do is open the door at the top of the stairs on the second floor, take the steps he'd previously spied through the glass transom. *Stairs upon stairs, more house delights—a barrel of laughs.* At the base of Hardship Mountain sits a stone bridge. Signs will lead to it, the book said. *What kind of signs, billboards? Hieroglyphic?* Once one reaches the bridge, all one has to do is walk it, for at its end are steps that lead to the Blessed Isle.

It all seemed simple, and that worried Billy. Simple, like a green mousetrap. He realized he hadn't heard anything for a while, and rushed to find Ricco on the floor between two stacks, shivering and clutching his satchel.

"Cats changed poison ... need to warn Fanny and others," Ricco sputtered.

Billy helped him up.

"You ... get ... what you wanted?"

"Later. I'll come back later."

"Books. At least bring Fanny the books I picked."

"We'll worry about them later."

But Ricco was adamant, so Billy carried both the books and Ricco to the grate they'd come through. He helped the shivering man down, then lowered the books and crawled in the passage once more. In twenty minutes they were back at the opening under the kitchen table.

"Ricco's hurt," Billy called out, tossing up the satchel of books. "His finger was poisoned by a trap." Billy stuck his head out of the hole and looked at Fanny. She was bleeding all over her arms and face. A large yellow tomcat's body sprawled on the floor; she kicked it aside and helped pull Ricco out. Billy heard a spitting near his ear as he climbed out and turned to see a hogtied cat on the floor.

Ricco was barely conscious. Fanny grabbed a butcher knife from the cabinet and held it high over the tied cat's tail. "Tell what make the cure, or you be a bobbed cat," she said, motioning with the knife. The cat licked its chops, taking Fanny's measure. It evidently decided she was more than willing to go through with her threat, for it spoke:

"Milk. All he has to do is drink milk. Pour some on the wound, too."

The cat was strangely purring as it spoke, Billy noticed. He wondered if it could be trusted, but walked to the refrigerator anyway, and found a half-gallon of buttermilk. Fanny scowled at the cat then poured the buttermilk over Ricco's finger, which was much easier than getting him to drink the stuff.

"These three was chasing a half-dead squirrel through the hall—regular cat torture fun—and wouldn't believe me about the backed-up drain. That's why they're here."

Three? Billy looked to see a third cat lying inert by the pot in the fireplace. A squirrel sat on the table, shivering under a dishtowel that Fanny had placed over it.

"Are you okay?" Billy asked the squirrel.

The hogtied cat gave something between a laugh and a yowl. "You expect a stupid squirrel to answer you?"

"I'm okay, thanks," the squirrel said. From the way it jumped at hearing its own voice, Billy wondered if it had expected itself to answer.

Fanny turned to the cat. "Live and learn, Mr. Puss. What we expect is for a stupid cat to be quiet. Only two ways that happen. You get thrown out in the yard and maybe some farmer pick you up and put you in his barn to torture field mice. You like that, or you like this?" She waved the butcher knife. "Cause that be your choice."

"Throw it out. That a lot more than it do for us," Ricco said. He was sweating heavily, though looking better. Evidently the cat had told the truth about the milk.

The cat looked from Ricco and Fanny's butcher knife to its two dead friends. Fanny picked the tom up by the scruff and threw him out the kitchen door toward the tombstones. It gave a yowl and Billy walked over to look. The cat worked its way out of the hogtying then shook off the miniature stunner holster that Ma Snelling had equipped it with. It ran to a tree, then stopped and began to lick its paw and wash its face. It seemed a normal enough cat now.

"Go outside The House, you change," Fanny explained. "Come inside, you change too." She looked at the squirrel and opened the window over the sink. "Going or staying?"

The squirrel looked at the dead cats, then at purple Ricco regaining his color. "Nice meeting you," it said, leaping from the table to the windowsill, then out. Billy worried that the cat would see it, but the cat had finished manicuring and was ambling off in another direction. It dawned on Billy that Bogus hadn't changed on leaving the house, and he wondered why aloud. Then he wondered about the electricity.

Fanny shut the window.

Ricco stood unsteadily and reached for Billy's hand. "No time for answering questions when we don't know answers. Take the flashlight and go on back.

Go get that information. We stay and dump these two in the stewpot. Nice meeting you, like the squirrel say, but you and Soapy come back some day, right mon?"

"Right," Billy said.

Fanny walked over and gave him a hug and a sandwich from her toolbox. If she had reversed the order, the sandwich would have been a pancake. He waved and crawled back into the hole. Halfway to the library, in the chamber with the two corpses, he heard the tiles screaking closed.

Chapter 37

"Too easy," Billy mumbled. "Too easy."

Ricco'd suffered a bout with a poisoned trap, Fanny'd tiffed with three cats, but nothing had confronted him personally since he'd left the extravagant mall. Being ever so aware of this inequity he was unnerved like a front-line soldier after days of absolute calm. Item one: on leaving Ricco and Fanny he'd easily accessed the library once more to locate the book on Hardship Mountain, copying down information undisturbed. The library's fireplace was even lit, which spooked him so much that his notes were in a scribble. Item two: once finished, he'd taken a key passageway behind an oversized set of encyclopedias and immediately wound up on the second floor, in the loft bedroom that overlooked the first floor. A blue rug saying "Welcome" had been exchanged for the green one saying nothing, draped on the railing. Item three: he'd heard voices and peeked over the railing to discover two teenagers, a boy and a girl dressed in hunter's orange caps, discussing whether they should nose around the house. They must have stumbled in from the outside, just as he had, just as the squirrel had. As they talked, Billy heard a scissoring sound so he hung over the railing to shout, "Get out of here!" and accidentally knocked off the green rug, which the boy and girl barely dodged before running out the front door, slamming it behind. The scissoring clacker sound simply ceased. Desist-o, vanished, caput.

Too easy. From the wood railing, Billy looked at the rug piled below in a green heap: it resembled a mound of lazy, cool moss. "Item four: Bad Form," he mumbled to himself, figuring the roof would cave in or compressing walls would squeeze him to sardine-size as punishment for knocking the rug down. Wasn't there a house rule about keeping rooms spotless? But once more nothing happened, so he simply walked toward the closet at the head of the steps. Heat from the desert room scorched his face. What would the young couple have thought if they'd discovered it? Whatever, he was glad he didn't have to return there. *But the devil you know's better than the one you don't know*, he reminded himself, turning from the open desert room to place a hand on the closed ivory door leading to the third floor.

Grabbing Frazzle Two he opened the door. Inside, stairs ascended steeply, encased by two claustrophobic walls painted the same fuchsia as Bogus's cards. The highest step—if Billy saw correctly—ended at another ivory door, itself topped by a dark stained-glass window with a daisy centerpiece filtering the stairway's sole source of light. A yellowish, sunlight light.

"Too easy, too easy," Billy chanted, grasping Frazzle Two. He took one step, kicking a heel backward to keep the door behind open. The walls didn't compress, spears didn't shoot out, so he began his climb. Click! He heard the door shut, as if it locked itself. He glanced back then ahead at the window's design: daisy or spider web? As brightly as its light lit the stairwell, he supposed real sunlight must be filtering through. Could that window lead to the roof? Here in The House, it could just as well lead to a star system. He closed his eyes; Bad Form alarms were ringing everywhere. He wouldn't be surprised to hear the walls breathing.

It was the vision of Soapy's blue eyes that kept him climbing. That and the fact that the door behind him was locked from the other side—*Tell the truth, scared uh-Billy.* By the time he reached the top step he was panting, and when he glanced back the steps had trebled, quadrupled. He inhaled three lucky times, readying himself. All his lucky breath rushed out as he twisted the doorknob and opened it.

Sunlight, yes. But no Hardship Mountain. Instead, inverting nearly immediately in the "room" below were miles of canyon cliffs and a singular, steep footpath descending from where he stood. The canyon was much too vast for him to locate any far wall—presuming there was one—but on nervously sticking his head inside the door he saw nearby walls to his left and right, walls of a stupid clammy blue plasterboard edged by a very narrow footpath and Wandering Jew plants that circumnavigated—he could think of no other word—the canyon as far as he could see. A receding line of gold doorknobs glinted both ways, indicating yet other doors, other steep, downward paths.

The whole thing was impossible, of course. This was much larger than the desert room on the second floor—the one he and Bogus had traversed. This canyon was thousands—millions?—times larger than The House itself—many jutting boulders alone looked as big as The House. The closest natural phenomenon he'd encountered to it in Alabama was Little Canyon, itself an anomaly for a state whose normal topography reflected a Southern who-cares attitude. What he was viewing was more like the real thing, the Grand Canyon, except that this psychedelic grand canyon incorporated patches of maroon, gold, Kelly green, robin's egg blue, and Sunkist orange, not to mention the purple border of Wandering Jew plant and the ridiculous morgue blue plaster wall. Still holding the doorknob, Billy leaned: the footpath directly below switch-backed to intertwine four circular patches of colors—patches that might encompass one or hundreds of acres, for perspective was hard to get a handle on. Occasional shadowy ravines peppering the path might slash downwards anywhere from hundreds of yards to miles. Again, his perspective was so overwhelmed that he couldn't tell.

He stared in reverential awe. Was a cloud moving below? He thought he spotted an eagle flapping, then a crow. The crow alit a hundred yards below on a lone cedar whose roots gripped two boulders, like the hand of a primal god gripping the eggs of the world.

Billy's brow wrinkled at the obvious. This was a canyon, not a mountain. Had he entered the wrong room? He slapped his pants' pocket for Ricco's Bad Form key that Bogus had passed along. Damn. There was a tear in his pocket; he'd lost the key, probably when he was tugging Ricco through the cave connecting the library and kitchen. Maybe things wouldn't be so simple after all.

With a second curse, he skimmed his library notes: *Only the path before you*

*will be your path; there will be a tree of knowledge, underneath which you must
spend the night; forks in the path will present themselves, trust your feet; when
the cloud of unknowing appears, meditate; to climb, you must often first descend
…*

The house's desert wisdom was about as sensible as a Bogus Dictum. A
second crow passed at eye level then swooped toward the cedar below to buzz
its fellow. Didn't early Christian mystics wander North African sands to live
atop pillars amid ruins, or in primitive caves? Didn't they pass their time
shouting spiritual riddles to one another or to the air when no other ear was
available? Billy imagined himself perched nude atop the cedar. Wise, the
sound of one riddle rapping. Billy, the sound of another.

A hot breeze hit his face, increasing the feeling that he was being initiated
into one of those early sects. He fully expected both crows to flap upwards
with yellowing hermit teeth and caw, "To know, you must first forget, O
clothéd biped." Or maybe it was a Zen sect he'd be initiated into: "What is
the sound, grasshopper, of one wing flapping?"

No sound, he thought. *No sound at all. Two wings are needed to flap, just like
Soapy needs me and I need Soapy … to fly.*

The second crow turned in a slow spiral.

*The hell with it. This is it, this is Hardship Mountain, one perverted House way
or another.* As Billy stepped onto the path a sheet of yellow fire enveloped
his skin. Not particularly painful, more discomfiting like a tickle, but when
he tried to step back, it swept to scorch and wither the Wandering Jews, and
his retreat was prevented by … by what? It was as if wind—invisible, firm,
and hot—held out a staying palm. As long as he faced the exiting door the
yellow burned intensely. He shook himself in a half circle and everything
stopped, the burning, the shaking, and the wind. He lurched, nearly falling.
The library notes slipped from his hand to be caught by a small dust devil
appearing from nowhere, then to be swirled toward a nearby gorge. *It's all
right*, he told himself, seeing limbs on a far-off pine shuffling with the dust
devil's progress. *You have them memorized anyway. Trust your instinct. It's all
right.*

So he walked down, hearing grit crunch under his feet. The sky soon turned a terrible, bright blue that glared—even when he concentrated on the ground he had to shield his eyes. Heat then blasted not just from wind, but from the sun hung somewhere in that brazen blue sky. Feeling sweat on his lips and dust in his nostrils, Billy pictured Fanny throwing water into the hall. He cursed himself for being so stupid as not to bring a jug of water, or even Maker's Mark. As he walked, beads of sweat turned to streams, streams turned into a constant sheet.

Though the singular cedar with its two boulders had first appeared near, the path followed switchback after switchback, and Billy realized how stupid he'd been to assume its closeness. An hour later he was once more drawing within sight of it. Then it disappeared; then, after one more switchback, it was there.

You have to spend a night under the tree, the note had read. Bull. He wasn't spending a night anywhere but in Soapy's arms. *Bad Form, Bad Form*—he could almost hear Bogus hissing this through sand, sweat and grit. Billy spotted a patch of green behind the cedar—the first relief from the landscape's yellow rock and sand. The green instilled hope of finding water.

What he found was a cemetery. Its stones were laid flat à la modern style, either a politically correct attempt to obliterate phallic tombstones or just one more contemporary veiling of bugaboo death. But there it loomed—polished, hard, and plain—the inevitable Capital D for Dally-Do-With-Daddy-Death. Three dozen flat, easily mown-over instances of the same.

No doubt the bones and rotting flesh beneath those small stones fertilized the Mecca of green above them. Another Zen/desert-monk message. But he did hear running water, so he walked among the grave makers, whose inscriptions gnawed with vague familiarity, until he came upon his mother's and father's stones, which made his throat swell. Then names tumbled with insistent regularity: a fifth grade teacher, an old girlfriend, two friends who'd died unexpectedly in a car wreck, a neighbor, a preacher, and another teacher. And then water, bubbling in a spring-fed pool

... beside his own tombstone.

"Natch," he announced to a scuttling black beetle with jaws like spaghetti tongs. In bright daylight the white medallion that had in the forest appeared to be a skull and crossbones now looked more like the mathematical sign for infinity. It really didn't matter what was on the stupid thing's back, it was those jaws that made Billy wince and touch his cheek. "Let's not let it come to that again, fella," he warned, chasing the beetle off with a stomp. At least the ground here was firm.

With a second glance at his own inscribed name, Billy knelt and drank from water's cool gurgle. The beetle ticked, in a too familiar sound. "I'm telling you: keep your distance, pal. I'm not dying of dying, I'm just dying of thirst." But the heedless beetle began scratching the dirt in front of Billy's tombstone.

After a last slurp Billy considered the stone. At least it didn't have a concluding date, nor did it have any ridiculous epitaph, as had Bogus's and Alexandra's. He bathed himself in the pool and searched for anything he might use to carry water while the beetle worked its jaws. There was nothing, nothing but himself, so he drank more, soaking his hair and clothes. The beetle's scratching reached a frantic pitch when Billy spotted a reflection in the water: it was the good-looking dame from Chaucer's time—what was her name? Lady Perrier Water? Smiling, he turned to see Mrs. Snelling, mightily heaving an uplifted sword ...

"The circuits blew last time, but it's for real now, you sap," he seemed to hear as the sword whistled downward.

Ninth Leg: Know Thyself, Redux

Chapter 38

Billy awoke staring up at high wooden beams and intervening dust motes, then sneezed. He was evidently lying on the musty floor to some warehouse ... wasn't he? Something was wrong though. His nose twitched. But smell wasn't it. He couldn't tell what time of day it was, since so little light filtered through the dirty skylights above. But that wasn't it either. Just how many skylights were there? His eyes shifted to take in hundreds. But that wasn't it either, the number of skylights. Something else was hugely and majorly amiss ...

"Ugh!" He slapped at a large bug—another black beetle?—crawling up his cheek, but hit only air. He slapped again and hit air again. A scuffling along the floor vibrated the back of his skull and his ears, but on trying to twist to ascertain its source, he couldn't. He was sure his neck and shoulder muscles had responded, but nothing had happened. Straining his eyes toward the top of his head, he gagged at what he saw.

It wasn't imagination. I was decapitated by Mrs. Snelling when I drank the water.

Help Help! Somdy helme!" His tongue thickly garbled the words after falling back on itself. He saw his standing body, dressed in a ridiculous white choir gown, fruitlessly grab in panic at where his head should have been. "Hel ... aghp!" The gargling frightened him so much that he stopped shouting for fear he'd choke. Through wisps of hair, he could make out his body standing within a few feet of his head, shuffling awkwardly, waving arms and hands over a raggedly cut neck and the bloody gown to encounter nothing but dusty air. His body's motions were becoming more and more spastic.

"Stop!" Billy called, afraid his panicking body would run away. Though it did stop, its skin quivered visibly and its feet pawed the warehouse floor, like a horse smelling danger.

"Pick me up! I'm at your feet. Pick me up and knock this damned bug off my cheek."

His body hesitated, then plunged awkwardly, its arms flailing far to the right of his head.

"To the left, to the left!" It again plunged, even more exaggerated this time. After several attempts, Billy corrected its movements until his body cradled his head under its left arm and brushed off the bug, which had once more taken a chunk of cheek.

Blinking, Billy saw that he was indeed in an endless warehouse, with dark wooden pillars stretching upwards maybe fifty feet. Between the pillars were what looked like makeshift horse stalls. It reminded him of a converted tobacco warehouse he'd visited in Kentucky that was used for antique shows after the Great Smoking Demise.

How strange to see everything from waist height! Like he was a child again! He didn't know whether to laugh or cry. One consolation: as far as his severed neck, there was no particular pain, only shock. What in God's name was going on?

"Turn," he told his body, not caring which way it went.

"Turn!" he shouted.

But his body couldn't comprehend the vague order, and Billy compared its inaction to a computer's refusal to insert one simple dot, to move one simple comma in a mis-typed command line without explicit directions.

"Turn to the right," he corrected.

His body did. He gave it more commands, facing the four winds. The warehouse looked the same wherever he faced: beams reaching forever high, open wooden stalls holding who-knows-what, occasional cross-lanes that no doubt led to other rows and other stalls. And dust everywhere, cutting much of the skylights' light. He sniffed—he couldn't really say he smelled aging tobacco leaves, but he couldn't say he didn't smell them either. There was an undercurrent of something in the dank air, maybe mold from the dust.

Or maybe blood from his neck.

"Turn left," Billy said, trying not to dwell on his neck and the implications. His body turned, to face him down a wide aisle. The stalls were about twenty square feet, the ones directly before him empty, though distant ones seemed to contain something—or at least seemed to emanate light.

"Lift me higher," Billy said. His body did. Then he realized that speaking was stupid. He'd never had do it when his body was connected to him, so why now? *Walk. Look for Soapy and Bogus. And Frazzle Two*, he added. But his body didn't react, maybe because it was no longer connected to his head. He tried again, thinking hard enough to start a mild headache.

The thought of a decapitated head with a headache was amusing so he laughed. His body shook in turn, as if sharing the joke, so some thoughts were getting through—or was it just vibration? Vibration, was that how his earless body was hearing? He concentrated again, but he couldn't get his body to respond to a thought-out command. He gave in and spoke.

"We need to search for the others and for Frazzle Two. The sword's probably nearby. Turn me in a slow circle."

His body did, but Billy didn't see anything. "Uh," he said, when something clonked his ear, "let me look at your waist."

His body twisted him, and there was Frazzle Two, safely tucked in his—his body's—rope belt. Should he pull it out? Why? What more could The House do than chop off his head? Billy blinked. *Better not ponder an answer to that*, he decided.

"Uh, walk straight ahead, turning left and right in a continual pattern as we pass the stalls."

His body responded, stepping forward and twisting Billy's head left and right.

"Slowly, you lummox! I've already got a headache!"

He felt his head being lifted inches as his shoulders shrugged. But afterwards he was rotated more evenly as his body carried him. These oral commands would present a futile situation in a fight with clackers or warehousemen—or with anything else he encountered, for that matter: he could never scream "Dodge left, strike right" quickly enough. If, that is, he was still in the damned House and if this warehouse was part of that same damned maze. He spat out a laugh. Where else *could* he be? How the hell else could his body hear without ears, much less live without a head? He was in The House, all right, but without Bogus, and without Soapy.

Somehow, Billy felt his heart skip a beat at Soapy's name.

"You said it, brother," he commented, surprised he could feel that palpitation. "Hey, look out for the box!"

His body stepped high over the box, which was empty, just like all the stalls he'd been passing. Yeah, there was no doubt that he was still in The House; this scenery fit the Good Form standard just fine.

He staggered along for an hour when the thought occurred that he should staunch the wound, that he might bleed to death otherwise. He glanced at a pile of old newspapers stacked against a stall, then laughed uproariously at the idea of stuffing paper into the bottom of his head and the top of his torso. If he wasn't dead by now, his expertise in Newsprint Bandaging 101 wouldn't make a hill-of-beans difference to his future survival as a headless wonder.

"Newspaper'd probably just choke us both to death," he told his body, feeling both alienation from and companionship with that same blundering creature. Then he thought, *Causal relations amongst rattlesnakes offer nary enough strife to alter one's life.* Yeah, it'd been a newspaper that had started this whole thing. He'd had enough of that mode of communication.

As time passed, there was no appreciable dimming of light, so he assumed it was midday. Spotting what looked like a crate of grapes before one of the skillions of stalls, he ordered his body to investigate. They really were grapes, Thompson's seedless, the crate stated.

But only one swallow made the obvious clear to Billy's head. His body caught on too and was stomping angrily as three chewed grapes dropped uselessly through his throat onto his toes.

"Uh, put me on top of your—my—uh, our—shoulders," Billy directed.

As long as his body stood perfectly still, and as long as Billy masticated with perfect patience, this positioning worked and the grapes found their target, his gut. One time his leg twitched and a grape went down his windpipe: Billy's head consequently tumbled off his neck in a spasmodic cough.

"Catch me!" he shouted. But his body had already done so.He realized that other actions had been carried out without a verbal command. Raspy breathing, for instance. And he'd felt his heart skip at the thought of Soapy. Maybe some instincts and motor responses were passed without speaking.

"Whatever," he commented, after positioning his head and once more chewing a grape, which happened to be half-fermented and made him feel pleasant, almost whole. It also reminded him of Maker's Mark and Bogus, and ... Soapy.

There, he did feel his heart skip a beat.

Since the gown had no pockets, he stuffed as many grapes as he could into his stomach, then heard a noise and whispered for his body to tiptoe and hold his head high in the air. Decapitation had some advantages. At one of the stalls he spotted movement, a blur of white, and indicated for his body to walk that direction ...

... to come upon a stall that held what would have passed for an idyllic clearing complete with chattering squirrels and buzzing bees, except for one thing. It was a scene Billy recognized all too well: his marriage ceremony to Linda. There stood his best man, Jack, who'd warned Billy he ought to think twice about the bride. "The gold digger from hell" Jack had called her when they were dating. There stood the preacher, his friends, his mother, Linda's mother and father, a jagged great-aunt whom even now he couldn't remember. Was she Linda's or his?

"Don't do it!" Billy shouted. His feet joined in by jumping up and down, and the gown billowed about him. "Don't do it! She thinks computer analysts are like doctors and lawyers. She thinks you're going to be Bill Gates!"

Despite his shout, the ceremony continued—with a hitch, so to speak. Only a few squirrels chattered among themselves in the stall's rafters as Billy screamed more warnings. Giving up, he watched himself kissing Linda, watched his friend Jack shaking his head and his mother weeping and ... and he wondered if everybody in the world had known what he hadn't. Well no, the old aunt was grinning. Two of us, then, who were complete blithering idiots. The wedding party disbanded, walking into the rear of the stall, into what seemed to be woods, there to simply disappear. Billy stared at something white lying on the stall's wooden floor. He urged his body forward.

A frilly white circle ... ah, Linda's flower bouquet. Who had caught it? Billy tried to remember the woman, a friend of Linda's he'd never seen before or after. Funny, when Linda looked at the wedding pictures, she'd thought the woman was a friend of his. All he remembered was the woman's heart-shaped lips and how appropriate he'd thought them for the occasion.

Billy's body swayed. Heart-shaped? It couldn't have been Soapy, could it? He pieced this recent depiction of the wedding with his much earlier memory, from a different angle and different time. Linda's supposed friend had stood to his left, that would be to his right from this recent view. With a jolt, he envisioned the wasp waist he'd just seen. And those bony ankles!

"Soapy!" he yelled. "Soapy!"

There was laughter from a far-off stall.

"That way! Run!" he told his body. His body began trotting in place—well not exactly in place, for it was turning a tight circle. "Over there, damn it! To the right!"

His body geared into action so well that he was barely able to stop it when it stumbled directly onto another stall, another scene, this one recessed so deeply in the stall that it was effectively night. Despite the scene's lack of light, he recognized himself and two "friends," blossoming into teen-hood. They were bending over his neighbor's porch, laughing. There! Tommy struck a match.

"Stop, you little jerks!" But just as happened the first time, Tommy and Lynn didn't listen. *Aw, don't lie to yourself, Billy Boob, you didn't tell them to stop the first time, now did you?* Billy blinked, realizing that was true. He angrily urged his body forward, willing it to chase away the three punks or ring the doorbell and spoil their fun, but the stall's beams took on independent life, growing limbs and tendrils to bar his way.

Fire flared on the porch and the boy named Lynn rang his neighbor's doorbell, shouting "Trick or Treat!" Then the three boys ran off into the rear of the stall. Billy watched helplessly as his neighbor, a woman in her early seventies, opened the door and screamed, trying to stomp out the model airplane glue, catching the hem of her gown on fire. A parent passing on the sidewalk ran to roll her on the dewy grass. Months before, at the beginning of summer, the woman had let Billy pick a quart of strawberries in her patch.

"You little jerk." Billy hit his own thigh and stumbled. "Following those two idiots. Are you ever going to learn to make up your own mind about anything?"

The scene faded, just as the previous wedding scene had. Billy felt too nauseous to move and blamed it on the grapes. He could smell fermenting alcohol rising from his stomach. Without being bid, his body began to walk as his eyes bulged, seasick—from the shifting ground or the fermenting grapes? Laughter roared from a distant stall, even as he pondered the cause of his queasiness.

The skylights retained pretty much the same brightness, so he held with his estimation of two or three o'clock in the afternoon. He heard an abrasive factory horn from somewhere.

It was nearly an hour before he came upon another active stall, one his past self didn't figure in at all. Instead it was just his mother and some woman he didn't know, in a small, antiseptic green room. The woman was evidently dressing his mother down—his mother had worked as a nurse after his father died—dressing her down for some stupid rule infraction. His mother tugged at her white nurse's cap. "Mom!" he shouted. After hesitating, he walked in, expecting the beams to once more stop him, but they didn't. "Mom!" he called again. But he was invisible and noiseless to the women.

The scene made him nervous because his mother looked so sheepish. Why didn't she just toss the damned silly cap on the floor and tell the supervisor bitch to ... Billy noticed movement outside a window. Some kids climbing the seats of their bikes to shake tree limbs. Oh yeah, this was the day he rode his bike way beyond where he was supposed to and stole crabapples from the hospital grounds and broke a major tree limb onto some visitor's car. Stealing apples from where his mother worked. Something Freudian in that, wasn't there? The Eve-us Complex? But Freudian niceties no doubt escaped this supervisor, whose voice had grown as abrasive as the factory horn. Billy grimaced: his mother had probably gotten chewed out doubly in one day, since one of the doctors had recognized him. No wonder she'd been so mad when she came home. All he'd thought about was his bellyache from the crabapples.

"Mom!" he shouted again, fearing to touch her.

No reaction. Seeing his mother's normally passive face wearing its normally passive mask, he ran from the stall, from the institutional green room.

Walking on through the afternoon, he gave up counting the scenes that were replayed. Between them all he trudged by empty boxes, securely bound crates, and weather-beaten ricks. Not to mention the eternal floating dust. He thought he spotted the sun once in a skylight, between scenes depicting the time he broke up with his high school sweetheart and the time he let a neighbor's poodle out of the fence as a joke and it got run over in the street. But it wasn't the sun, it was a high-beam lamp that was quickly extinguished.

"Hey! Hey! Anyone up there?"

No answer, just dust motes.

"Whoever you are, this isn't fair! Every damn thing in my life hasn't been bad, damn it!" he yelled. "What about the time ..." Cackling laughter broke out when he couldn't think of whatever time he'd started to come up with. The laughter seemed to be situated in the roof, among the skylights and beams.

Miraculously, after what seemed years, an ocher glow touched the stalls. He sneezed from the dust. As his left hand itched his nose, he thought of the day's horrible scenes, realizing they'd presented themselves in a timeline pretty much reversed. It was like his marriage with Linda had seeded those delinquencies and all his pettiness, from the jerky comment he'd made to their preacher down to the summer before kindergarten when he refused to play with the girl in leg braces. He was much too pure, for both of them. He might have caught some disease, that being faith and good will from the preacher or car wreck–itis from the girl. Where was that girl now, besides in this warehouse he called his mind? He hoped she was a successful discrimination suits advocate. *But don't sue me*, he pleaded, *sue Linda. It's all her fault, from the marriage on back.*

"Bullshit." He jumped, despite knowing it was his own voice. It *was* bullshit.

Time didn't flow backwards, and even if it did, he could hardly blame Linda for his own weepy personality. Might as well blame Mr. Schroeder or an allergic reaction to dust. Devil-dust made me do it.

No, just one seed sprouted this mess he called his life: the tangled vine of Billy F. Wise. His eyes drooped toward the sword stuck in his belt—his rope, that is. He wanted to pull the sword out and fall on it, kill himself and his body, or maybe use the rope to swing—well that wouldn't work, would it? His body and his head were already separate. *As separate as you were from that old lady on the porch and your mother and billions—(Oh don't be so cocky, Billy Boob)—lots of other people.* Billy blinked back tears—from the dust, he was sure. He heard laughter again, but ignored it.

"Let's sit on that crate," he suggested to his body. "Maybe the warehouse's emergency squad will show up—that's a joke," he added.

Instead of laughing, his face turned stiff from tears, as if someone had squirted a tube of super glue on it. Billy wondered stupidly if it would be rigor mortis'ed into a frown. Good! A frown would frighten off any strolling bureaucrat inventorying the dead. That's where he was, in a warehouse of the dead! The house's final joke, to drop him uncounted among the remains.

He again thought of the pizza parlor job and his recurring dream. Was this what Ma Snelling had meant to happen the first time, in the forest with the never-setting moon? *My final judgment, recapitulating each scene of my life. The millstone hung around my neck. Except there is no neck.* He blinked back tears. *Another staged show, Billy Boob, except you're doing the staging, solo: Billy, the professional weeping cynic.* He stared at the light—as murky, gray, and dust-mote ridden as it had been from the first—and he closed his eyes...

Chapter 39

He'd heard about newspaper workers falling asleep while they stood waiting for the presses to roll, but had never believed it. Now he awoke and found himself slumped on the crate where he'd sat down hours ago. Above, the skylights were doing their inevitable job. Below, the dust motes were doing theirs.

Noise came from a nearby stall. He listened carefully and heard a voice familiar from his first job in the pizzeria, the voice of a friend whose father had urged him to join the Marines. Billy jumped from the crate, screamed as his head dropped onto his feet, then breathed heavily, remembering his situation. The young man's voice droned on.

"Pick me up," Billy whispered. His body did so. "Turn around and walk in the opposite direction." Billy didn't want to hear that particular conversation finish, for the boy that Billy had encouraged to listen to his father and join the Marines had returned from service a paraplegic, missing one leg and one arm where Viet Cong shrapnel shredded the left side of his body.

Bullshit, bullshit, bullshit! Billy thought as he walked. He damned sure didn't want to spend this entire day rehashing his life like some old codger poring over yellowing photo albums. He didn't and he wouldn't. But the boy's voice followed through the rafters: "My dad . . . what do you think I should ..." Billy struck at a stall's supports with his fist: grievous pain bounced between his knuckles and his neck, jumping somehow into his head. It left him shaking.

In a new stall he saw himself drunkenly retching in a fraternity house's yard. He remembered how he'd managed to burn a hole in an expensive rug inside the frat house by showing off and smoking a cigar. His nose twitched from the mixture of vomit and cigar smoke he could still smell.

"Move," he told his body.

It did, but to no use, for shadowy movement in another stall indicated a teenage scene when Billy had bullied some poor teen more slovenly than him. He could see himself pushing the kid with his knuckle. He'd never done anything like that before ... another stall, showing a scene when he was a child. He was rubbing tobacco from a cigarette butt in some poor child's eyes.

Billy blinked. He'd never thought of himself as a bully; in fact, when he thought of himself in any way it was as a victim. After all, hadn't Linda ... the young boy screamed and cried until an adult came running from a house to pull Billy off.

There it was, in dust-mote and white, so to speak. *Bully*, just one letter's difference from *Billy*. His head ached, more from the truth than from any cut Mrs. Snelling's sword made.

"Okay, so I've been a jerk. Who hasn't?"

He turned back, only to see the friend in the pizzeria agilely flipping pizza dough in the air. How many times did he wish he could do that after returning from the Marines?

"Damn it all, what the hell happened to free will?" Billy shouted, unsure whether he was addressing the friend who'd joined the Marines or himself, unsure whether the anger and hurt were from the pain of his neck or the pain of his memory. Free will seemed lost, for the same pizzeria conversation followed him from stall to stall, no matter which way he walked, followed until he heard its bitter last: "I think the Marines would be a great personality builder." Yeah, they'll teach you falling, crawling, drooling, shivering and countless other manly activities to conduct in symphony from a wheelchair. But how was he to know? The guy could have come home with the Medal of Honor, right? Free will works forwards and backwards, if that makes sense.

No matter which way Billy walked, which aisle he tried, he stumbled upon another scene from his life and stood mesmerized at seeing himself and some friend—or enemy—replaying the Saga of Billy the Boob, Billy the Bully, Billy the Butt, Billy the Braggart, Billy the Belittler. In short, Billy the Ballast.

The worst came when he watched himself once more receive a telephone call from a hospital's social worker, telling him his mother had been admitted in the early morning and they'd been trying to reach him all day—admitted? How had she been able to hide the cancer from him? How had he been so pig-headed as not to see it? In the same damned town as her and she'd lain in her own dying mess for nearly three days before a neighbor phoned the police and an emergency squad broke in. He'd planned on visiting her that weekend. He had. He had. He had ...

What was happening with time? What was happening with him?Damn this House, damn this stupid job that isn't a job. He looked at the flowing gown. Was he a choir director now? If so, the solo was meaningless. He had to find the key that would lead back to Soapy and Bogus.

Chapter 40

Did he sleep? He must have, though it seemed that voices called tinnily all night, just as when he was a child lying with his stupid crystal radio set plugged into his stupid ear. "Billy, why on earth did you … Billy, I'm so ashamed that you … Billy, how could you … Billy! Billy! Billy!"

This was why people killed themselves: the possibility of quickly ending a bad, screeching musical comedy was just too appealing.

"Billy!"

He turned, since the voice seemed distinct, but there was nothing other than stalls and dust.

"Bill Wise!"

"William Francis Wise! Get in here!"

"Billy!"

"Billy!"

Shouts, shouts, shouts. Voices, male and female, young and old, cascading like white-water rapids. He got up and started to run. Now the empty stalls he passed weren't empty, but held dark gray shadowy movements. Now he started seeing straight razors, automatic pistols, bottles of pills, knives, revolvers, shotguns, bottles of bleach, bridges, tall building roofs, boxes of rat poison, jagged broken fifths of whiskey, X-acto knives. Then came fill-in-the blank suicide notes. Was he delirious?

He tripped, his body barely able to protect his head from the floor. Looking back he saw a spilled carton of ivory-handled straight razors.

"Bill Wise!"

"William Francis Wise! Billy! Pick me up! Slide me across!"

"Billy! Do it! Just do it!"

"End it!"

"Just do it! You know you'd be better off!"

"And so would everyone else!"

"Just do it."

One of the razors skittered with a life of its own to touch his foot, opening to reveal a glistening blade. "Billy, pick me—"

Another skittered across the floor, already opened. "Pick me, Billy. Look how shiny and sharp—"

"No!" Billy shouted, kicking at the razors. "No! No! No!"

When he awoke, the warehouse floor was barren, as if janitors had swept and cleaned. No razors, no dust, no nothing. No stalls. Even the tobacco-must smell was gone.

"Dai-umn!" Billy exclaimed on sitting up, conscious of a collar of stinging pain encircling his neck. Reaching, he realized his head was attached. That normal enough thought required an exclamation point, which he belatedly placed by cautiously twisting his neck. *Attached*! He searched gingerly to make sure: a hideous inch-wide welt greeted his fingertips wherever they travelled over his neck, a welt which tickled in every spot he touched, the way recently healed wounds do. A welt, but his head was certainly attached. And he was once more wearing a shirt and blue jeans. Had he passed some test? Did Ma Snelling take pity? Billy looked up at the rafters, empty now. What was the sense in worrying over all that, anyway? It was like the blank in Bogus's * + * The Society of * +* card.

Billy stood, with another yelp of pain, and walked. The stalls reappeared, but they were all empty.

When his neck began bleeding in so many places that he feared his head would once more fall off, he slumped against a post. As he did, he heard voices again. Then they disappeared. He was desperately hungry and thirsty. There was a screak, as if a metal door in need of oiling had opened. Billy looked to a distant blue glimmer. Squinting, he was sure it was some type of lettering. He walked as fast as he dared until he saw a blue EXIT glimmering.

More House humor. As far as he was concerned, The House had written the book on Bad Form.

No, it didn't say EXIT, it said EMIT. Whatever, it was different than the rows of stalls, so taking the marriage councilor's advice he followed instinct and walked forward until his growing reflection told him he was staring into a wall-sized mirror angled from a warehouse wall. On reaching it he saw that EMIT reflected a blue sign on an opposite mirror that read TIME. Underneath that blue sign was a black opening.

He turned. EMIT? He turned. TIME? Three empty handcarts, their yellow paint chipped, stood as if awaiting a shipment. Was he stuck in some galactic warehouse of good and bad deeds? Of all instances of time? Some Einsteinian, webbed universe? Looking up at the ceiling beams, he saw skylights stretching limitlessly. He leaned against the mirror and almost fell through. Its blackness was open, just like the blackness under TIME. Or was TIME the mirror? He stuck a hand in that one. It was open too. Which one to take, EMIT or TIME? *Trust your feet*, the instructions to Hardship Mountain had read. He entered TIME ...

Sunlight blinded him. He heard a crow cawing and tried to focus, succeeding at last. After minor stumbles, he stood once more by his grave, once more by the cedar and the small burbling stream. He was again in the canyon. He lunged for the water and drank, careful to keep Frazzle Two ready in case Mrs. Snelling showed again.

Chapter 41

Licking his lips, Billy touched the cedar's shaggy bark. The library notes had indicated he should spend the night. As far as he was concerned, he'd spent three nights. What had the stupid warehouse and his decapitation all meant? Everything he'd seen had to do with his life, like an intense regimen of psychoanalysis. *A test. I was supposed to learn about my self from overgrown horse stalls.*

"Yeah, and what I learned is that Billy F. Wise ain't so wise," he announced. "Is that what gave me my head back?"

A small chuckle emitted from the cedar. He peered into a knothole, wary of getting too close.

Bad Form, Bad Form, a bird overhead seemed to cry.

"Tough titty, tough titty," Billy mumbled, being as adult as he could. Of course, the knothole was empty and uninformative, so he turned to walk down the path he'd started on before the great warehouse escapade. He heard one more faint, irritating laugh as he did.

Soon he was walking on a cliff's path. The cedar disappeared completely after the first switchback. A hundred or so feet loomed above and just as much below. The path was relatively smooth, made of hardened sand and occasional gravel. It was of a width comfortable enough that any good ol' boy tailgating his camper toward an Alabama game could have driven it. Still, within—what? twenty minutes?—Billy began to wheeze, and this caused him to consider whether the house was pulling another fast one, whether he was somehow really steeply climbing while he believed he was steeply descending.

"Very symbolic, if that's so," he said, touching the rock wall and expecting more laughter. But there was none. "More symbols than a Bible class," he mumbled, just to hear a voice accompanying the crunching gravel beneath his boots, even if it was his own. It didn't take long before crusty humor and philosophic speculation gave way to tedium, hunger, and heat.

He spotted something slithering among sudden overlapping sandy rocks on the path. "Bogus?" He stepped forward gingerly.

"Bogus?" he repeated. For answer, a low, nervous rattle.

A college teacher had lectured that in a fit of anger Freud commented that not every cigar and not every tall building were symbols of the phallus, that some things were simply … things. After calling Bogus's name once more, Billy took Freud's advice. Billy left the rocks and their rattling, dark recesses, giving them wide berth, walking as close to the edge of the switchback as he dared in passing them. Looking down in sudden inspiration, he screamed Soapy's name.

"Soapeee, soapeee, soapeee," echoed back.

He walked on, crunching gravel again and moving away from the edge.

One of the colorful patches he'd spotted from the canyon's rim began swirling as he rounded another switchback. This patch—still at least a quarter mile below—emitted a pleasant, almost pulsing hypnotic blue, reminding him of the warehouse's TIME-EMIT sign. He watched as it turned: maybe it was a tie-dyed cloud.

"Look out! She's laughing at you and she's everywhere!"

Billy froze and gazed to where the voice seemed to have originated, but saw only bare cliff wall. The canyon was completely windless at this level, though the blue patch still stirred below.

"Hello?" Billy called.

"Sh. Look out! Stay alert. She's everywhere."

He spotted a bald, completely nude creature squatting atop an outcrop of rock. The flesh-colored creature was no more than a foot tall and almost looked as if it were taking a dump. Billy gawked.

"Mr. Snelling?" His voice rose and echoed.

"Sh. She's everywhere." With a stick, the miniature man thumped the rock he sat on, then motioned with his left hand to indicate the area about him. As he did, thunder clapped, probably from the blue swirl, and the small man half-tumbled, half-floated down the rock to land behind Billy, his fall softened by fluffy angel's wings attached to his scrawny shoulder blades. They looked dirty; worse, they looked stapled on.

"Mr. Snelling? Mr. Snelling, are you all right?"

The elfin man shook the wings, tossing dust in a puffy cloud. "I'm fine. Can't stay long. I just wanted to warn you that she's everywhere." Mr. Snelling slapped at the dust. "Here, in the dust, in the rocks—" he stomped his small foot, barely making a scritch—"everywhere, just like I used to be. Ah, sweet bye and bye. Well, easy come, easy go, eh?" Mr. Snelling gazed up at Billy for a response, got none, so he continued: "Listen, you're doing right, young man, by not following House Rules and etiquette. After all, she's not, so why should you?" Mr. Snelling gave an embarrassed laugh and rubbed his bald head, which glowed like a billiard ball. "Of course, she won't see it that way, so you need to be careful. Get Soapy out of here. Tuscaloosa's a great idea. *She's* hopping mad about that, let me tell you. *She* knows damned well that no one, I mean *no one*, will believe that Sophia has made her home in Ala-bubba-bama." Mr. Snelling's voice had shrunken with his size, and every time he emphasized a word it came out more of a bat's radar shrill than anything intelligible. He tilted his head, whose baldness reflected sunlight in a glare, and gave a pained grimace, as if his kidneys hurt. "At least, we're all *counting* on that being true. These are crass times, crass, so the whole wide world's melding into one unlikely lump despite Lady Wisdom. But enough. You have to hurry, because *she's* got something very bad planned for Soapy. Very bad indeed." Mr. Snelling stood on his tiptoes, and as his wings twittered off more dust he recited in a sing-song, "Bad Form, I warned her; you can't do that, I warned her; it'll upset the whole universe worse than quantum theory and those quarks and that jokey God Particle already have done, I warned her. But she's not to be reasoned with. She's in a spiraling tiff—" Mr. Snelling dropped flat-footed and with a tiny smirk motioned for Billy to lean closer—"in a tiff, you see, because right before I resigned the executive chair, I reached out of the house to kill twenty-four high school football coaches at some sportball meeting. Oh it was lovely, so symbolic, even in the way I accomplished it! Their tour bus was passing a sausage factory and I just burst a huge vat of grease to drown them all." Mr. Snelling's wings shimmered in ecstasy. "I admit it was stupid to do that just before the transition; if I'd done it a year ago, she would've taken over and had her little vengeance on four or five libraries or a publishing firm—maybe she'd have given Salman Rushdie dysentery, who knows? But she's beyond reason now. I mean, she's *always* beyond reason. That's her whole problem with Soapy, who is reason personified—" Mr. Snelling let out a nervous giggle, pulling in bare toes as if he expected a plague-ridden rat to grab them—"but Mrs. Snelling's gone beyond even Machiavelli this time."

Mr. Snelling's small wings fluttered, much as a ingénue girl's eyelashes might on prom night, and his sighs added to the effect, though what he said came out in drag-queen anger: "Well, *I'm* to blame, but *I'm* telling you, Billy Boy: those twenty-four big-gutted yahoos spitting tobacco, pinching waitresses, farting and haw-hawing on education money and time—a wasted mind's a terrible thing! That money could have ..." Mr. Snelling began choking as if a fishbone had caught in his throat, and right before Billy's shocked glance he turned beet red. With a final, stupendous hack that belied his size, the elfin angel fluttered his wings until he regained color.

Billy was about to pat him on the back and ask if he was okay when a swooping eagle pinioned the little creature. Billy got in one whack with Frazzle Two, but sliced only tail feathers as the bird took flight to carry Mr. Snelling over the lower cliff side.

"Let him go! Let him go!" Billy shouted.

As if it heard, the eagle dropped Mr. Snelling, who fluttered his wings in a spiral. But just before he gained control of his flight, the eagle pinioned him once more.

"You bastard! You can't do that!" Billy shouted.

But the eagle clearly could do that, over and over.

Billy threw two stones downward, but the eagle easily dodged both. Once more it let poor Mr. Snelling drop. Billy saw him spiral crazily downward, saw the eagle snatch him, leaving a scattering of angel feathers. Then the pair headed directly for the blue patch, which was now churning like a building tropical storm on Channel 9's weather radar. Billy angrily tossed another rock, managing only to pull a shoulder muscle.

SIC SEMPER SIMPERERS!

SIC SEMPER!

SIC SEMPER!

These voices, for there were many of them, shouted all about him. When he gripped his sword they laughed shrilly. With a pop, thousands of doll-sized Mrs. Snellings danced over the cliff's surrounding rocks. With the flat edge of Frazzle Two, Billy slapped at something crawling into his left pants leg. Not another beetle but a tiny Mrs. Snelling tumbled out, clutching tufts of his leg hair in her miniature hands.

"WAKE UP! THE SOAPY BITCH IS JUST USING YOU, BONEHEAD. SHE'LL LEAVE YOU THE MINUTE YOU GET TO TUSCALOOSA. WHY SHOULD SHE STAY WITH SOME NICKEL-DIME, SIMPERING COMPUTER ANALYST?"

Despite the voice's immensity, Billy raised Frazzle Two, but a clattering along the cliff's wall distracted him. Seeing a mini-avalanche of rocks and gravel bounding toward him, he ran as best he could. Everywhere he ran, the avalanche met him. As suddenly as it started, it stopped. Wheezing, Billy appraised himself: his arms were cut and he had five knots on his head, but no major damage. It was like Mrs. Snelling—in the guise of her tiny selves—had been toying with him, just as the eagle had toyed with the tiny Mr. Snelling.

Billy looked for the bird and Mr. Snelling, but couldn't see them, and instead of any more Mrs. Snellings, there was only settling dust. Rubbing an especially bothersome bruise, Billy walked on.

Was Mr. Snelling dead? Would Mrs. Snelling actually have him killed over twenty-four football coaches—if that ridiculous story could be believed. *More house symbolism, no doubt. Let me guess: those coaches represent good versus evil, ignorance versus knowledge.* Billy kicked at the ground. Were the Snellings themselves opposites, him capital G good, her capital E evil? Then what would happen if one should die, where would that leave the other? The sound of one morality flapping? Impossible.

"You can't kill him, you know!" Billy shouted.

No answer.

Rounding another switchback to overlook a deep, shadowy ravine, Billy stopped to watch the blue swirling patch. *What I just thought about the Snellings doesn't make sense. Mr. Snelling was the one who knocked me out when I was with Chaucer. And killing football coaches? Come on. It's not like he's Mother Theresa in drag...*

"Don't worry about it. Just walk. You have to reach Soapy."

Billy raised Frazzle Two as soon as the first two words had been spoken. He almost, in fact, out-reacted himself, for he teetered from the edge of the path to prevent falling into the shadowy ravine.

"Don't worry about it, I said. Just get to Soapy."

With a glance down into the ravine, Billy saw a chalk-white figure crumpled atop a jutting rock. A gossamer wing fluttered in a breeze. *My God, she has killed him.* But he heard a cough and turned to see Mr. Snelling perched on a shrub whose roots clutched at two rocks. The tiny Mr. was preening angelically clean feathers.

"Mr. Snelling? I thought—"

"Thought is admirable in its place, young man, but you need to get on with things. *I think, therefore I am* was Descartes' shtick. Take his word for it. Walk. *I walk, therefore I am.* That was Gassendi's answering argument, every bit as valid. Hop to!"

Mr. Snelling disappeared, leaving Billy just mouthing the *Uh* in *Uh, what in the world are you talking about?*

"Walk!" a voice shouted as Billy stared at the barren shrub that had seemed to speak to him.

Like Gassendi, whoever that was, Billy walked. But also like Descartes, he didn't stop thinking: The second Mr. Snelling in the shrub didn't have a scratch on him; it was like the eagle had never touched him. But those talons had been plenty sharp and that crumpled white shape at the bottom of the ravine ... *She's everywhere*, Mr. Snelling had said, meaning, Billy presumed, Mrs. Snelling. Everywhere? Well then how about here? Billy kicked at a stone.

R-OUCH! it replied in a growl.

Billy rushed ahead, suddenly feeling not so clever, suddenly afraid to think, suddenly afraid to look back. *Billy F. Wise, you're the dumbest man alive*, he told himself, heading for a bend in the switchback …

Chapter 42

... Soapy looked up from her book. Billy had dragged himself around the switchback and there she was, sitting on an outcropping flat rock, reading. As simple as that.

And there they were, at the bottom of the canyon, by a large lake whose waves lapped like an ocean's. Spray hit his face as he stood stunned at the sight of the lake, at the sight of Soapy—both rosy from a setting sun.

"Uh ..."

Soapy primly laid her book on the flat rock and looked up as if the pages held a stock report, as if Billy were arriving for a business consultation. Then her smile broke and she jumped down and ran to hug him, her long white cotton gown trailing on wet sand. Ridiculous, but charming and titillating too.

She stopped short and stared at his cut face and arms. "What happened? Are you all right?"

"Fine. Now that I'm with you I'm fine." But even as he spoke he remembered the talking rock he'd kicked, the broken remains of a Mr. Snelling lying in a ravine, and Mrs. Snelling's cruel games.

Soapy tugged at his face and gave him a heart-shaped kiss. "Fine? Didn't you say you were fine?"

Billy looked at the twinkling from her oceanic blue eyes. Had he known Paradise before now? "Uh, fine."

When Soapy giggled, Billy grabbed her; and the feel of her spine underneath his grip, the push of her small nipples pressing his chest obliterated any pain or doubt. *Fine*, he told himself. *I am fine. We are fine.* He wanted to smell her hair, bury himself in her white cotton dress, anything ... but he stopped to lick his lips. He couldn't close his eyes for fear. Looking anxiously about, he turned to gaze into her blue, blue eyes.

"Soapy, the place I just came from, and what just happened to Mr. Snelling ..." As the sun winked behind some cloud, he proceeded to explain everything that had happened for ... well, he wasn't sure for just how long it had happened, but he explained anyway.

"The warehouse of time. Then it's real and not a rumor," she said.

"More than real enough for me: I saw my mother."

Soapy squeezed his hand.

"And after that ... Soapy, Mrs. Snelling ... I thought she killed Mr. Snelling. I mean, I guess she did in a way, so why didn't she just kill me back on the cliffs with a real avalanche instead of tossing down pebbles? Or why didn't she just leave me with my head chopped off—dead, for instance." He ran his hand over his neck, but the welt had nearly disappeared.

"She wants me to leave, to go with you to Alabama, that's why."

Billy shook his head. He wanted to believe whatever those blue eyes told him, but he was afraid. "Mr. Snelling says she wants to kill you. At least I think that's what he was getting at between all his babbling."

At that, Soapy pulled from Billy's grasp. "Kill me? Me?"

"That's what—well he didn't say it exactly, but that's what I gathered. He said he warned her it was extremely Bad Form."

The waves picked up in the lake until a fine spray chilled the two of them. Billy shivered and Soapy led him to the flat rock she'd been sitting on. He recognized the area from what he'd seen at the bottom of the Plexiglas barrier in the corridor many, many days ago. Or was it so many? The multi-colored canyon surrounding them faded from purple into plasterboard blue-gray. Soon enough, Billy looked to its rim to see a storm cloud, barely visible, lit by a rising moon. Moon? But no doors or walls or Wandering Jew plants were in sight. More of The House's magic, no doubt.

"Soapy, I was wondering on the way down here ..." He paused to lick his lip and tasted spray from the clear water in the lake.

Soapy smiled. Her heart-shaped smile bamboozled him, as always, leaving him grasping for some obscure word. Underneath that smile, what was she thinking? The rock she'd led him to was warm, despite the lake, despite the coming storm and night. With an all-knowing, secret smile like hers, it wouldn't surprise him if she'd installed a miniature nuclear reactor inside the rock to warm them. But then, with a smile like that, they wouldn't need a nuclear reactor.

"I was uh wondering," he continued, touching his palms first to the rock, then giving them a better home on her thigh. "I was wondering about Mr. And Mrs. Snelling and The House. Mr. Snelling seems so good at times, but—" Billy gestured inarticulately with his right hand—"but he told me that he drowned a bunch of football coaches in grease, and as infantile as that sounds, I don't think he was kidding. He uh said they weren't even in The House, but somewhere in America, at some convention. And that yellow cat whose eyes look so evil, that Mr. Whateverhisname who Mrs. Snelling appointed to head that Department of New Education? He was purring on Mr. Snelling's lap during my interview just like they were the closest of pals. I know it was him." Billy listened to the water lapping, then spoke: "And just now, up on those cliffs, Mrs. Snelling was playing with me like she was a kid—a damned mean one, but a kid nonetheless."

Billy blushed at a memory of his punching a boy to goad him into a fight. Then Billy looked at Soapy, hoping she wouldn't smile or blink or otherwise throw him off track and into more Uh-land thoughts. "What I'm getting at is this: Mr. and Mrs. Snelling aren't really complete opposites, like you'd think at first. Are they?"

Soapy, pressing Billy's hands with her own, pursed her lips and shook her head. Waves beat against the sandy shore.

"And they run The House ..." Billy looked out over the large lake—evidently it had been the swirling blue spot he'd seen.

There. He knew it would happen, he was diving into Uh-land and all Soapy had done was purse her lips and shake her head. The lake was so immense that white caps glistened in its distance, so immense that he couldn't see its opposite shore. He thought: *A huge natural phenomenon like this and like the canyon. And the train and all those other rooms with who-knows-what in them. So to say that Mr. and Mrs. Snelling run The House—what does running The House really encompass?*

"Uh, Soapy, I started to wonder if they were like mini-gods or something."

"Something," she answered softly, her voice echoing the lapping waves. "Something."

Billy's eyes drooped like the moon being swallowed by an approaching cloud; he felt himself riding a current whose warm trough was pleasant, he felt Soapy's arms behind his neck guiding him down. When he looked up he saw her smile, he saw the rock they'd been lying on close upon itself behind her back like it was gliding silently on rollers, cutting out two stars persistently twinkling through gathering clouds ... No, one of the stars wasn't twinkling, so it was a planet. Venus? The planet of love? He tried to raise his arms but they were as numb as his legs from his long walk, so they fell with a tired plop he barely heard before he was asleep, half-hypnotized by his own heavy snores. Or was that distant thunder?

Chapter 43

Billy lay on his side. At his back were velvet cushions, warm and pressing; at his front was the musky smell of Soapy, emanating from her breasts and nipples, her hair, her lips, her firm spine, her eyes that he couldn't see, her lashes he could occasionally feel as they blinked in the dark, and from her fingernails that caressed him in a tickle. Emanating. From her whole being. They were that close. He breathed in deeply. Emit. Time … But as Soapy exhaled he shook any thoughts loose. "Mmmmmmmmm," he said instead, thinking that the most complete word in the English language, much more satisfying than, for instance, *wait*. He only wished that he could say it in capital letters: "MMMMMMMMMMMMMMMM MMMMMM!"

"Are you finally awake?" Soapy pressed the length of her body against his.

He tried to concentrate on each point of contact, but found himself delirious. Toes, knees, hips, mons venus, belly, breasts, nipples, lips, nose, cheeks, eyelashes, forehead, hair—and her fingers and nails everywhere.

"Soapy," he whispered.

He rubbed his nose under her neck and inhaled. They rolled, bound on either side by the velvet pillows. Her buttocks were incredibly smooth and firm. They rolled onto their sides, and she placed her left leg over his. Heat and moisture surrounded him; he envisioned a tropical rainforest, his body brushing among vines, large sheeny leaves, trickling water, heat, and a pervasive musk. Their tongues licked, their arms pulled, their mouths opened, ready for—

Cannons fired, kettledrums crashed. Billy and Soapy separated quickly,

Billy groping for Frazzle Two. But what started as a prelude to war or the finale of the *1812 Overture* switched to the lone trumpet of Copeland's "Fanfare for the Common Man." Literally. It literally played, unbelievably, from the hollowed-out boulder surrounding them. Then the voice Billy had recently come to know too well spoke in disharmonious shouts:

NOT IN MY HOUSE, YOU SLUT! YOU SLUT, SLUT, SLUT!

Klieg lights snapped on—Billy could feel their instant heat on his back as one wall of the rock became a makeshift screen and the following message scrolled out:

MEMORANDUM

TO: ALL EMPLOYEES

FROM: DEPARTMENT OF NEW EDUCATION

RE: GOOD FORM

GREETINGS! WISDOM WILL WIN! A NEW HOUSE RULE, NUMBER ELEVEN, IS HEREBY APPENDED TO THE ORIGINAL AND GLORIOUS TEN: NO LOVEMAK-ING DIRECTLY BEFORE DAWN. THIS RULE IS INSTITUTED IN DEFERENCE TO THE PROVEN FACT THAT THE RELEASE OF SEXUAL TENSION INSTILLS SLEEP, AND SLEEP IS AN ENEMY TO WORK. THE COMMON MAN FINDS FULFILLMENT IN WORK FOR THE COMMON CAUSE. WISDOM DECREES THIS TO BE WISE.

Cannon again, then the trumpet solo for "Fanfare for the Common Man." The makeshift screen darkened, though the klieg lights remained lit. Billy felt himself sweating under their glare and covered his personal Frazzle Two with both hands lest it get sunburn.

Soapy, though, was hitting a pillow and laughing—so hard that Billy first thought she was hurt. She gripped her side and laughed more, pointing to the wall where the memorandum had appeared, then to Billy's embarrassed hands covering his half-erect penis, then to herself. It was infectious. Billy, seeing the ludicrousness of the situation, also began to laugh, starting with a confused chuckle then crescendoing to rolls of guffaws echoing Soapy's own until tears were rolling down his cheeks and hers both.

STOP IT! voices shouted. *STOP IT! THE ELEVENTH COMMANDMENT IS SERIOUS BUSINESS.*

Once more the wall lit the same memorandum. This time, Billy and Soapy took turns shouting the memorandum's lines, playing straight man to one another and rollicking with laughter.

"No luuuuvmaking die-rectly before daw-un," Soapy intoned.

"Yes, for sssss-sss-ex-ual ten-shun in-stilllls sleeeeep, and sleeeeeep iz an enema to work. . . ."

<u>STOP IT!</u>

<u>STOP IT!</u>

<u>STOP!IT!</u>

The hollowed boulder they were cocooned within shivered until fist-sized rocks cleaved from its ceiling, which was not that far above them. Billy and Soapy crawled toward one another, still giggling. A rock dropped harmlessly between them and cracked open to shout *Stop it!* while taking on the form of Mrs. Snelling angrily waving a crumbling finger. Soapy tossed a pillow on top of the miniature Mrs. Snelling, cajoling her, "No finger-twittering before dawn ..."

"It instills, sleep, and sleep is an enema to work!" Billy joined in.

The pillow scuttled across the boulder's floor, blindly colliding with the boulder's interior wall. After more wobbling, a tiny Mrs. Snelling emerged from under the pillow. "You slut!" she shouted at Soapy before spinning like a top to face Billy. "You penis head!"

When Soapy and Billy laughed in response, Mrs. Snelling rushed them, but Billy struck with Frazzle Two, sending her halves in separate directions, spinning once more as two pieces of rock. There was a rumbling and the surrounding boulder groaned like an old man, splintering into thousands of Mrs. Snellings. "Slut! Penis Head! Penis! Sluthead! Slit! Pithead! Pit! Pit! Pity!"

"No cursing before dawn," Soapy proclaimed.

"For cursing is an enema to work!" Billy shouted.

They both laughed. They laughed. They laughed, grabbing their sides.

The voices garbled into meaninglessness, then silence. Then Billy and

Soapy could barely hear the waves of the lake as dawn broke amid heavy white mist and settled like a father's calming palm. Then the rock no longer existed.

Billy chuckled and felt grass underneath his legs. Were they still by the lake? Water lapped, but in tiny, inconsequential waves, not in the great night roar of a stormy lake. A bird whistled, as if surprised by the morning sun.

Twe-oh-wee.

They were on an island, and at their feet lay fallen persimmons. Billy picked two up and offered them to Soapy, who was looking about, letting out another giggle. She took a persimmon and tasted it, giving a heart-shaped smile at its sweetness. A fish broke the water, a squirrel caught a limb overhead, and once more a bird whistled. *Twe-oh-wee.* Billy recognized the area for the small island behind his Tuscaloosa house. They were home.

Final Leg: Sweet Home Alabama

Chapter 44

They became wet from swimming—not submarine walking this time—from island to shore, but since fall afternoons burn in the Deep South, the pond's water was warm with slimy algae. "That way." Billy pointed toward the rise that would lead to his house. *Uh*, he thought as his feet plodded and clumps of algae fell, *I'm walking in a forest where I saw a unicorn, and I'm walking with Lady Wisdom, who's thousands of years old but looks twenty-four, and I'm walking with her to my house and we're going to get married ... Uh.*

For once that word offered a perfectly reasonable beginning *and* ending.

They reached his modest rental house, which Soapy investigated minutely, starting with the master bedroom—whose bed, Billy noted, still held his and Bogus's impressions from the night they'd slept there. He wondered where the snake had toted the computer cable, figuring he might just need it to hang himself if he had to keep staring at Soapy's slender figure next to an unmade bed. When she turned and gave her heart-shaped smile, he backed out of the room. *Wait.* What a stupid concept.

"This one will be for all my books," Soapy said when they entered a second room where Billy'd placed a couch from Goodwill and a TV from Wal-Mart. Flicking the TV's remote control, she gave the screen an electronic snap. Pursing her lips at a puerile sitcom joke, she shook her head until the bland sitcom faces foundered into a dying, wriggling blue line which itself disappeared into a burning blue dot. So much for Wal-Mart's twelve-month guarantee. Billy blinked, his new secret code for *Uh*. Should he blame Lady Wisdom for the TV's demise instead of Sam Walton's successors? He sniffed ozone from the dead TV and watched Soapy's blue, blue eyes as her ivory nails disdainfully dropped the remote control into a trashcan. Clunk. Her eyes were hawk-like from reading, her nails honed from turning so many pages. Billy tried to imagine just how many books Lady Wisdom might own, how many bookshelves she might need. Well, at least now the room was conveniently cleared of one hindering bit of furniture. Studying the old tongue-in-groove wood ceiling he envisioned hanging shelves from it. Would he and Soapy have to open the attic to accommodate the incoming library?

"Your house is yummy," Soapy said, taking Billy's arm. "The rest of it can wait, though, since I'd like to see my new hometown, too. Can we?"

"Uh, do you want to go to the university's library?"

She gave a wry look. "When in Tuscaloosa, do as the Tuscaloosans do."

"Well you sure won't be going there then. Uh, maybe there's a football game. Time got so screwed up in the house that I'm not sure what day of the week it is here, but we can always go check the nightlife to find out."

"Nightlife?"

"Drinking and stuff. An America tradition to waste time when there's nothing on TV." He nodded toward the dead TV. "Which it doesn't appear there will be." Suddenly Billy opened his palms in question. "Hey, I thought you were Lady Wisdom and were drillions of years old and would know all this multi-cultural stuff. Nightlife and wasting time, I mean."

"Wasting time's as old as Noah and Socrates, Billy. They were both dreamers and wine drunks. But then again, there's wasting time and there's wasting time. And time well spent is time saved."

"Lord, another BD."

"Beg pardon?"

"Another Bogus Dictum, another confusing, pithy saying. Well, you are his daughter ..." Billy pinched his nose to distract himself from Soapy's leg, where a piece of algae clung to her calf in a most alluring manner. "Uh, his BD's were close to BM's. I told him so too."

Soapy laughed. "Bowel Movements?"

"See, you have kept up with the times."

Soapy brushed off the algae and with a double-take bent to peer under a large cherry secretary. She pulled out the lost computer cable, which Billy promptly carried, along with the algae, to the kitchen's trash.

"Still," Soapy said, following him, "new jargon requires assimilation, and assimilation requires time." Reaching for Billy's hand after he dropped the algae and cable, she pressed it between her breasts. "Time, Billy. I'm not a computer."

Instead of feeling a heartthrob, Billy felt sizzling electricity, and saw a mysterious blue-eyed dazzle. *Ah, more magic.* Then he corrected himself: *Not magic, love.* He leaned to kiss her. And then he re-corrected himself: *If there's any difference.*

"I really would like to see Tuscaloosa," she insisted, accepting and even returning the kiss, but removing his hand when its roaming became too cartographic. "I've heard so much about it. Let's wait just a bit on the hanky-panky."

Wait. He cursed that word.

Chapter 45

Driving toward Tuscaloosa, Billy worked up nerve to broach a sad subject. "I don't uh know how we got out of the house and away from Mrs. Snelling and her cats, but I sort of thought uh Alexandra would be coming with us."

"Mrs. Snelling kicked us out of the house for laughing, that's how we got out. I knew she would; she can't stand laughter. Have you ever known any mean-spirited person who could? But laughter or no, Alexandra won't be coming. She's dead, Billy. Even the house and all the laughter, magic and love in the universe can't change that."

"But you told me on the phone—"

"I thought Dad explained that to you."

"He did, but the new Alexandra, why didn't she come with us? She's your sister too, Bogus told me. And he's your dad, right?"

"Right. He's my dad and all the Alexandras have been my sisters, but—"

A small deer jumped from bordering scrub brush, paused, then raced across the highway. Billy stopped the car and peered expectantly for a pink bridle, rolling down his window to listen for jangling bells. But all he heard was the itching of cricket legs.

"Billy, don't get any romantic notions. It's not her. That deer's a deer, not a unicorn. The reason the new Alexandra didn't come is simple. She was killed too. By the cats, by Mrs. Snelling, by idiocy in general. It's rampant in The House now."

Billy stared where the deer had hopped a barbed wire fence. "Death and idiocy come awfully easy in The House—especially death." He gripped the steering wheel.

"No easier than here." Soapy motioned at the road. "What if a deer panics and smashes into our windshield? What if we run off this road into a thirty-foot drop like we passed minutes ago?"

"Yeah but—"

"No buts. Billy, when you were in The House death was just easier to see. I don't mean anything magical; I mean that you had a tighter network of friends. But death's everywhere, always. Read your newspapers. How many drunks kill themselves or others on highways just like this, how many innocent people get gunned down while walking by a convenience grocery?" She tapped the windshield to indicate an approaching car. "Speaking of death, don't you think we ought to drive on?"

A car slowed and blinked its lights. Billy waved an okay and started forward. Reaching Tuscaloosa, they passed, by Soapy's curious count, ten barbecue houses, seven hamburger drive-ins, and thirty-four beer joints. She commented that Socrates and Noah had nothing over Alabamians.

At a red light, which Billy explained meant *Stop your car*, something he figured would be hard to learn from a daily newspaper, Soapy gazed at a video store's brightly lit display window, its posters depicting half-nude, blemishless women and biceped, blemishless men holding various shiny, semi-automatic, blemishless weapons. Soapy sighed.

As they drove by Bryant-Denny Stadium—empty, so it was either a weeknight or an away game—Soapy craned her head out the window. "I expected big, but ... do they hold drama festivals here when the footballers aren't playing?"

"*Footballers* isn't a word. You need to know that if you're going to live in Tuscaloosa. They're called football players."

"Football players. Okay. But does the university use this stadium to put on dramas like the Greeks did, when the football players are—"

"Are you kidding? Soapy, the ground inside that stadium is sacred. Dozens of employees manicure it. Thousands of scabs get formed on vestal twenty-year-old knees from scraping it. Hundreds of thousands, even millions of semi-virginal adolescent throats have turned hoarse from victory chants while facing it. Untold tears from defeated players, fans, and cheerleaders have watered it. There's no way the university would let pansy actors act on it. Doing that would be—"

"Let me guess," Soapy interrupted, smacking her lips at Billy's rant. "Bad Form."

"Exactly."

Soapy sighed again.

"Regret coming here?" Billy asked.

"No, I love a good battle."

"Well, Tuscaloosa, Alabama, USA, is going to give you one."

Soapy pinched his leg hard enough to make him bark.

The nightlife he wanted to show Soapy was at a restaurant and bar called Storyville, close enough to campus to attract students, yet adult enough to attract faculty, staff and occasional townspeople. He was so enamored with having Soapy by his side that he didn't consider the possibility of running into anyone from work. In fact, he was so enamored that he'd completely forgotten work. But the waitress hadn't more than served his Maker's Mark and Soapy's Cabernet when in walked Janet Gateman and several women from Purchasing.

"Billy!" Janet said, approaching their table. "You look better, much better. Was it my chicken soup or hers that cured you?" Janet glanced archly, or so Billy thought, at Soapy.

"Uh ..."

"My name's Janet Gateman," Janet said, holding out her hand.

Soapy smiled. "I'm Soapy Riddle. Nice to meet you."

Janet turned with a dramatic flourish. "Billy, guess what? They found who stole the computers. Two fraternity kids—you won't believe the story they told."

From the way Janet sang out, Billy knew he *would* believe it. The three other women from Purchasing congregated, already laughing at what she was about to tell.

"They both swore that a wrinkled old lady who chewed tobacco paid them to move the computers. Supposedly she told them she was the department head and couldn't get any university help because it was late on a Friday. They swore she paid them in silver dollars to load the computers into a university van. They said a huge fifty-pound yellow cat sat next to her the whole time. They thought she was a zoology professor or something."

"Something all right," one of the other women said.

Janet shifted her hips and looked from Soapy to Billy. "Well ... *ciao*, Billy." She walked off, leading the three women to a back room in the restaurant.

Ciao? Where'd she pick up that? Janet was Birmingham-born, not exactly jet set. Billy twisted to spot a silken-haired professor he recognized from the Foreign Languages Department. The man waved at the four women, stood to give each a lusty hug, reserving a special wet kiss for Janet as they sat at his table.

Billy smiled. Oh well, *ciao* to chicken soup. He'd have to make do with—he gave a start. "Soapy. You *were* in that kitchen reading Nietzsche, weren't you? And you *were* cooking corned beef and cabbage in there, weren't you?"

She nodded, not altogether enthusiastically, so he dropped the subject, realizing that the time he was referring to was when Alexandra had been killed.

"Why'd you ask?" she said after a sip of wine.

"Because she—" he nodded toward Janet Gateman—"showed up in the same kitchen with chicken soup. Only she thought she was in my kitchen, in my home."

"Mm. The House and Mrs. Snelling were busy that day."

"Uh, Soapy, what are you going to do here in Tuscaloosa?"

"Not me, Billy, we."

"What are we going to do?"

"Get married. If we do it at a herpetarium, Dad might even show up."

The idea of Bogus posing as a regular snake distracted Billy only momentarily. "And after we're married?"

"After that I'll do what Lady Wisdom has always done: spread wisdom. Can't be accomplished in The House now, with the cats and Mrs. Snelling raging, so I'll have to do it here. I've been away long enough from America anyway."

Long enough? He tried to think of some American renaissance in thinking, which left him staring into his Maker's Mark. Not wanting to be cynical on their first real date, he let the subject drop.

"You should be embarrassed," Soapy admonished, as if she'd read his thoughts. And maybe she had, for she continued: "America's spawned plenty of wisdom: Edison, Melville, Lincoln, Dickinson, Twain, Carver, both Roosevelts. And what about the suffrage movement, the peace movement? And computers?"

Billy wondered aloud if, on the other hand, Mrs. Snelling had been around during the Salem witch trials or Jim Crow or the McCarthy blacklist era. Soapy gave no answer. "Well riddle me this then," he pressed, "just which one of you was around for the invention of the atomic bomb? Which for the computer? You know that its first use was for perfecting a hydrogen bomb, don't you?" He frowned, thinking of Ricco, Fanny, and Bogus still caught in The House with Mrs. Snelling and the cats. Then he felt something touch his foot. Soapy. She'd signaled the waitress and was ordering an appetizer tray of cheese and fruit. Practical Soapy. No reason why Lady Wisdom couldn't be practical between spurts of genius, was there? When the waitress left, Billy renewed his argument, on a different level.

"Soapy, I promised Fanny and Ricco that I'd try to smuggle books into The House. The libraries there have been locked up, you know. Mrs. Snelling ordered that."

"Who's Fanny?"

"Huh?" Billy looked at the TV over the bar, where he'd spotted familiar movement, an odd slink wrapping about the set. "Uh, she's Ricco's girlfriend ..." Billy leaned, rising from his chair as he counted three tan-and-ivory hourglasses slithering around the TV's controls. "Uh, she wants to go to night school. Better herself." He stared and sat back. Nothing now, except the screen showing a bimbo actress being interviewed by a bimbo announcer playing with his short moustache. Oh yeah, there was one thing: some vet had left a mottled camouflage cap beside the set.

When the waitress bought their cheese and fruit tray Billy spotted a purplish tint under a slice of apple. The waitress saw it too and pulled out a soggy, fuchsia * +* The Society Of * + * card.

"What in the world?" She was bleached-blonde, probably a college student. "Aristotle B. Riddle and The Society Of," she read. "The Society of What? It's blank after that. Isn't that odd? Some weird secret society like the Knights Templar or something." Glancing at Billy and Soapy, she held the wet card so they could see. "The Knights Templar fought during the crusades. I'm taking an introductory history course. It's sort of hinky." She shrugged and took Billy's empty glass, offering to bring him another drink. As she walked away, he noticed her drying the fuchsia card on a napkin and sliding it into her apron.

He glanced at a grinning Soapy and it dawned on him. "You're at it already, aren't you? Turning would-be bimbos into graduate students."

Soapy smiled her heart-shaped smile. "Not me. That was Dad. Curiosity comes first, then pluck, then wisdom. Aristotle Bogus Riddle, Alexandra Riddle, Sophia Riddle. Curiosity, pluck, wisdom. Ever since the Garden of Eden. Hey, wanna know what Dad told Eve? 'Get smart, Babe. Eat the apple and get smart.' " Soapy raised her palms. "That's it, Mr. Snake's whole evil, wicked message."

"But—"

"—Excuse my Alabama vernacular, but nothing pisses a god or goddess off more than to have his or her loyal subjects getting smart. It doesn't bode well for blind worship."

"Then your dad's the devil?" Billy started to take a sip of whiskey, but found his glass wasn't there. He eyed Soapy's wine, but was nervous about its deep red color.

"You haven't been listening, pea-brain." Soapy turned and stared at the TV behind her. "No wonder." The bartender had raised its volume to blast-off. Soapy flicked her finger and its sound wound down to a buzz and its color wilted into a bright blue wave pattern, just as the set at Billy's house had done.

"I thought you were supposed to turn into a normal Southern Belle once you got here. No more magic. That's what Bogus said."

"Dad doesn't know everything. That's my department." She raised her wine glass in a salute: "At least I'm drinking, am I not? What's more Southern Belle than drinking a nice red wine?"

Drinking Southern Comfort and Coke with two cherries, Billy thought, keeping that concoction to himself for his stomach's sake. And Soapy's too.

"Maybe if you buy me a pink corsage I'll even chew tobacco and go hunting with you."

Billy made a face. "Okay, enough jokes. If Bogus isn't the devil, just who is he?"

"I told you already, he's curiosity. But not just personified like in an English class. For real. That's why he doesn't have any worries about Mrs. Snelling. No one, not even the Snellings, can get rid of curiosity."

"And Alexandra?" Billy asked.

"Alexandra is courage or pluck. Either of which can be killed easily enough, as we all know from reading newspapers. Myself, I can be exiled, which is what's happened."

"Can you be killed?" Billy asked lowly, looking about.

"Ah, you're still thinking of what Mr. Snelling told you. Interesting proposition. It's been tried, you know, by the Roman Catholic list of proscribed books, by fundamentalist book burnings, Hitler's brown shirts, Stalin's secret police, by Ayatollahs—and I dare add by politically correct people everywhere. Still ... killed? Forever? Let's hope not. Unless it's from too much of this stuff." She lifted her glass. "But, *in vino veritas*, right? So here's to Pluck, the Riddle who goes to night school, reads by candlelight—"

"And gets killed," Billy said.

"But always comes back," Soapy added.

Janet Gateman walked from the back room to their table. "One of the girls happened to have this in her purse. We thought you'd get a kick out of it." She handed him a piece of paper that read:

MEMORANDUM:
    TO: ALL PURCHASING EMPLOYEES
    FROM: MR. SCHROEDER
    RE: UNITED WAY CAMPAIGN

IT HAS COME TO MY ATTENTION THAT OUR OWN WILLIAM F. WISE, THOUGH SICK IN BED AT HOME, HAS PUSHED THE UNIVERSITY OVER THIS YEAR'S PLEDGE TO THE UNITED WAY. THIS MAKES OUR DEPARTMENT PROUD. WHEN MR. WISE RETURNS FROM CONVALESCENCE, PLEASE LET HIM KNOW HOW MUCH WE APPRECIATE HIS GENEROSITY.

Billy laughed, remembering his pink phone conversation on the train's toilet.

"This was how we all knew you were really sick. What else could make you give to United Way, other than a high fever?" She smiled grandly at Soapy. "Well, *ciao*, again. I have to get back. You can keep the memorandum. I'm sure we'll get more." She rolled her eyes and Billy laughed.

He kept chuckling after she left, but Soapy, sober-faced, was staring at the back of the memorandum. He turned it over:

MEMORANDUM
    DATE: TODAY
    TO: WISE AND WISDOM
    FROM: DEPARTMENT OF NEW EDUCATION, MR. TOM POWDER

CONGRAUTLATIONS! YOUR DADDY HAS DIPPED HIS LEWD WICK AGIAN AND A NEW DARLING ALEXANDRA'S ON TEH WAY. WE CAN IETHER SEND A BABY CURL OR A BABY HEAD, DEPENDING WHETHER OR NOT YOU TWO PALY OUR WAY.

"Paly our way," Billy said. "I've seen that before. Will they really . . ." He pointed vaguely at the word *head*.

"This says Mr. Tom Powder, but it's from Mrs. Snelling," Soapy said. "You can bet she means it."

"How'd they get this note out here, into Tuscaloosa?" Billy glanced angrily at Janet Gateman, who was laughing with the language professor.

"It doesn't have anything to do with her. The Snellings can do whatever they want. They're God."

"God? Those sick-joke prunes? God's supposed to be an old man with a white beard and—"

"—and soft palms chocked with Milky Ways? Look around, Billy. Did a Pennsylvania chocolate factory create this universe?"

Billy didn't bother to look; instead, he took a sip of Maker's Mark the waitress placed before him. He was appreciating Bogus's taste in whiskey more and more. "Then what about Bogus and Ricco and Fanny? If you're exiled here and the libraries are closed there, what hope is there ... there?"

"There? What about here? Sports metaphors splatter American universities like a grease gun on automatic, but students and professors manage. Computer chips get built, dissertations written, research accomplished."

"Maybe ..." Billy said dully.

"No maybe, my husband-to-be; think positive. Cats may be top dogs for a while, they may kill even Ricco and Fanny and several Alexandras, but curiosity will always kill the cats." Soapy crumpled the memorandums. "That's an important BD to remember. BD, not BM."

Billy could smell the wine on her breath. Or maybe her breath always smelled so intoxicating.

She reached for his hand. "Tonight, Billy Wise, Lady Wisdom takes a vacation. Tomorrow the library and Internet, but tonight Lady Wisdom wants to be a bimbo. Aren't you curious to see icy Lady Sophia in that state?"

"Curious?" Billy bit his lip.

"Yes, curious. And believe me, it *will* kill the cats."

There was a yipping and Billy looked back at the foreign language professor, who'd donned a maroon beret to bark like a French poodle. The guy had written six books and had another on the way. And Janet, she was no slouch at work ... Billy realized Soapy's foot was tapping his own. He tapped hers back as she offered him a bite of apple. Chewing it, he answered, "Yeah, I'm curious. Let's finish this and go paly around."